PHOENIX

STEELE SHADOWS RISING

AMANDA MCKINNEY

HH TISEVICH

Paperback ISBN 978-1-7340133-6-8
eBook ISBN 978-1-7340133-5-1

Editor(s): Nancy Brown
Cover Design: Damonza
📷: Wander Aguiar Photography

https://www.amandamckinneyauthor.com

DEDICATION

For Mama

ALSO BY AMANDA

THRILLER NOVELS:

The Stone Secret - A Thriller Novel

A Marriage of Lies - A Thriller Novel

The Widow of Weeping Pines

The Raven's Wife

The Lie Between Us

The Keeper's Closet

The Mad Women - A Box Set

ROMANCE SUSPENSE/THRILLER NOVELS:

THE ANTI-HERO COLLECTION:

Mine

His

ON THE EDGE SERIES:

Buried Deception

Trail of Deception

BESTSELLING STEELE SHADOWS SERIES:

Cabin 1 (Steele Shadows Security)

Cabin 2 (Steele Shadows Security)

Cabin 3 (Steele Shadows Security)

Phoenix (Steele Shadows Rising)

Jagger (Steele Shadows Investigations)

Ryder (Steele Shadows Investigations)

Her Mercenary (Steele Shadows Mercenaries)

BESTSELLING DARK ROMANTIC SUSPENSE SERIES:

Rattlesnake Road

Redemption Road

AWARD-WINNING ROMANTIC SUSPENSE SERIES:

The Woods (A Berry Springs Novel)

The Lake (A Berry Springs Novel)

The Storm (A Berry Springs Novel)

The Fog (A Berry Springs Novel)

The Creek (A Berry Springs Novel)

The Shadow (A Berry Springs Novel)

The Cave (A Berry Springs Novel)

The Viper

Devil's Gold (A Black Rose Mystery, Book 1)

Hatchet Hollow (A Black Rose Mystery, Book 2)

Tomb's Tale (A Black Rose Mystery Book 3)

Evil Eye (A Black Rose Mystery Book 4)

Sinister Secrets (A Black Rose Mystery Book 5)

And many more to come...

LET'S CONNECT!

Text **AMANDABOOKS to 66866** to sign up
for Amanda's Newsletter and get the latest
on new releases, promos, and freebies!
Or, you can sign up below.

https://www.amandamckinneyauthor.com

PHOENIX

A man who cheated death.
A woman hired to pick up the broken pieces.
And an obsession strong enough to kill for.

They told him he'd been given a second chance at life. Told him to count his lucky stars, to stop and smell the roses. Kind of hard to do when your body is bound by chains and cuffs. That's what it felt like, anyway, when Phoenix Steele woke up from his coma to a life full of restrictions. Once known around town as the fearless, indomitable heir to the Steele fortune, the former Marine was suddenly labeled unstable, short-tempered, and loose cannon. Unwilling to accept his issues, Phoenix instantly clashes with his assertive therapist—the town's most eligible bachelorette.

No one knew overcoming the odds like Dr. Rose Floris. Determined not to be a statistic, Rose lived her life under carefully constructed routines—until a gruesome murder and a series of mysterious events reveal she's become the center of a madman's obsession. Suddenly, Rose's world is turned upside down and she finds herself under the watchful eye of her new patient, a broken man she's been warned not to trust.

As the tables begin to turn on their client-patient relationship, Phoenix realizes he must battle his own demons before he can save anyone, including the woman who's become his own obsession...

An obsession he'd kill for.

1

ROSE

*L*ightning lit the sky, a momentary reprieve from the darkness of the kitchen around me. I twisted my long, black hair between my fingers, my eyes widening with the flash of light. A fear of what might be illuminated sending a chill colder than the temperature up my spine. I can still remember that moment. I was wearing my favorite purple nightgown, a pair of holey pink socks. The kind with the little pom pom ball on the back. Purple, to match the gown that hadn't been washed in weeks, but I didn't care. It was mine, it fit, and made me feel like a princess. Night after night, I'd pretend it was a glamorous gown and that I was trapped in a castle by an evildoer. A *really* evil one, with slitted red eyes, squared chin, pointed nails, the works. I still can't watch Nightmare on Elm Street. Heck, that movie might as well be a biography at this point, because Lord knew, I'd seen hell up close in that house. Evil, as sure as my beating heart, in human form. But dream after dream, no white knight came to save me. No one saved me. The crazy thing is, despite that, I continued to dream. Between matted lashes, swollen eyes, and years that dragged on, I still dreamed. Why? It's that little light that children carry inside them. The light that for some ignites a happy, fruitful path, but for others, dims or fades all together when the pain of the world around them becomes too great. Although the latter was my path, I continued to dream. Incredible thing, the human mind is. The spirit to thrive. To survive. Looking back, that little light was what saved my life.

A loud *pop* of thunder sent my heart slamming against my ribcage. Windows rattled above me. I hugged my knees to my chest, pressing my back against the wall, the thin sheetrock like ice through my nightgown.

I knew how fragile sheet rock could be.

I knew from experience.

Then, the sleet started. First, a delicate pitter patter, quickly turning into a loud buzz against the roof. You've probably heard of thunder snow before. This was thunder sleet. To this day, I've never seen weather like it. Typical early spring in the south. That year, winter desperately clutched on with its icy grip. Unrelenting.

I closed my eyes imagining the ice falling from the sky, sparkles of silver against streaks of lightning, carrying on the wings of the wind. Free to fall where it wanted, free to fly away.

Free to melt away in a silent surrender.

I imagined myself as that ice, fading away. Away from the pain, the torment, the life I'd been thrown into, the series of circumstances that shaped the woman I would become.

For better or worse.

The definition of evolution is the gradual development of something, from a simple form to a complex form. There are three main types of evolution: convergent, parallel, and divergent.

Convergent evolution occurs when species of different ancestors begin to develop similar traits in response to their habitat. Think of birds, insects, bats. Each very different species, but each sharing the ability to fly. Parallel evolution happens when two independent species evolve separately, without sharing any of the same traits or adaptations.

Divergent is the most commonly addressed and debated form of evolution. This happens when two species share the same ancestor but each gradually becomes different over time. The first study of divergent evolution dates back to 1895 when a young explorer named Charles Darwin visited the Galapagos Islands where he studied finches, noting how their beaks were different according to their diet. Same ancestor, but different species over time.

I, Rose Floris, was a walking example of divergent evolution. Of environment and predation pressures, or, the effects of being preyed upon.

Natural selection.

The weak are destroyed.

Only the strongest survive.

Adapt, or die.

I understood this concept from a very young age.

Sure, to most, evolution meant advancement, growth, progress. But for me, it was something deeper, something darker. A necessary adaptation to the environment I'd been thrown into.

My definition of evolution? A will to survive, no matter age, circumstance, environment. And that will, I've learned, is the strongest part of the human body.

You might have heard of children being compared to clay.

They can be molded and shaped at a young age with the end goal of becoming a productive, functioning adult. I remember watching children at the playground with their parents while mine left me in the car to make a quick run down the back alley. The gleeful giggles, the joy in the smallest things. Their prideful smiles as their parents cheered them down the slide. Appreciation for life, for family, for things.

Happiness—an adaptation of their environment.

Not for me. For me, my adaptation was silence. Fading into my environment so that I was neither seen nor heard. Becoming as much of "nothing" as I possibly could. It was a type of survival, and one that, unfortunately, goes overlooked.

In school, I learned very quickly that the misfits were the only ones who were assumed to have a difficult upbringing. The more rebellious the kid is, the more defiant, the more obnoxious and crude, the ones who get into physical altercations—those were the kids that had it worst at home. Not true. There was an entirely different species of children who had it much worse than little Johnny with the bloody knuckles.

Those were the quiet kids.

The ones in the shadows, in the corner. The ones who never made eye contact.

The ones with bruises under their clothes.

That was me.

To be silent, to *not* fight was to survive. A complacent acceptance manifesting in silence, while unrelenting anxiety churning inside your stomach evolves you into something else.

Yeah, I knew evolution all too well.

And that night, I witnessed the effects of environmental impact on human life. Natural selection? I sure hoped so.

The house had been quiet for hours. Cheryl had given up on looking for me sometime around sunset, as she usually did. Funnily enough, they never looked under the kitchen table, which had become my nightly refuge until they'd go to bed.

Rain began to mix with the sleet, a steady deluge, a white noise buzzing around me blocking out everything else. It was those moments that I took my chances. Few and far between, but I took them when I could. My gaze fixed on the refrigerator only a few feet away. Anxiety bubbled inside me, knowing that eating without approval would lead to another run in with the sheet rock. *Feed me more, then,* I'd think. Simple.

The rain picked up, pellets of ice sliding down the windows. My eyes darted from the doorway, back to the fridge, to the window, then back to the doorway.

Confident that the storm would block out any noise I'd make, I pushed away from the corner, maneuvering between the chairs under the dining table as I had done so many times. A snake, slithering through the darkness. More lightning, more thunder to drown out any mistake I might make.

A waft of cold air swept past me as I slinked out from under the table. I froze like a groundhog peeking up from the ground. Exposed, vulnerable.

But hungry.

I was *so hungry.*

It had been seventeen hours since I'd eaten—yes, I'd counted—a crust of a microwave pizza I'd been tossed. They liked to mess with me like that. A cliché power trip. I know that now.

My pulse hammered as I forced myself forward, shuffling on my knees along the cold, tiled floor. Stay low, stay small. Low so that they couldn't see you. Small, in case they did. The smaller the target, the harder to hit. Heck of a lesson for a child.

My hands trembled—I'm talking *earthquake* trembled—as I reached for the handle.

And that's when the front door flew open.

Lightning outlined his silhouette like the villain in every little girl's dream. Freddy, indeed. Rain swirled around his untied boots as he stumbled inside. I dropped to the floor, spun around and slammed my back against the cabinets, praying he didn't see me.

His scream was something out of a horror movie, echoing off the walls and lingering in the air as if to punctuate the shock.

I stilled, wondering what could entice that kind of reaction from a man who was the one who typically did the scaring.

Boots shuffled across the living room, a low, panicked repetitive muttering of something I couldn't make out. My thoughts spun, every instinct in my body telling me that something was wrong. Very, very wrong.

"Rose!" My name exploded from his lips. It wasn't the first time he'd screamed my name, but it was the first time it sounded like *that*.

"Rose!"

My heart kick started into panic mode, my gaze darting around the kitchen, stopping on the window above the sink. Could I make it? Could I escape?

"Rose!"

I surged to my feet, my nightgown catching and ripping on a nail sticking out from the cabinet.

My legs moved like rubber though the kitchen, a sick need to both see what was happening in the other room, and to prevent myself from another night in the emergency room after "falling down the stairs."

I stepped into the doorway of the living room.

A low, haunting melody accompanied the end of a movie streaming on the television. His back was to me, shuffling from side to side, frantic mumbles against the music.

And as my gaze shifted to the couch, my stomach plummeted.

That's when it happened.

That's when my life took a turn.

Natural selection. That was my personal theory, anyway. Because evil like that didn't have a place on earth. Evil like that faced its own demons.

And demons always win… unless you face them.

And I'd faced mine. That night, I'd faced mine.

I was eight years old.

Eight years old when I'd decided enough was enough.

2

ROSE

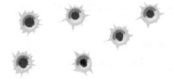

Twenty years later...

a blast of cool air whipped through my hair, the sweet scent of rain and budding flowers filling the cab of my SUV. It was springtime in the south, although you wouldn't know it. Days and inches of rain had plagued the small town, causing intermittent flash flooding and more cases of seasonal depression than I'd seen in my entire career. And, no, light therapy did *not* include the neon sign above the local bar, I had to remind my male clients. The weatherman had promised it would be the last cold snap before warmer weather. Little did we know at the time, Mother Nature had much more than cold air in mind for the next few days.

The late morning sun peeked out from the thick, grey clouds that had been hovering overhead for days. My face lifted to the sky, taking a moment to appreciate the beams of light shooting through the canopy of trees above us. I squinted, the elusive light reflecting off water dripping from the budding leaves, the branches heavy and swollen with the barrage of rain we'd gotten over the last week. Somewhere beyond the miles of forest we were in was a glorious rainbow.

Maybe I'll catch it next time, I thought.

My SUV hit a pothole, mud splattering onto the windshield as it bottomed out.

"Road needs some work." This growl from the passenger seat, the first words my boss had muttered since checking his seatbelt—twice.

With my grip tightening around the steering wheel, I peered down to the dirt road where most of the rocks had been washed away. It had been five days of storm after storm, with midnight temperatures dipping low enough to allow black ice to form on the mountain roads in time for morning commute. The first responders had been working overtime, even recording a PSA for the small-town folk reminding them to drive with caution, and threatening to close down the mountain that housed Banshee's Brew liquor store. I hadn't seen an accident since.

Springtime in Berry Springs was always a crapshoot. Never knew what you were going to get, and that day, it was another morning of freezing temperatures, with highs expected to reach sixty in the afternoon. Impossible weather to dress for, by the way.

"Well... can't rain forever." I replied in a tone that reminded me of the snooty local librarian who ended her sentences with 'so,' punctuating her point and leaving no room for retort. I liked that woman.

As if on cue, thunder rumbled in the distance.

"Rose... watch out," my boss said.

"Wh—" A pitched squeak cut off my question. I cringed

as a low-hanging branch scratched down the side of my brand-new BMW.

Son of a—*Shake it off, Rose,* the voice in my head scolded. *You've got this.*

It was the faceless voice in my head that had become so prevalent over the years. A separate entity, almost. Thorn, I called her—the thorn to my Rose. And, let me tell you, Thorn was one unrelenting, unforgiving, judgy *B.* She was also the reason I'd graduated with honors with a doctorate in Psychology by the age of twenty-five, while having a full time job. A record, according to my college advisor. Thorn was the light, that fire inside me that pushed me to better myself, my situation, my circumstance. Thorn was the reason I'd gotten a job at the prestigious Kline and Associates Clinic for Therapy. She was also the reason we were on this journey—success, to be determined.

As the branch made its final squeal, I glanced over at Dr. Theo Kline and forced an easy, breezy *well-what-can-ya-do* smile—a kind of casual shrug-off that didn't come easily to me. He shook his head. I humored him, although I wasn't quite sure why. I always had a feeling the guy could see right through me.

It had been eight months since I'd danced my acceptance to his offer to be part of his team. Little did I know four months of that time was going to consist of a very humbling "training-phase" where he personally monitored my client sessions. Yep, my boss would lurk in the corner of the room while new clients poured their hearts out on my couch, judging my response to every tear. But I fought through the awkwardness because a job with Kline and Associates was exponentially better than my previous job. Nothing like practicing psychology at an elite private college where the frat boys' biggest challenges included paying off their teachers and finding new Adderall dealers. Sitting across from America's entitled youth and listening to them piss and moan about their elitist problems had made me question my patience for the job. I'd learned how to spell pachydermatous forward and backward at that desk, trust me on that.

I clicked through the radio stations in an effort to break the silence and ease the nerves that were starting to creep up.

"You like country?"

Theo wrinkled his nose.

"No? That's blasphemy in these parts, Dr. Kline."

He didn't laugh.

I turned to another station. "How about rock?"

Nothing.

"Pop?" I grinned and looked over at him. "A little Biebs to get the blood flowing in the morning?"

"Slow down there, Andretti."

My heart skipped as the one-lane wooden bridge, shimmering with a layer of ice, came into view. I gently tapped the brakes—that's what you're supposed to do right?—and coasted over the dilapidated bridge.

"Calm down, Rose."

I cleared my throat, willing my pulse to slow. "My adrenaline, noradrenaline, and cortisol levels are fine, thank you very much." Because that was a normal response for a mental health professional.

"I'm not suggesting you're on the verge of a panic attack, I'm just saying... relax."

"I'm fine."

He snorted and checked his cell phone. "What time is the appointment?"

I glanced at the clock feeling a twinge of panic. Between

the rain, pitted road, and my shifty passenger, we were running late. And I was never late.

So I lied.

"I told her we'd be there around ten."

"Around ten?"

"Yep. 'Round ten." I kept my eyes on the road.

"'Round ten? Is that an official calendar invite option? Because my whole life just changed."

Pleased with his smartassery, Theo refocused on his phone, scrolling through emails or reading the latest medical study he'd surely forward to me, then force me to discuss during my lunch break. Because that was Theo, always analyzing, thinking, dissecting. Always working. Especially since his messy divorce months earlier—or so the waitress at Donny's Diner had told me.

Theo was a short man, mid-fifties, shaggy brown hair with grey at the temples, and a scruffy beard he'd trim only after the sunflower seeds he always munched on started catching in it. He had a dry sense of humor and a closet made up of three colors: brown, dark brown, and plaid. He was a handsome man—if you liked that earthy, nerdy type —even with the wrinkles that aged him beyond his years. That day, he was bundled up in a brown hat, plaid scarf, an oversized wool coat, and faded leather gloves. He looked more like a modern day version of Sherlock Holmes, amplified by a permanently cocked brow as if he was always in deep thought. A deep, passive aggressive, *I'm-smarter-than-you* thought.

It wasn't the best start to the appointment I'd planned for weeks. He'd already tried to cancel twice—the latest due to the impending storms—but I'd urged him along with some song and dance about how unpredictable weather in the south can be, and topped that off with an offer to pick up lunch on the way back. Sold. Honestly, I would have thrown in breakfast the next day, too, because there was no way I was missing that appointment. The date had been selected months ago, arrangements made, weeks of preparation—none of which he knew about. I had gone above and beyond, crossed all my Ts and dotted all my Is to make sure that morning went off without a hitch, and I wasn't going to let a few raindrops and black ice stand in the way.

Girl power. You've got this, Rose. Go get 'em. Or, *git,* was perhaps more appropriate to the surroundings. I'd dropped my southern drawl the moment I'd boarded the Greyhound bus out of town. Only eight months back and I'd already caught myself addressing a group of cowboys as "y'alls." Dammit.

I forced Thorn out of my thoughts and focused on the road that was getting narrower by the minute. Sprinkles had started to fall again, and if the darkening clouds were any indication, another deluge was about to hit. After taking a hairpin corner slower than a bale of baby turtles, I turned into a long driveway next to the red sign I'd pounded into the ground two days earlier.

Massey Stables

I wrinkled my nose as Thorn judged my paint job. There was a splatter of mud in the corner, and the arches on the "M" weren't perfectly parallel but I'd deal with that later. Painting was never my thing... unless it was to cover up bruises. That, I could do in spades.

My nerves began to build as we drove down the

driveway that cut between two treeless fields, green with budding grass.

Two horses grazed in the distance with red plaid blankets tied to their backs. I'd picked those out myself.

I took a silent inhale, reminding myself again to relax.

I knew my selling points.

I knew my audience.

Most importantly, though, I knew my numbers. My facts —my best friends. No one beat me when it came to an argument based on facts. A childhood rooted in chaos tends to lend itself to an adulthood that gravitates toward things that are steady. Constant. Predictable. And nothing was as black and white as facts. You could count on them. Take them to the bank, so to speak. And that's what made me different at my job as a psychologist, made me excel at it. In a world that revolved around *feelings* and grey areas, I broke things down into bite size chunks based on facts and figures, then tackled those points head on. I wasn't afraid to combine proven tactics, or try new things. As I was doing right then.

A smile tugged at my lips as the red carriage stable came into view, the new shutters and fresh coat of paint that had taken forever to complete—and stains on my clothes that took even longer to remove. Not to mention a wicked case of tennis elbow, which I learned is not exclusive to the sport. That was another fact you could take to the bank.

Pride swelled in my chest as I rolled to a stop under a massive oak tree.

The stable was small—humble, a better word for it—but it got the job done, and that's all we needed at that moment. Sometime in the future, I planned to add more stables, paddocks, acres of trails, and if I could come up with the money, a riding course. In my dreams, I had myself as the owner of my own therapy clinic right next door.

I just had to get the ball rolling first.

The brief moment of sunlight we had was long gone and had been replaced by a grey haze over the fields.

Theo's gaze fixed on the stable. Either the guy was waiting for a maître d to open his door, or he wanted to bring home the fact that he was less than enthusiastic about the meeting. I assumed the latter.

"Ready?" I said in my most confident voice, then pushed out the door without waiting for a response.

It was my show.

And *you got this, girl.*

Briefcase in hand, attitude in my step, I rounded the hood, slipped on a pile of horse manure and fell flat on my ass. I'm not talking a sweet, little "whoopsie" slip, I'm talking desperately-grabbing-at-the-air, feet-flying-out-from-under-me, hitting-the-ground-like-a-sack-of-potatoes, falling on my ass. As if that wasn't humiliating enough, the universe continued its chuckle by sending my briefcase into the air and landing upright on my hood, right in front of Theo's face.

Classic.

Gritting my teeth, I jumped up, swiping the fresh dung from my new, charcoal grey Von Furstenberg power suit— the one I'd gotten specifically for that meeting. The one that had single-handedly used up half my spring wardrobe budget.

And worth every penny, I might add.

I plucked the briefcase from the hood as the passenger door slammed shut. The grin on Theo's face told me he'd seen the entire thing.

Cherry on top.

"Ah, heck of an entrance. Hello, there," a familiar voice called out from the stable, the tone immediately calming my anxiety, as it had done so many times before. I turned as June Massey crossed the driveway. I smiled. She'd pulled her long, grey hair into a slick bun, with not a strand out of place. This sleek do was in contrast to her trademark messy braid, more often than not, interwoven with hay. Her blue wide-rimmed glasses had been swapped out with more conservative, wireless frames. Perhaps most shockingly, the woman had put on *makeup*. In all the years I knew June, I'd seen her in makeup only a handful of times. Her usual faded Levi's and muck boots had been replaced with starched khakis—a line down the middle to prove it—and a white blouse under a plaid suit jacket that rivaled any eighties-era Murphy Brown blazer. Despite the football pads on her shoulders, she looked a decade younger than her sixty years. June had done herself up, and it was the first time I wondered if she was nervous, too.

Always give them your best self, her voice echoed in my ear.

She seamlessly passed me a hand towel as her other hand stretched toward Theo. Bless that woman. I wiped down my thigh and backside, the moisture already seeping through to my thong as I made the introductions.

Horse poop on a thong. Heck of a way to start the day... or a perfect hook for the next hit rap song.

June fell into casual small talk as she led the way into the stables.

I tossed the towel into the barrel next to the stables and followed June and Theo through the double sliding doors—noting a knick in the paint—where June had set up a refurbished wood table and matching chairs just past the entry. The newly-swept concrete floor was gleaming under the fluorescent lights. The buzz of three space heaters broke the silence, and based on the warmth, they'd been running all morning. To the left were four small stalls with wooden gates, and a tack room on the end. To the right, an open space which, weeks ago, had been packed with mismatched plastic bins, cleaning supplies, medical supplies, wheelbarrows, bedding, hay, and in June's case, multiple boxes of Christmas decorations. All that, though, had been sifted, sorted, organized and tucked away into a newly-added wall of metal cabinets. Three polished saddles hung next to our table with mounting blocks below. Nice touch.

I winked at June, and was met with a wink back, then said, "June, would you like to give Mr. Kline a quick tour before we begin the meeting?"

"Of course, Miss Floris."

I grinned at her formality, then waited until they were in conversation before darting to the sink to scrub my hands, wipe down my heels, and spray my four-figure suit with disinfectant. It was like pouring salt on the only Twinkie left in the house because you were on a diet. Heart-breaking. I listened to the pride in June's voice as she explained that each of her horses were rescued from bad situations and personally rehabilitated, an irony that was not lost on me. After that, we settled around the table.

I felt the heat start to rise up my neck, that familiar stress-sweat spreading over my skin. No, my adrenaline, noradrenaline, and cortisol levels were *not* in check anymore. I was a mess. And that wasn't like me. But the thing was, that meeting wasn't only about me, it was about June and so many others in need. I *believed* in it. And reminding myself of that was the kick in the ass I needed.

I yanked my shoulders back and pulled out my folder with color-coordinated tabs. Then, I angled myself toward Theo, and began.

"As you know, I've brought you here today to discuss my

desire to add an Equine Assisted Therapy program at your clinic—"

"A new department you're proposing to head up, which would involve me hiring another therapist to pick up the slack—something that wasn't in the budget this year," Theo countered, not to my surprise.

"Not necessarily," I countered back. "I can incorporate this new program with at least half my current client list while we work out the kinks. Then, word will get out, and the influx of new patients that this program will bring to Kline and Associates will more than cover the cost of a new therapist." I slid him the business proposal I'd worked weeks on. "As you can see here, the startup costs are very minimal due to the fact we will partner with Ms. Massey and use her stable and her horses. The program will run primarily on volunteers, with Ms. Massey as the director and myself as the therapist. You already pay me, so no additional cost there. We already have a website and can add the program to our current marketing materials, so there are no additional costs there, either. As you know, the hardest part with any new company or service is getting your name out there initially—we already have that. Kline and Associates is the biggest mental health clinic in the area, and has a stellar reputation. The greatest cost will be maintaining the grounds and providing medical care for the horses. Lastly," I clicked my pen and pointed to the paper. "This is my suggested fee for the program, per patient, and an estimated profit and loss statement for the first year. I broke it into two columns, one without hiring an additional therapist and one with. Both columns include the amount of new business we would need to not only break even, but make a profit." I circled my projected first-year net revenue—which was nothing to sneeze at. "But that number is nothing compared to the number of people we will help with this new program."

With that point, a spark of energy, an excitement, shot through me. I slid him another document, this one with bulleted facts and figures. My favorite document, of course.

"As you know, over twenty percent of Americans have some sort of anxiety disorder, including PTSD, ranging from children to aging adults. Equine Assisted Therapy, or EAT for short, is proven to improve symptoms of a wide range of issues including depression, dementia, genetic disorders, developmental delays, traumatic brain injuries, behavioral issues, the list goes on and on." I tapped the paper. "There are several studies marking the improvement of brain functioning, via MRI imaging, of patients who were part of EAT studies. One study included a group of children with ADHD, and another a group of veterans with documented PTSD. It's really promising stuff. Exciting."

June smiled.

Theo crossed his arms over his chest. "Okay, so tell me *how*. How does it work?"

"There are different buckets of techniques within equine therapy that we would apply, based on the patient's need. The most common would be applying it as cognitive therapy. This would be used to treat anxiety, PTSD, behavioral issues, etcetera, and would involve addressing the patient's anxious response to new situations, such as the horse. This EAT technique works because of two main components: Horses mirror human behavior, and are hyper sensitive to their environments."

He cocked his head.

"Let me explain further. The therapy begins with introducing the patient to a new, uncharted experience—interacting with the horse. This will trigger symptoms of anxiety, which the horse immediately senses and responds in the same way, mirroring the patient's anxious demeanor. This forces the patient to push through the emotions, because in order to work with the horse, the patient has to foster a calm interaction. There is no other way. The patient has to shift focus from their own anxiety, to the horse's, and will notice that the horse will not calm until they do. This teaches them to acknowledge and identify *automatic thoughts*—the trained behavior of anxiety—with the end goal of learning how to control that automatic response. But that's only part of it. The key here is the horse is a safe zone for them. It's not a judgmental family member, a friend, or someone who makes them feel like they aren't good enough. The horse is unbiased and forgiving. The horse doesn't talk back. The only way to make the horse calm, is for the patient to be calm. To learn to *control* their behavior. Then, repeat, repeat, repeat, until the new learned behavior replaces what was once debilitating anxiety, anger, panic, or whatever the case may be. The therapy retrains their brain, thereby retraining their thoughts and behaviors. It's amazing, Theo."

I handed him another document.

"Beyond cognitive, there is Practicing Therapy which involves carrying out actual duties and chores with the horses where the patients will participate in new activities, new experiences that they would usually avoid. This includes bathing or feeding the horses and gives them a sense of accomplishment, aiding in their self-confidence and self-esteem. Last, is Play and Communication Therapy. This is geared toward creating relationships in group play settings and building communication and language skills. This is the most common form of equine therapy for children. Again, the key here is that horses are not 'judgmental humans.' They are smart, gentle, forgiving creatures who mirror human behavior, which makes them ideal in therapy."

I was on a roll, so I kept it up.

"The closest Equine Therapy facility is three hours away, and according to my visit there, has to turn patients away. Offering an EAT program in Berry Springs would not only bring new patients to Kline and Associates, but would help people who might not turn to therapy in the first place. It's different. It's not the dreaded, cliché couch-time, 'tell-me-about-your-feelings' stuff." And then I brought it back home with, "Kline would be the only registered EAT provider within a hundred mile radius, which would increase our patient roster exponentially."

"And how are you going to do that?" He asked. "Ensure that the patient roster increases exponentially?"

"By going on a good ol' sales route. I plan to pitch our program to the area VA hospitals first, then physical and occupational therapy clinics after that, and finally, to foster care facilities and children's shelters." A lump caught in my throat.

June quickly picked up the torch. "I've already met with my bank to begin the paperwork on turning my stable into a non-profit organization."

I nodded. "And I've already completed my application to obtain my equine therapy certification."

"Back to school, sales route... all this with your current client portfolio?"

"I can do it."

"Yes, she can." June nodded. "And I can help."

Theo leaned back and focused on me. A solid minute ticked by as I stared back on pins and needles.

This was met with—

"Where're you taking me for lunch?"

3

ROSE

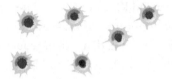

$\mathcal{M}$y car slid in a puddle of mud, the bumper grinding to a halt on the sidewalk. I shoved the vehicle into reverse and cringed as it grinded off the concrete. A duo of cane-toting, Wrangler-wearing cowboys shook their heads as they passed by, rain pouring off their cowboy hats. They both eyed me through the windshield and I swear the one with the handlebar mustache muttered, *"damn women drivers."* The other spat a wad of tobacco into the ditch.

My next thought involved a chainsaw and can of motor oil, but I digress.

I looked at the clock—3:37 p.m.

I was late. For the *second* freaking time that day.

After having lunch with my boss where the meeting continued but the final decision remained unclear, I'd dropped him off at the office before hauling butt to my house to change my dung-stained clothes. I'm devastated to report that the blessed power suit took its final resting place in the trash can. After wiping the tears, I'd gone into my closet where I tried on not one, not two, but three separate outfits. I settled on another power suit, this one in my trade-mark black, a wool pencil skirt with matching jacket, paired with a teal paisley-print blouse and black pumps. It was my "I'm super confident" suit, and Lord knew I needed to look my best to be the featured speaker at career day at the local high school. Because if anyone knew how cruel kids could be, it was me. Heck, I'd almost knocked back a shot of tequila before leaving the house.

After that blessed event, I was stalled in traffic from an accident on my way back to the office.

A business proposal in the morning followed by public speaking in the afternoon sent my usually well-maintained anxious resting-state into an all-out frazzled mess. And I didn't do frazzled well. I didn't do anything I couldn't control well. Especially the dent in my bumper that I'd just gotten.

Would go well with the scratch from earlier, at least.

Muttering curses I hadn't heard since my last appoint-ment with my Tourette syndrome client, I grabbed my purse, briefcase, my skim-milk latte, said a Hail Mary and stepped out of the car. A million little rain bombs pounded my head, sure to flatten the blowout I'd gotten the day before.

"Dammit, dammit, dammit," I chanted under my breath as I did a little tip-toe jog across the sidewalk, cradling my new Louis Vuitton while scorching hot coffee spurted out of the lid like a volcano of destruction.

"Shit, shit, shit..." Because dammit no longer fit the situation.

"Aw, good day, dear. You really should wear a rain coat, you know that? Gonna catch a cold with this damn weath-er," a low, gravelly voice called out behind me, reminding me of a cartoon bullfrog with four cigarettes hanging out of its mouth.

An Army veteran, Chester Jenkins was a chain smoking, whiskey drinking legend in Berry Springs. The former proctologist turned baker—a questionable move nonetheless—could tell you stories that would send your heart into your throat, or your dinner onto the floor. Born and raised in Berry Springs, Chester knew everyone, their neighbors, and their dogs by name. With four failed marriages under his belt—typical for a proctologist, he'd tell you—Mr. Jenkins was a walking file cabinet of town gossip, easily unlocked after his morning Baileys.

Fighting the internal battle of good versus evil, I kept walking but glanced over my shoulder. Wearing his usual flat cap, Mr. Jenkins' beady eyes pinned me from behind a red scarf wrapped around the bottom of his face. His wool coat was two sizes too small, barely covering the fifties-style baking uniform that no one demanded he wore. On his feet, a pair of black orthopedic shoes as square as the bricks that lined his bakeshop. In his hands, two grocery bags. In his trunk, three more.

Good won. I stopped and turned around. "Need some help, Mr. Jenkins?"

"Oh, I'll manage." He stepped onto the slick sidewalk teetered like a seesaw.

I sprang to action, my briefcase and purse slipping from my grip as I grabbed his arm—a split second before my high heel caught the edge of the sidewalk. The coffee flew from my hand, a spray of eight-dollar boiling liquid raining down on us before bouncing off the sidewalk, soaking my heels. My hip caught the corner of the curb, and in a display I wasn't proud of, I started wildly grasping at the truck next to me before sliding into the muddy, wet ditch.

Two falls. One day.

As if that wasn't bad enough, my skirt was around my

waist by the time the mud settled. Or coffee, I should say. Yanking down the hem, I focused on the man next to me, who'd managed to remain *on* the sidewalk.

"Are you okay Mr. Jenkins?"

He nodded as he pushed to a stance. "More than I can say for that purse of yours."

I followed his gaze to Louis, my newborn purse, laying against the muddy wheel of the truck—a ball of chewed tobacco stuck to the side.

"Dammit," I whispered, then grasped Chester's hand as he attempted to help me up. I sent a blazing look to the two cowboys chuckling from behind the window of the bakeshop. I repositioned my skirt, then picked up my purse and briefcase in one hand a grocery bag in the other.

"You sure you're okay Mr. Jenkins?"

"Yes, yes, damn heart medication got me a little wobbly, is all. I'm fine." He handed me another bag. "You might not be so fine, though. Your three-thirty appointment has been at your clinic for forty-five minutes already. Was there before I went to the store."

"Forty-five minutes?"

"Yep."

I glanced at the office, windows darkened against the bleak afternoon. If my current luck had anything to do with it, my new patient had probably seen my little tumble on the sidewalk. Nice first impression.

As had everyone else who'd driven by.

Kline and Associates was located off Main Street, down a steep hill lined with quaint shops that catered to tourists. Soaring pine trees enclosed a small commercial lot at the end of the cul-de-sac which was home to *Mulberry Maverick* —Mr. Jenkins' bakeshop—and a cigar shop named *The Back Porch.* At the end, my office. It wasn't lost on me that a mental health clinic was the bookend to two shops that made their money off of addictive indulgences. Coincidence? No way. Smart business move? Absolutely. Like selling Girl Scout Cookies outside of a gym. Genius.

I opened the door to Mulberry Maverick, a place I had a love-hate relationship with. Jenkins could bake, no doubt about that, and my waistline had responded accordingly. Every morning—every *single* morning—the man had a ham and cheese croissant and donut holes waiting for me as I got out of my car. Crack, is what those little balls of sweetened dough were, and based on the amount that went out his door, I wasn't the only one who thought so.

Jenkins had turned his bakery into the local hub for every retired cowboy and military veteran in town, with fresh coffee always on tap and a continuous flow of Willie, Waylon, and Merle floating from the jukebox. Leather booths lined two big windows that overlooked the city admin building where patrons could watch the comings and goings of the day while arguing about politics.

In the afternoons, the scent of freshly baked bread mingled with the sweet cigar smoke from the shop next door, luring my emotionally vulnerable patients to each of their doors like a siren's call. So much for indiscretion. Word is, patients of Kline would swing into the cigar shop, then into Mr. Jenkins' bakeshop where they'd continue their "therapy" over a cup of coffee—free, if I had to guess, considering gossip was like gold to the old man. Although booze wasn't on the menu, it was common knowledge that at least half his drinks were served with some version of pure grain alcohol, making him even more popular. Mulberry Maverick? Should be called *Spill the Tea*. That was the thing about small towns, and Berry Springs was no different.

Nestled deep in the Ozark Mountains, Berry Springs was the quintessential small, southern town where people still called each other sir and ma'am, and the only way to get a decent seat in church was to arrive thirty minutes early. It was a farmer's town, with more cows than people, and where dressing up was considered felt cowboy hats and bejeweled boots.

Springtime was the beginning of tourist season, the town's main source of revenue. People from all over the region traveled to Berry Springs to hike, camp, kayak, tour the local winery, and even hunt—preferably not together. It was a town where time seemed to freeze. Working from dawn until dusk, Monday through Saturday, was capped off by sweet tea on lazy Sunday afternoons.

It was a way of life that, quite frankly, made me itch.

I knew I was different, and not just because I'd been told that my entire public school career. I was different in Berry Springs because I hadn't married at eighteen and pushed out two strapping young boys. While I had long, black hair against pale skin, the gals of Berry Springs wore their spray-tanned curves with pride, curled their bleached hair with hot rollers, and bought Aqua Net by the case.

My black designer clothes and handbags stuck out like sore thumbs. But I didn't care. I'd been called worse than a city-slicker, trust me on that. I fully understood that my "fancy-schmancy things" were filling a deep rooted emotional need, and that was just fine with me. I accepted it and smiled every time the credit card dinged. You see, when you grow up with nothing to call your own, you tend to grip onto material things once you have the means to get them. Okay, fine—more like grasping onto them with bloody fingernails. Freshly manicured, of course.

I ignored the side-long glances from the cowboys as I

followed Jenkins behind the counter where I set down the groceries.

"You look particularly nice today, Miss Floris, aside from the mud of course." He handed me a pack of napkins. "Got a hot date after work?"

"Not sure what you mean by *particularly*..." I winked and wiped myself down, the paper-thin napkins only smearing the mud. "But the only date I've got after work is with that batch of cinnamon rolls you've got cooling on the rack back there."

He winked back. "Swing by after five and I'll send you home with some."

"Count on it."

Just then, the door opened.

"Morning, Mable, sit where you'd like." Jenkins focused back on me. "How old are you now? Thirty? Careful, honey, that you don't slide right into spinster territory."

"One, this isn't the nineteen-fifties, and two, I'm twenty-eight, thank you very much."

He lifted his palms. "Oh, sorry to offend the modern-day feminist."

I rolled my eyes.

"You need to settle down with a good man, Rose. All I'm sayin'."

I busied myself by pulling the milk from the grocery sack, mentally counting the number of times he'd said that exact sentence to me.

"You need someone besides me watching over you." He paused. "Speaking of watching, have you seen that creep around, anymore? The one that would sit outside your office and wait for you?"

I stilled, a chill snaking my spine. "No. That's been taken

care of. And I've told you, you don't need to worry about me, Mr. Jenkins."

"I do, and I will. It's how I was raised. I chased him out of the parking lot a few times. I'll always keep my eye out for you, you know."

"Well, it's not needed, but thank you."

"I keep telling you, you need to date my son."

"Your son is gay, Mr. Jenkins."

His brow cocked. "A woman with your kind of beauty can turn any gay man straight."

"Thanks... I think?"

Jenkins fisted a hand on his hip. "You know, you never did tell me what happened with that last guy you dated."

"You got anything else that needs to go into the fridge?"

He handed me the butter. "Fine, I understand. Keep your secrets. Want my opinion?"

"Why do I feel like you're going to give it anyway?" I hollered as I set the milk and butter in the fridge.

"You were too good for him."

"Thanks." I smiled and squeezed his shoulder. "I gotta go. I'm late."

"Yes, you are. Grab yourself a new cup of coffee. You're going to need it for your new patient, darlin'."

"What do you mean?" Hook, line, sinker.

He scowled as he lined bags of flour on the counter. "Gluten free. Never in a million years did I think I'd be buyin' flour without gluten." He shook his head. "These damn kids and their kooky health crazes these days. Back in my day, we were lucky if even—"

"Back to my new patient... what do you mean I'll need coffee?"

A second passed as he appeared to be gathering his thoughts, or choosing his words carefully. I wasn't sure which. It was the first time the man didn't vomit gossip and I couldn't help but wonder why.

"Ever seen that movie Raging Bull?" He finally said.

"No."

"You're about to."

I frowned, blinked. Uh, come again? My attention was pulled to the whispering cowboys by the window.

"Raging Bull? Try One Flew over the Cuckoo's Nest."

"Kid had it comin' if you ask me. The Mighty King always falls."

Then, the woman piped up. *"That playboy finally found the only thing his billion dollar bank account couldn't get him out of."*

"You've heard of Steele Shadows Security?" Jenkins said, pulling my attention back to him.

I nodded. No one passed through Berry Springs without hearing of the family-owned company that had turned into one of the most prestigious private security firms in the country.

"Your new patient's one of them. Used to be, anyway."

Used to be? Playboy? *Humph.*

An oven dinged from the back reminding me of how late I already was. As much as I wanted to understand what it was about my new patient had gotten the bakeshop so riled up, I wouldn't allow myself to be that late for the appointment. Raging Bull or not.

I pecked Mr. Jenkins on the cheek. "I'll swing back by for those rolls."

"Sounds good, dear."

Jumping from under awning to awning, I darted down the sidewalk then pushed open the mirrored door that read *Kline and Associates.*

"Whoa. *Girl...* what the... Hang on..." Zoey, our eccentric, hipster office manager with more piercings than a tribal leader jumped out of her seat, her overly lined eyes scanning me from head to toe. Guess that answered my question about my appearance.

"Oh my *God.*" She jogged around the desk. "What *happened?*" She snatched Louis from my arms, her attention shifting to the designer bag.

"He fell."

"Oh, no. No, no, no." Ignoring me, she turned back to the desk and began yanking tissues from the box, sending a few flying into the air as she wiped down the handbag. Dramatic, on all counts. As was Zoey. With fire-red hair, the woman spent her paychecks buying vintage designer duds —a slap in the face to her former husband, the son of a senator. He'd tried to change her eccentric ways after they'd married, and in return, she'd taken half his bank account. Zoey had been with Theo from the beginning and despite her eye for detail, she was notorious for dropping the ball on small tasks. The woman's age had become a mystery to me. Some days, the glittery eyeshadow and pink lipstick made her look barely old enough to buy a bottle of wine. Then there were the days she'd drag herself into the office like a stray cat. Those days, the woman was easily pushing forty... and that's being generous.

I grabbed a few of the tissues, popped off my heel and dabbed the saturated insole. There wasn't much worse than wet high heels.

Once satisfied with the bag, Zoey set it on the counter and turned back to me. Her face scrunched in disgust, her nose ring twinkling in the dim lobby lights.

"Girl... you look..."

"I know. It's been a day. Don't." I blew out an exasperated breath, then shook out of my suit jacket, wet, dirty, and smelling of old coffee. I smoothed my blouse as Zoey squatted and wiped down my skirt like a prelude to a cheesy office porno. I found myself glancing out the window, as if the cowboys hadn't gotten enough of a show with my legs split on the sidewalk.

"How did the horse therapy meeting with Theo go?" She asked as she stood.

I sighed. "I don't know."

"He didn't give you a thumbs up?"

"More like the middle finger."

"Dammit. Well, go flash these mile-long legs to him and try again. If I know anything about you, you'll find a way to make it work."

She was right, and those were the exact words I needed to hear at that moment.

"Okay..." Zoey stepped back and surveyed my outfit. "Got most of the mud off. Good day to wear black."

"Where's Cameron?"

"Had an appointment..." she lowered her voice and leaned in. "And by appointment, I mean a lunch date that he still hasn't made it back from."

"Does Theo know?"

She shrugged. "He left a bit ago."

"Where to?"

"Not sure."

My boss had left his door cracked enough to seem accessible to anyone walking in, but closed enough to let us know to stay out. It was no secret that the boss didn't care for our new energetic, charismatic therapist, fresh out of college who looked like he'd stepped out of GQ magazine. Cameron Evans was a trust fund baby with a revolving door of women that rivaled any Sephora store.

"Do we know her name?"

"Do we ever?"

"Good point." I glanced at the clock. "Crap, I've gotta—"

"Yeah, your new client's been here for forty-five minutes. Got here early."

I looked around the lobby. "Where is he?"

"I let him in your office. He wasn't exactly... patient."

Raging Bull...

I grabbed my purse from the counter and as I started to turn, Zoey grabbed my arm.

"What?"

She plucked a tube of lip gloss from her pocket—because who doesn't carry a tube of lip gloss in their pocket?—and slathered some on my lips.

I wrinkled my nose, smacking the slimy paste. "Ugh, this tastes like sugar and mint."

"Yeah. It freshens while it plumps."

"Do I really look that bad?"

She yanked down the neckline of my blouse and pushed up my breasts, and for the second time, my gaze flickered to the window.

"No. You look fine..." Her grin curled to her ears. "You're just gonna want to look better." With a wink, Zoey stepped back and nodded to my closed office door. "Go get 'em, tiger."

Frowning, I turned toward my office, nerves tickling in my stomach. I didn't know what the heck I was about to walk into, but between Mr. Jenkins' warning and Zoey's fondling, I wasn't sure I wanted to.

Little did I know, that single meeting was about to change the course of my life.

4

ROSE

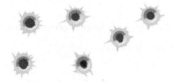

a fter taking a quick second to review my new patient's file, I stepped into my office—and stopped dead in my tracks. The dark silhouette faced the window, sitting in *my chair*. His back was to me, his feet kicked up on the windowsill as if he owned the place. He appeared to be staring at the rainy mountain landscape outside.

The first thing I noticed was the size of his feet, two dirty cowboy boots crossed at the ankles, a trail of mud running down the wall. I literally cringed. He had brown, shaggy hair that looked like it hadn't seen a pair of scissors in months, and a neck as thick as a tree trunk. A tattoo peeked out of the collar of a black leather jacket stretched over the widest shoulders I'd ever seen.

I blinked. Although he had to have heard the door open, the man didn't move. Yep, my new patient, whom I'd never met, had made himself right at home behind *my* desk in *my* office chair. Had he gone through my stuff? Pilfered through *my* space? My mind began spinning with all the confidential information he could have read on my desk. Totally unacceptable, and totally inappropriate.

Little did I know what kind of inappropriate this man had in store for me.

"Thanks for showing up." The faceless voice was jarringly low. As smooth as the icing on Mr. Jenkins cinnamon buns, and as loaded as a ham and cheese croissant. The man was pissed. At *me*.

"Excuse me?"

He kicked his boots off the window, plopping them onto the floor with a thud, leaving enough mud to fill the Grand Canyon. Another cringe.

"You're late," he said, still not gracing me with the front part of his body.

No *way*. This was not happening. Who did this guy think he was? I bit the inside of my cheek and squared my shoulders. *Professional, professional, you need this job, be professional,* Thorn reminded me.

"I apologize, Mr..." I glanced at the name typed on the file in my hands. "Steele."

"Phoenix."

The chair swiveled and a flutter of butterflies rippled through me.

And I thought the voice was jarring...

His eyes were the color of a tropical ocean, a baby blue, almost iridescent, if not for the heat that spilled from them. The lines of his face were sharp with defined angles, a mirror to the disinterest he wore like a beacon, blinking brightly, making sure I knew he didn't care to be there. Days of unkempt scruff covered his clenched jaw line, pulling my attention to a pair of lips that had me licking my own. Circles shaded his puffy, aqua eyes with wrinkles at the edges suggesting he was a good decade older than me, possibly pushing even forty. A grey T-shirt fit snugly under that leather jacket, defining a pair of pecs I could only assume were as hard as the expression he was pinning me with. I felt my weight to my tiptoes, like a magnet being pulled, assessing him with a frowned expression that I knew was giving me away. Because under all that weather-beaten, overtly masculine appearance, narrowed eyes, and locked jaw, there was a strikingly handsome man. Hidden, almost as if on purpose.

I'd never seen an aura before, but the man vibrated the air around him in a hostile, dark cloud like an animal warning of its presence. I could actually *feel* him in my office.

A Mighty King. Fallen.

He held a plaque in his hand—my diploma—gripped loosely at calloused fingertips as if letting me know what he thought about it. Not much. He'd taken it off the wall, where I'd so proudly hung it months earlier. This little power play ripped me out of my hypnotic gape. He was playing a mind game, and I didn't like it. Ballsy, too, coupled with the fact that he'd settled behind my desk.

This was my first indication that my new patient was going to be like all the other macho males that crossed through my door. Too *manly* to take care of the most important organ in their body—their brain, to be clear, because trust me, I'd done the leg work there. Too prideful to speak to a female doctor. As if my vagina somehow made me less capable. They were my worst patients, my headache patients. The patients that made me want to throw myself out the window.

Good thing I knew how to deal with them, though, and it was time to show this one who was boss. To watch him fall in line as the others always did. Because I was the doctor, and he was the patient, and that was how it was going to be.

"Phoenix," I repeated his name as I crossed the room,

both tone and step colored with attitude. "As I said, I apologize for being late—"

"Accident on the south side of Shadow Mountain?"

I cocked my head. "Actually. Yes."

"Should've taken the cut off before Snakepit Road, then looped around."

My gaze shifted to the stack of mail on my desk, some with my home address on them. Sneaky bastard. I narrowed my eyes and leveled him. "Mr—"

"Phoenix."

"Phoenix," I said between clenched teeth, my patience from my crappy day waning. "If you wouldn't mind, please take your seat on the couch and we'll begin."

He stared at me a moment, the slightest curve touching those lips as if my authority was humoring him. A subtle, cocky expression I assumed came as naturally to him as his next breath. It was a look that made women either fall to their knees, or take a few steps back.

Not this woman.

This was *my* office, *my* territory.

He was *my* patient.

He tossed my plaque on the desk before standing.

Jerk. Agreed, Thorn. Agreed.

My chin tilted upward as he stood, unfolding himself from the chair that seemed so tiny underneath him. The man was massive. I guessed six four—at the very least. He stepped toward me, eyes locked on mine in a way that sent another tickle of butterflies through my stomach, a weird mixture of attraction and nerves incited by an intimidating presence that seemed so innate to him. I felt like a bunny encountering a wolf in the woods. Cautious, wary, curious.

I forced myself to keep eye contact as he brushed past me, his hips sweeping past my own leaving a spark of heat on my skin. It was then that I realized my pulse had picked up sometime during our interaction.

Phoenix Steele was throwing me off my game. I needed to get a grip and reverse the roles between us that had somehow switched to his favor.

I stepped behind my desk, taking a quick scan of what else he might have seen—or, taken, for that matter. But everything seemed to be in its designated spot, including my cleaned, empty coffee mug that read *I'd Rather Have a Margarita*. This, a cheeky little gift from Zoey after our first outing together as budding work friends. That night had ended with her head hanging out of a taxi and me with a stamp on my forehead that read *do not serve*. A few folders sat to the side, each color-coordinated and labeled. Above that, a cork board covered in post-its of the million to-dos I'd yet to cross off. Lastly, a Bob Ross desk calendar—another gift from Zoey. A blinking light from below my desk caught my eye. My computer was on, and I always turned it off when I left for the day. It was number three on my "walking-out-the-door" checklist. I frowned, looked at my laptop and monitor, both black, then at the piercing pair of eyes watching my every move.

Holy smokes, the guy was *intense*.

I cleared my throat and flipped open the folder labeled *Phoenix Steele*.

"Would you like some water?"

He lifted the bottle he'd helped himself to from my mini-fridge—*under my desk*.

"Okay, then. So. Have you been to a counselor before?"

"Is your last name really Floris?"

I blinked. "... Yes."

"You're Italian, then."

"No, I'm American. My grandparents are Italian."

"Both sides?"

"Just one."

He plucked a green crystal from a decorative bowl I had on the coffee table. He turned it over in his hands.

"Vesuvianite," he observed.

My brows raised. "That's right."

"A mineral found at the base of Mount Vesuvius."

"Hence the name."

"Hence." He mocked me. "Have you been?"

"To Mount Vesuvius?"

"Yes."

"No."

"To Italy."

I shifted. "No."

"So you just think they're pretty, then."

"Vesuvianite is said to have healing properties. To override the energy of the ego and aid in spiritual growth and forward movement." Note to self to get an entire truckload for this guy.

"If you believe in that sort of thing."

"If you believe in that sort of thing," I repeated, rather condescending.

"Floris." He repeated my last name as if deciding whether to believe me or not. The emerald green stone sliding through his fingertips. "Rose Floris?"

Where the heck was he going with this? "That's correct."

"Floris means flower in Italian."

"Yep."

"... So your name is Rose Flower."

"... No. My name is Rose *Floris.*"

We stared at each other, one trying to deflect, one trying to reign in her impatience. Seriously, I was *beyond* not in the mood.

Turn the tables, I told myself.

"Anyway, as I was saying, or asking rather, have you ever been to a counselor before this?"

"I thought you were a doctor."

Geez. "I am. Let me rephrase. Have you ever been to a psychologist before?"

"No."

"Psychiatrist?"

"I don't believe in Psychiatry."

"Why not?"

"Throwing drugs at a problem only masks it."

Narrow-minded macho male. Check.

"There's a lot more to psychiatry than prescribing drugs." And little did he know, my evaluation was the only thing that was keeping him from seeing a psychiatrist. If I decided that medication would assist in his therapy, I had been advised to give the referral. And from what I'd seen already, I was guessing this guy could use more than just a truckload of vesuvianite. More like a steady flow of valium in the veins.

He leaned back, letting me know he disagreed with my comment, and had nothing else to say about it.

"So we've established that this is your first time visiting a psychologist. Good. Let's review why you're here first, and then—"

"I'm here because the local healthcare system saw an opportunity to pull a few more pennies from my pocket before leaving me alone."

"Is that what you think?"

"That's what I said." He leaned forward on his elbows. "And let me guess, your next question is going to be 'how do you feel about that'?"

The sparkle of attraction I'd had was quickly evaporating. In fact, it had already disintegrated.

"We won't get into those questions yet, Mr. Steele."

"Phoenix."

I ignored him and began flipping through the pages of his file. "I'll review why you're here, according to your medical file, because it's important that we start out on the same page. Will that work for you, Phoenix?"

The snarl of his lip told me if there had been any attraction on his part as well, it was also long gone.

I grabbed my reading glasses from the drawer, slid them on, and focused on the file that I was ashamed to say I'd only skimmed when Zoey created his account. Typically, I'd take at least thirty minutes before an appointment to review notes, but that day had been, well, horse crap.

"According to Dr. Buckley at the Berry Springs Medical clinic, and your neuropsychological evaluation, you are suffering from mild PTA, or post-traumatic-amnesia, and PCS, or post-concussion syndrome, including a decrease in fine motor skills, intermittent confusion, and behavioral changes as a result of a traumatic brain injury. Does this sound correct to you?"

His gaze had drifted to the floor—the first time they hadn't been fixed on me. His toe began to *tap, tap, tap* against the hardwood floor.

I continued going down the list. "According to your assessment, somatosensory issues include dizziness and occasional double vision. Motor issues include hemiparesis, or occasional weakness, as well as slowed performance," he literally twitched at that one, "and cognitive issues include attention, concentration, judgment and reasoning. Finally, the behavioral issues noted are decreased inhibition, impulsivity"—another twitch—"inappropriate behavior, anxiety, anger, and irritability."

Highlighted in yellow under the list read: *List not exhaustive, patient participation unwilling and unforthcoming with any and all symptoms.* In other words, Phoenix had continually told the doctors he felt "fine."

I continued, "Due to this, Dr. Buckley referred you to a physical therapist to rehabilitate your motor skills, and referred you to me to address the behavioral changes you are experiencing. Does all this sound right?"

He'd picked a spot on the table to focus on. I was surprised the wood didn't burst into flames.

"Does this align with what you understand to be true, Phoenix?"

"On second thought, call me Mr. Steele."

"Mr. *Steele,* does this align with what you understand?"

He looked up, those blue eyes narrowed to slits again, but this time, a deep flush started working its way up his neck.

"Let me tell you what I understand. I understand that I no longer have a driver's license or my concealed carry license, both of which were taken from me after I woke up from a coma. I understand that in order to get these things back, I need you to check a little box that says I'm cleared. That's what I understand, Miss Flower."

"Doctor Floris," I growled back.

We glared at each other like two boxers about to throw down. Street fighters is probably a better description.

Be the one in control. You are *in control. Focus on the facts.*

"Your driver's license has been suspended by the DMV at the recommendation of Dr. Buckley until you complete therapy, your gun license—"

"—concealed carry." He corrected.

My head was officially about to explode. "Your *concealed carry* license…" I literally did air quotes with my fingers. "…

was suspended because federal law prohibits possession of a firearm by a person who has been adjudicated as mentally defective, whether temporary or permanently."

"You think I'm mentally defective, doctor?"

And that was my first little alarm with Phoenix Steele. Behind that tone, an anger began to simmer. One that my gut was telling me only released into a volcano of fury. There was a feral look in his eyes now that had goosebumps prickling my skin.

Unstable? Without question. And I *did not* like loose cannons.

I cleared my throat. "Based on your medical file, I think it was a wise decision to place you in therapy, Mr. Steele."

His hands curled into fists on his knees as he stared back at me. It was the first time the nerves of the little bunny looking at the big bad wolf turned into a trickle of fear.

I shut his file and switched angles. This man would not scare me.

"Okay. Fine. Let's cut through the pillow talk, then, shall we? You were shot in the head, Phoenix. A traumatic experience for *anyone,* and something that warrants a little couch-time for *anyone.*" I nodded at his file. "Even a former special ops Marine, current CEO of Steele Shadows Security, and a stand-in father to three younger brothers—"

He surged to his feet, a wild expression contorting his face that had me both scooting back in my chair, and rethinking my own *concealed carry* license. I remained calm, still, with an impassive expression on my face even though my heartbeat had just skyrocketed.

Phoenix stalked to the front of my desk, gripped the edge and leaned forward, inches from my face.

"You don't know anything about me, Dr. Flower." He seethed. "You don't know anything about my family. And I'm not going to talk about me getting shot in the head, or about them. If you want to know what happened, feel free to ask ol' Jenkins next door, or have breakfast at Donny's Diner where the topic is served up like the daily fucking special." His grip on my desk had his knuckles turning white. "Let me make one thing clear. I'm not here to talk about the past. I'm here to get my independence back."

"You've made that very clear, Mr. Steele." My tone was calm, but my nails were digging into my thighs under the desk. "And you're in luck, because the therapy I do is based on CBT—Cognitive Behavioral Therapy—and does not focus, or dwell, on the past. It focuses on the now."

He blinked and I swear I caught a flash of relief on his face. Only a flash.

I continued. "It's also clear that your independence relies on my final evaluation, and the sooner you accept that, the sooner you can have it back. We have the same goal here, Mr. Steele. I'm just trying to get you, your life, back to normal. To do that, I've got to take a look under the hood—and I need you to let me."

"If that's the case, Miss Floris..." My name rolled off his tongue like a taunt. "I'd be more than happy to give you a look under my hood." His gaze dropped to my breasts, lingering, while he licked his lips. A lump caught in my throat as my pulse roared in my ears.

He reached into his pocket and slid me his wallet. "Or, you can take a look in there, if you'd like, *doctor.*"

My eyes rounded in total, complete shock.

A bribe.

A freaking *bribe!* The smug jerk was offering me a bribe. What. The. Hell? I'd just walked into my own version of Goodfellas.

The *gall* of it. That I'd even consider it. That I was that desperate. That weak of a human being. That he could control me like that.

I forced my hand not to tremble with anger as I slowly pushed the wallet away, leaned back in my chair and crossed my arms over my chest, my gaze never leaving his.

And that was my first experience with Phoenix Steele's erratic, impulsive behavior that had landed him in my office in the first place.

Like a flash of lightning, he obliterated my desk with one swipe of his arms, sending my phone, files, computer monitors clamoring onto the floor and my heart slamming against my ribcage.

I froze in shock.

Chest heaving, he resumed his grip on the now-bare desk and leaned in, this time, so close I could feel his breath.

"No money?" His voice was low, menacing. "Okay. How about I give you a look under my hood right here, right now, on this desk?"

One hand began undoing his belt, the other slid over my hand.

My mouth *dropped*. Unhinged.

Rage mixed with adrenaline shot through me like liquid acid. My body trembled as I rose from the chair, facing the bastard nose to nose.

A rumble of thunder sounded in the distance.

"There's not enough money in the world for me to take a look at what you've got in your pants, Mr. Steele. And if you ever talk to me like that again, I'll personally remove your balls, shove each one down your throat, and ensure no woman ever takes a look under that hood again."

5

ROSE

*Y*ou've heard the term white-knuckle before. Well, that night, the phrase took on an entirely new meaning. More like iridescent knuckles. The sweet little afternoon rainstorm had turned into a monsoon. Rain so thick you couldn't see more than a few feet in front of you.

It was after eight o'clock by the time I left the office. To say that my meeting with Mr. Phoenix Steele had set me on edge was an understatement. Don't get me wrong, I've had plenty of difficult patients in my office over the years—not all men by the way—but none that had destroyed it.

Or bribed me with money and sex.

It had taken me ten minutes to calm down after he'd stormed out, and four times that to put my desk back together. Zoey had ran in after Phoenix had barged out. I'd lied and told her I'd tripped and there was nothing to worry about. I wasn't sure why I didn't tell her the truth other than I was still in shock that it happened at all. A weird part of me was embarrassed that I couldn't handle a patient. That I had allowed it to get that far. Also, the fact that a billionaire

CEO having a mental breakdown in my office would be too tempting for Zoey to spread all over town. Call it professionalism, but I couldn't let that happen—even though the jerk totally deserved it. I did, however, tell Zoey not to book any more appointments with 'said jerk' until I could review his file in more detail. And by "review his file," I mean find him another therapist. Because no woman should tolerate being treated like that. I'd never walked away from a client in my life, and believe me, there had been dozens that I wanted to, but I'd never been spoken to like that by one, either.

I wouldn't stand for it.

Aside from all that, I was sure the guy wouldn't come back, anyway. My guess was that he'd never set foot in a therapy clinic again. All that pride, of course.

After that blessed appointment, I'd spent hours catching up on emails, reviewing cases, and returning calls that had been sitting in my mailbox for days. I was restless, edgy, hyped up. And when Mr. Jenkins had delivered a Bloody Mary and box of cinnamon buns to my office with a note that read '*Go Home*', I'd decided to close up and do just that.

When I'd purchased my first home—*real* home, not apartment—eight months earlier, I'd underestimated the drive from the office. Not the length of time, but the difficulty of it. My new home was located on the peak of one of the tallest mountains in Berry Springs, with a narrow two-lane road snaking up to it. It was seven minutes from Main Street and my office, but any kind of weather, other than sun, added time to the drive, including the year-round fog. Jagged cliffs hugged one side of the road and steep ravines the other. Someone had attempted to put up guardrails on the shoulders, but those had been destroyed by what I assumed were accidents that didn't end well.

That night, it had taken me twenty minutes to get home

and when I'd finally made it up my long, curvy driveway, I was beyond exhausted.

Rain blurred the small, rock and log cabin against a black landscape that in sunlight showed miles of mountains in the distance. In good weather, I had a postcard-perfect view from my deck. That night, oak and pine trees that enclosed the house sagged under the weight of the rain sparkling off the branches in my headlights.

Despite the dilapidated wraparound porch and crumbling shingles, the realtor had called it a craftsman home. I'd called it the most beautiful thing I'd ever seen, but was sold when I saw the sweeping windows that overlooked the mountains. There was just something about it. Something about it that felt like *home.* And that feeling was as foreign to me as Sunday dinners and family traditions.

I'd purchased it on the spot and began renovations the next month.

It was my little place, *my own,* and I loved it.

I rolled to a stop under the carport, an addition I'd added after I purchased my new BMW SUV. New house, new car, and the best part was that I'd saved up enough to put half down on both before signing on the dotted line.

Things were going well.

At least that's what I'd thought.

I cut the engine and blew out a breath as I peeled each finger off the steering wheel. After grabbing my purse and briefcase from the passenger seat, I got out of the car—and stopped cold.

I stared at it for a moment, the vibrant colors of purple against the dark wood of my front door, the deep green petals.

An exotic orchid in full bloom.

The craziest thing was that my first thought went to

Phoenix. I quickly laughed that thought away, though, because *Mr. Steele* didn't seem the apologizing type, especially to a woman. He also didn't seem the type to send flowers for any occasion... unless they were Venus flytraps, of course.

No, I knew who they were from. They were a dramatic reminder of a decision I'd fought over sleepless nights. A part of my past that I wish would *go away.*

A gust of cold wind whipped my hair around my face, sending a chill up my spine. I glanced around the woods and down the driveway that disappeared into the trees. A solid minute passed as I stood there listening for any reason to justify the weird feeling that I wasn't alone.

You're being ridiculous, I told myself.

I sighed, crossed the deck, my heels echoing into the dark night. My immediate instinct was to kick over the flowers, but instead, I picked up the chilled vase. The smell hit my nose like a high-dollar perfume.

No—like a hundred pounds of guilt.

Right there in my hand.

Juggling the load that included more than the weight in my hands, I unlocked the door, stepped inside and kicked it closed with my foot. Water sloshed out of the vase and onto the floor. Cursing, I set the flowers on the table next to the door.

I needed a drink.

Leaving a trail of heels through the living room, I beelined it to the kitchen with singular focus.

I ripped the cork from my favorite Bordeaux like a rabid hyena and poured a man-sized glass. I closed my eyes, inhaling the earthy smokiness swirling in my glass, then sipped.

Heaven in a bottle.

I turned my focus to the flowers pulling my attention like a beacon from my doorway. Clutching my wine glass at my chest, I leaned against the kitchen doorway and doubted, for the millionth time, the decision I'd made eight weeks earlier to end the relationship. A part of me hated him for not letting go, but a part of me liked it, culminating in a confused mixture of self-doubt that had landed me in the mess in the first place.

Damn the self-doubt.

I mindlessly swirled the wine in my glass, staring at the flowers until I noticed the white envelope tucked between the petals.

He'd left a note.

Fan-freaking-tastic.

Well, I didn't have to read it, did I?

I stuck my nose in the air, pushed off the doorway and clicked on the living room light. Then, I rearranged the pillows on my couch. Then, the Vogue magazines on the coffee table—by month this time, not volume number. After a few more minutes of trying to convince myself that I didn't care what the card said, I gave up and walked over to the flowers, eyeing the arrangement like a newborn baby.

I set down my wine, plucked the envelope, and read the three simple words.

I miss you.

Those three little words heavier than the metal he used to listen to, that I despised.

My shoulders dropped.

What was wrong with me? Why couldn't I just love him? Every other woman in town did.

Why did I run from every relationship I'd ever had?

Why couldn't I allow myself to give someone a real shot? A *real* shot.

I knew why. In my heart, I knew the answer. It was a part of my past that no amount of CBT could cure. A culmination of a series of events that had shaped who I was. The evolution of the terminally-single woman.

That was me. And a psychologist, in an ironic twist. Those who can't do, teach. Right?

I tossed the card on the table and decided the only way I was going to relax was if I finished my wine in a scorching bubble bath. I made my way into the bedroom and flicked the lights, and received my second surprise of the evening— a brown teddy bear sitting in the middle of my bed.

I didn't own a teddy bear. Had never owned a teddy bear. True story.

The bow around its neck was a velvety red with gold sparkles along the edges, the beady black eyes staring into my soul.

I glanced at the orchids by the door, then back to the stuffed animal. My eyes drifted from window to window as I set my wine on the bureau and crossed the room.

I stared at the stuffed animal for a few more seconds before picking it up.

I hated it.

Immediately. I hated it.

There was no card, no sweet, little *To/From* stitching on its furry little feet. Nothing.

Frowning, my thoughts spun with all sorts of scenarios. First, why would my former fiancé leave exotic flowers on the front porch during a thunderstorm, but put a stuffed animal on my bed? Then, my thoughts froze on one epiphany—my former fiancé didn't have the keys to my house. I'd changed the locks after ending the engagement.

I chewed on my lower lip, a nasty habit I'd developed when I was nervous.

Maybe I'd forgotten to lock the door when I came by to change earlier in the day? No. I always locked my door.

Had someone broken in?

My heart started to pound. I set the bear on the bed, then went through each room of my house—all three of them—checking the doors and windows. Each was locked, with no obvious sign of forced entry. I contemplated calling the police, but considering I'd called them twice in the last handful of months, I decided against it. Both times had ended with them implying I was crazy, and me feeling even crazier.

I stopped in the middle of my living room, my gaze landing on the bookcases that flanked the fireplace. I squinted, staring at the two vesuvianite bookends that I was sure were out of place.

Were they out of place? Or was I going crazy?

I made my way back to the bedroom and stared at the bear.

I didn't know who it was from, I didn't know how the thing got into my house, but knew I didn't like it.

I also knew the little warning bells in my head were going off a mile a minute.

6

PHOENIX

*T*he wind sliced through my jacket, an assault of icy raindrops against my already-drenched clothes. Spring be damned. After wiping the rain from my forehead, I repositioned the flashlight on the log behind me and took a quick survey of the woods, knowing I wasn't the only animal lurking after nightfall that deep in the mountains. It was that time of night between twilight and darkness where a muted blue glow settled between the trees. It had been a bleak, depressing rainy day with relentless downpours as the hours passed. The temper tantrum I'd thrown in Dr. Rose Floris's office had been nothing to the thunderstorms later that afternoon. There was no sun to slink behind the mountains that day, only a blanketed sky promising more erratic seasonal weather to come, and hopefully, more rain to scrub the image of the assertive, pain-in-my-ass doctor from my thoughts.

Rose Flower—as I'd dubbed her in my head—had hair as black as raven's wings and as silky and shiny as the fender on my Harley. Her eyes, wide and almond shaped with dark irises that had me questioning how many shades of black there were. Heavy, hooded lids lended themselves to a resting look of skepticism, while endless black, feathered lashes gave her an unintended sensuality sure to make even the most committed monk question his vows. The lines of her face were sharp and defined, suggesting a beauty of some sort of eastern European descent. Her body was long and lean with just enough curve to grip onto under the sheets. And when she'd finally opened her mouth, she'd spoken with a sharp, confident tone as bold as the designer suit she'd had on. The woman was stuffy, uptight, and sexy as *fuck*. But all that paled in comparison to those lips. Those fucking lips. Plump, pouty, and crimson red.

The color of Rose.

The color of her cheeks after my dumbass had bribed her with money and sex then exploded like a rabid ape in her office. Which, over the course of the evening, I'd decided was for the best, because Rose Floris, in all her judgy, condescending, brain-analyzing glory was everything I never wanted in a woman, including the fact that she had the upper hand. And I *really* hated that. Not just because I wasn't in the habit of letting a woman get the upper hand of anything on me—unless it came in the form of whips and chains, of course—but because this particular woman *knew* she held the key to my independence. This *psychologist* had control over me. Of all freaking people, a head doctor.

The hits just kept coming.

A bead of sweat rolled down my temple as I grabbed another nail. *Focus,* I reminded myself, the buzz of rain like an orchestra of bees in my head, the pricks of pain like stingers between my temples.

Damn headaches.

Focus, Phoenix.

With every swing of the hammer, raindrops snuck past

my collar, little devil's fingertips sliding down my back. The sensation was temporary, though. I focused on each one, at the exact spot on my spine where the feeling faded to nothing, reminding me of the science experiment I'd turned into. As if I needed a fucking reminder.

Numbness. Complete loss of feeling in random spots of my body. That was one of the many *symptoms*—as they called them—that had slipped by good ol' Dr. Buckley and his team. My team of "medical professionals," as they liked to call themselves. I called them overpaid assholes with a God complex. The overpaid asswipes who'd decided to take away my freedom—my *life*—after skimming the results of a few bullshit mandatory tests.

"Temporarily mentally deficient", the tests read.

Un-*fucking*-believable.

A rumble of thunder sounded in the distance.

I gritted my teeth and pounded the nail, the smooth rhythm I'd established began to waver.

It was coming. That mood swing brewing in my gut like licking flames, igniting me from the inside out. My pulse started to increase as I warned myself to get a grip before it happened, but in an ironic twist, this only ignited it more because I knew I couldn't control it.

These types of mood swings were new to me—not the anger, the rage; trust me, I was very familiar with those emotions. Hell, I'd built an entire career on them. No, the type of anger I'd felt since waking up from my coma was an entirely new kind of mad. An immediate, uncontrollable wave of white hot fury that gripped ahold of me like a bear trap, vibrating until it exploded out of me. Tossing a computer on the floor? *Ha,* that was nothing. Only a touch of what this new—impulsive was the word they'd used— Phoenix was capable of. And honestly, the doctors had no idea how bad it really was. Of course they didn't. They'd never been shot in the head before.

I couldn't help but wonder if this was the universe's way of doling out karma. My old life had finally caught up to me. After all, not many people had killed as many men as I had. Mission or not, I'd ended their lives. How many? Countless. I knew because the nightmares played on loop since waking up. Good thing I never slept. Another symptom. Loss of sleep. They didn't document that one either. Meticulous bastards.

My jaw clenched as I connected with the nail, again, and again, each hit harder than the last.

Yeah it was coming.

It started with a rush of heat over my skin as what I assumed resembled a hot flash, giving me an entirely new respect for the enigma of the female body. It was beyond me how women even got out of bed in the mornings. Complex creatures, they were.

After the hot flash, the shakes would come. Trembles, whatever. At that point, I'd tell my brain, *'It's coming, you crazy bastard; stop,'* as if the organ was independent of my body. But then, adrenaline would flood my system like a drug. And that was it. I was at the mercy of the rampage I'd thrown down.

It was a force greater than myself. I hated it. For someone who demanded control, *not* being able to control my body was maddening. This new fury was an unre-strained, uncontrollable temper tantrum that overcame rational thought, or whatever incoherent thoughts made up whatever the hell my brain had become. Everything became a fog, static on a television, when it began to brew. Not confusion, just... nothing. It was as if my brain had cleared, an emptiness allowing the emotion to flood inside and take over.

And it did.

Holy *shit* it did.

When it would happen, I didn't exist. Only the rage.

More often than not, it would be a verbal onslaught of insults and threats I hadn't heard since my days in the barracks. But sometimes, most recently it seemed, it became physical. I'd destroy anything and everything in my path. The Incredible-fucking-Hulk. Although the difference there was that Hulk turned back into a nice guy after his temper tantrums.

Not me.

Afterward, I'd snap out of it, usually at the hands of my brothers, either physically restraining me, or coaxing me off the ledge as if I were a toddler. I hated that. Beating me to a pulp, that I could handle. Talking to me like an infant? I wanted to tear them limb from limb.

Things would slowly begin to register, and the first thing I would notice would be that look in my brothers' eyes.

Irritation, exhaustion. And the worst—pity.

Then, they'd hang around for a while, making sure I was "okay." They'd even altered their schedules since "the incident" to ensure I was never alone at the house. They'd changed their lives to accommodate me.

I, the oldest Steele brother and heir to the Steele family fortune, had become a drain on the family.

They probably thought I didn't notice the looks, hear the whispers. I did. If anything, my hearing had reached super-human levels. Go figure. It didn't make sense. I didn't understand it. All I knew was that every day, there was something else in me that didn't work quite right. Or, at all.

The doctors told me the symptoms I was experiencing

were consistent with traumatic brain injuries and would subside within six months to a year.

A *year.*

I was familiar with TBI. Any soldier who'd run black ops for decades usually was. But now I knew that no one could really understand until it happened to them. It's hard for me to explain how screwed up it is—ironic, by the way. You wake up and you're just suddenly... different.

During the course of a casual conversation, I'd have moments of confusion where memories simply weren't there. I got lost mid-conversation and had no idea what the other person was talking about. This wasn't an abnormal occurrence with Gage—my unfiltered, hot-headed, scattered brother whose conversations typically included the size of a woman's breasts. But this never happened with Axel, my neurotic, laser-focused brother whose every word had intent and meaning. Gunner, on the other hand, I could handle because most of his conversations revolved around the words, 'let's go clean our guns.' That I could do.

Although no one said it, my role as CEO of Steele Shadows Security was on hold until everything got back to normal. Days that used to be spent catering to clients and bar hopping were now spent doing whatever manual labor I could find around our thousand-acre property. An endless job, thankfully. Getting my hands dirty, swinging an axe or a hammer, was the only thing that made me feel like myself. The *old* me.

Then, the sun would fall and darkness would come. Some nights I wouldn't sleep at all, resorting to pacing back and forth for hours. In the dark. In the silence. Those nights were the bad ones. I could *feel* a hole in my head. An empty, black hole that used to be *something,* was no more. Hours and hours I'd pace with my eyes on the mountains in the distance, waiting for the light. For another day as this 'new me.'

Another day of questioning who I was, who'd I become.

Another day of being treated like a ticking pipe bomb.

The mental stuff was bad, I'm not going to lie. But I took solace in the fact that neither my brothers, nor my doctors, could actually step inside my brain and know what was really happening in there. Hell, Gage would have me in a strait jacket in a padded room in seconds flat.

The worst part were the physical issues I'd been experiencing since waking up. I learned that the area of my brain that was injured controlled my fine motor skills. Fantastic.

Before "the incident," I could outrun, outmaneuver, outfight, and outshoot anyone in the military. In peak physical shape, I benched a solid four-twenty, could squat five-fifty, and deadlift a clean six-thirty. I was a machine, a trained weapon who didn't back down to anyone or anything. There wasn't a battle I couldn't fight, a brawl I couldn't dismantle, a woman I couldn't bring to her knees.

Funny how things can change in an instant.

The first time I noticed something was up was within an hour of waking up from the coma. I'd gripped the rails of the hospital bed—cage, more like—and attempted to pull myself up to a seated position. *Attempted* being the key word. My grip wavered and I fell back into the pillows. I couldn't close my fist. I'll never, ever forget that moment. It was the first moment of fear—real, ice-cold fear—I'd felt in years. The thought of not being "physically able" terrified me. It wasn't me. I prided myself on my strength and to lose any of it was an assault to my psyche worse than any confusion or temper tantrum. I remember looking at my hand, turning my palm over and staring at it as if it wasn't part of my body. My hand was no longer my own, simply a casualty to circumstance. Then, the pain began to register. Damaged nerve endings, they'd said. Fuck you, I'd said back. It would come in waves, a hot searing pain like acid. Again, they said all this would fade over time, but the thing was, I could handle the pain. The intermittent inability to grip something was unacceptable. I felt it in my legs too, my knees, a foreign sensation suggesting they could buckle at a moment's notice.

I'd never hated my body. My weapon. My temple.

I did now.

I'd fought many battles in my life, both on and off the battlefield, but nothing like this. This was a new kind of enemy. One that I couldn't overpower with my fists. One that I couldn't destroy with a grenade. One that I couldn't walk away from.

So what did I do? I pushed it all aside. The pain, the confusion, the weakness. Why? Because that was the only way I could deal with it, the only way I could cope. Mind over matter, right? I'd grab my tools and head to the woods to mend fences. Escape to nature where I pretended nothing had happened and I'd try to get back to the Phoenix Steele I knew.

Exactly as I was doing at that moment.

A swift gust of wind kicked me off balance. A distant *crack* had my head lifting, the sound echoing through the woods around me. I glanced up at the pine tree above me, its branches bending with the weight of the rain. Branches were beginning to break.

I positioned another nail on the wood, noticing the throbbing prickles at my fingertips. I drew the hammer back and connected but the nail didn't split the wood. Again, and again. The nail didn't budge.

The damn thing wouldn't budge.

I checked the tip of the nail like an idiot. Yep, it was sharp.

I cleared my throat, a murmuring commentary telling me to keep my cool. With a slight inhale, I repositioned the nail, blew out the breath, then slammed it again. This time the hammer tumbled out of my hand, landing on my boot.

I surged to my feet, lips snarling to stifle a scream. My breath came out in rapid puffs of steam around my head. I began to pace to release the energy building inside me. Pacing, pacing, pacing, I squeezed my hands into fists, talking myself off the ledge.

I can do this, I told myself.

I can do this, I can do this, I can do this...

Clenching my jaw, I plucked the hammer from the muddy ground, kneeled back down at the fence and pounded that damn nail until it went in. Seconds faded into minutes, minutes faded into an hour as I worked on that fence, all rational thought replaced by the need to meet my goal. To finish what I'd started—which should have taken twenty minutes. Twilight faded into an inky blackness, the rain a deluge as I hammered nail after nail, picking up the hammer each time it slipped from my weak grip to start again.

I would not give up.

I'd removed my jacket sometime after the first half hour, welcoming the precipitation against my skin. I had tunnel vision. Nothing else mattered other than mending that damn fence, a normal job for old Phoenix, a challenging one for new Phoenix.

I was into my third hour when a familiar snort pulled me from my focus, a big, black nose nudging my shoulder. I set down my hammer and turned to Spirit, my four-year-old

Arabian horse. Her milky white body seemed to glow through the darkness.

"You find what you went looking for?"

Another snort.

"Good." I stroked her coal-black mane, slick with rain, and found myself picturing Rose Flower's hair.

"Got a little chilly on us tonight, didn't it, girl?" I glanced at the fence, then back at Spirit.

A moment ticked by.

"Okay. I hear you. Let's get you back to the barn."

After collecting my tool bag and jacket, I pulled myself onto Spirit and together, we made our way through the woods, slow and steady through the cold rain. I focused on the smooth rocking of her steps, an easy rhythm we'd established over the last few weeks, unlike months ago when I would take her on sprints through the fields. We didn't need directions, we didn't need light. This was our land and we'd walked it together countless times since "the incident."

That slow, easy rhythm.

I gripped her reins as she soared over a wooden fence before making our way across the open field. I listened to the sound of the rain, the thump of her heels on the ground, the silence, the stillness around me.

I closed my eyes and tipped my head to the sky, letting the rain slide down my face, feeling each drop, focusing on the sensations that I could feel. I pulled off my T-shirt and tossed it into the air.

Wash it away, I thought. *Wash it all away.*

A deep breath found me, followed another. I was searching for that sweet scent of budding flowers, that indescribable smell of spring that was absent this season. Or maybe it was just me.

Spring was supposed to be a time of renewal, rebuilding. Out with the old, in with the new.

Reincarnation, some might say.

I hoped so.

What had I become?

What if I never returned to normal?

What if this was my new life?

I opened my eyes and the question returned. The same, haunting question that had kept me up every night.

The same question that I pushed aside, put into a box, and padlocked.

7

PHOENIX

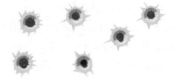

*a*n orange light flickered in the loft window as the barn came into view, a massive brown silhouette against the swirling rain.

Home.

Yep, that's right, home.

My new home.

Twenty-four hours after the doctors had released me from their death grips, I knew I couldn't stay in the family home anymore. My brothers, our staff, the housekeeping, all fussed over my every move. My *every single move.* I couldn't take a piss without someone monitoring me. Axel followed me around with a bottle of prescription pills in his hands, Gage with a bottle of Johnnie Walker, and Gunner with a therapy schedule longer than my dick.

All that was annoying as hell but it was the looks that broke the camel's back, so to speak. The side-long glances after I'd deny the pills, deny the food and drinks, deny the therapy. The entire house walked on eggshells around me because I was a loose cannon. I'd literally seen Gage cover his dick during one of my rants. I shouldn't have been surprised, though, it was his most prized possession after all.

My prized possessions used to be my guns. Couldn't touch those anymore, thanks to the almighty doctors.

So, at two-oh-seven on day two of being home, I packed a bag and snuck out the back door while my brothers gathered in the kitchen to debate my future over a case of Shiner. I walked to the stable, set up shop, and never looked back. Since then, I'd added a mini-fridge, a microwave, and a cot in the loft. Better than sleeping in hay, which if I'm being honest, I didn't mind that much. It reminded me of the old days. My glorious military days running specials ops, kicking in doors, living each day like it could be your last.

A life that seemed so long ago.

And it wasn't like I was living in squalor, anyway. The Steele stable was nothing short of obnoxious, with six horse stalls, an office, a utility room, washroom, and an overhead loft with a large loading door that overlooked our land. Our dad had renovated it a year before his death, and while he kept the old, weathered look outside, the inside was as opulent as my dad's taste. The walls, floors, and ceiling were a polished oak, the stalls a shiny black iron. Handcrafted stone pillars lined the walkway, stretching to the ceiling where flickering iron chandeliers hung from the center beam.

It really was ridiculous. As was the main house that sat just up the hill. Our father had built an eight thousand square feet log cabin mansion, complete with staff quarters, elevators, a theater, indoor and outdoor pools, an outdoor kitchen that could accommodate the US curling team, and a gym bigger than most grocery stores. Below the house were basketball and tennis courts, multiple fighting cages, and an indoor and outdoor shooting range.

You're probably getting the picture by this point that we had some money. That's correct; lots of it. And while my father's lifestyle might rub some the wrong way, the man had grown up dirt poor and worked his ass off to make a better life for himself and our mom. He'd made sure my brothers and I knew hard work and the value of a dollar. When my mom and dad both died, those lessons stuck with me. Which is why I'd worked tirelessly alongside the contractors who built the main house while my brothers played war in the woods.

Blood, sweat, and tears made up every inch of the Steele property and I was proud to call it my home.

No matter where I slept.

I guided Spirit into the stable then pulled the doors closed behind us, wind and rain swirling around my legs until the door latched. It was going to be a cold night. Although the stable had a HVAC system, I didn't use it. The horses were fine as long they weren't out in the elements, and I didn't want to be the cause of a massive spike in our electricity bill. Lord knew I'd already inconvenienced the family enough.

A chorus of snorts rang out, dark brown snouts appearing from each stall. We had four horses total, including Spirit. Two quarter horses named Butch and Cassidy, and a thoroughbred as black as ink named Midnight.

Spirit was mine.

One of our old military buddies had rescued her from a frozen pond in Utah, and when he realized she was feral— craziest horse he'd ever met, were his exact words—he'd given her to a group of cowboys who'd thought they could take her on. They couldn't. She was on her way to the glue factory, so to speak, when my buddy called me up, knowing we owned acres of land. I drove through the night to pick up her crazy ass and had her tamed within a week.

I admired her, her spirit.

It's funny, although my brothers would each take a bullet for me, it was Spirit that felt like my rock since "the incident."

I'd just laid hay in each stall when I heard the growl of an ATV outside. I groaned as the front door slammed open with a totally unnecessary force.

It had to be Gage.

"Holy *shit*. It's colder than a penguin's tit outside. Where the hell is spring?"

I dropped the hay, then straightened. "It is spring, and penguins don't have nipples."

My younger brother cocked his head as he strode down the middle of the stalls. "First, where's your shirt? I know you haven't seen a woman in a while, but," he glanced at Spirit, "I'm pretty sure this romance is illegal in several states. And two, there's no way that penguins don't have nipples. No way a population that dense can arise from nipple-less women."

"One, I lost the shirt. Two, don't ever talk about Spirit like that again. And three, there are two females to every male penguin, most of which engage in prostitution, polygamy, and in some cases, necrophilia."

"Sounds like a party. How do you know this?"

"National Geographic played on loop in the hospital."

"And you'd think the nurses would be more sensitive to the fact that showing nipples the size of dinner plates would send their patients into a sexual frenzy."

"Only you, Gage. Only you." I eyed the cooler he had in

his hand.

He lifted it. "Gunner made a batch of his famous chili tonight. Celebrating the last cold snap or some shit like that."

My brow cocked. "You bring the sides?"

"Chili isn't chili without saltines, cheddar, and pickles. And beer."

Sold.

He helped me lay down more hay, and after grabbing my jacket and tool bag, he followed me up the stairs to the loft —otherwise known as my bedroom. I motioned to the small wooden table I'd spent half the day building with discarded lumber. Hay bales sat on either side. My cot was set up next to the trap door that I kept open most nights, watching the stars twinkle hoping to fall asleep.

"I like what you've done with the place."

I ignored the quip and tossed my coat on my dresser—a wooden bench—and hung the toolbox. Priorities.

"Going to dip into the thirties tonight," he said.

I nodded to the space heater as I pulled on a clean T-shirt and swapped my muddy boots for a dry pair.

A moment passed and I could feel his gaze on me, assessing, as everyone did when they saw me. I turned my back fully to him. He got the message and began unloading dinner.

"Took a trip to the hospital today," he said.

"Finally getting that rash taken care of, huh?"

"Yeah, Ax gave me some of your old ointment."

"Funny."

"No, this visit was personal."

I looped my laces and turned, eyes narrowed. "How so?"

"Ax and Gunner and I decided it was time to confirm who was spreading our business."

"*My* business. My business is *my* business. Stay out of it."

"Your business is *our* business. Just as ours is yours. It's always been that way, brother. This is no different. I won't have some loose-lipped son of a bitch spreading your confidential medical information. Considering who we are, that information should have been locked tighter than a nun's—"

"Stop."

"Oh, so you don't want to know who it is?" He chided.

I waited.

"Our assumption was right." He said.

My hand curled to a fist.

"It's him. Pretty-boy Josh Davis."

"How do you know this?"

"I have a source."

"Who?"

"One of the nurses."

"Who?"

"My business."

"*Who?*"

"Big-bootied B."

Big-bootied B was the name Gage had given my main nurse who he may, or may not, have slept with in the stockroom. Regardless, she was hell on wheels, a southern spitfire, and the only nurse who could handle me.

"She said Josh paid one of his mom's friends to take a peep at your file."

My jaw clenched. Josh Davis was the spoiled, worthless son of a state senator who'd paid his son's way into Kings Point. As if that wasn't enough reason to hate him, throw in a good ol' southern family rift. Apparently, our dad had done business with Josh's dad, and somewhere along the lines there had been a falling out between both men—over money, of course—causing bad blood between our families. Money and evil. Hand and hand. Things got worse when Josh and I served together in the military, our hatred for each other coming to a head during a failed op where Josh abandoned his post to save his own ass while two of my men died, one while dragging the other out of a burning building. Josh Davis took credit for dragging the dead man out, and I'd almost been kicked out for standing up against him. Turned out his daddy had more strings than a drag show. Josh was awarded a bronze star and was honorably discharged from the military to take a cush desk job managing his daddy's construction empire.

When I'd heard someone was spreading my business all over town, my first thought had gone to Josh, as had Gage's apparently.

I leveled my brother with my gaze. "What happened next, Gage?"

The corner of his lip curled into a cocky little smirk.

"Gage..."

"Let's just say ol' Rumpleforeskin won't be able to make it into town for a while to spread your business."

"You slit his tires?"

He snorted a laugh. "Come on. Child's play. What am I, eight?"

"No, you were eight when you slit principal Mortensen's tires."

"Teach him to confiscate my slingshot."

"No, that taught him to start searching everyone's backpack for pocket knives."

"But not underwear."

"You're something else, you know that?"

"Thanks."

"Anyway, what did you do?"

"I sweetened his gasoline."

"You put sugar in his gas tank?"

"His, and..."

"And?"

"You know that subdivision he's building down Apple Ridge road?"

"Tell me you didn't..."

"Every backhoe, bulldozer, and truck on that site, bro."

"Dammit, Gage."

With a triumphant smirk, he tossed me a beer from the cooler and opened one for himself. "Sit," he said. "Cold chili is blasphemous in this house. Or barn, I guess."

I shook my head. What was done was done, and couldn't say I wouldn't have done the same for him. So, I sat and sipped, as he began scooping out the chili. We dug in like a pair of starved war prisoners.

"So. How was therapy?"

I swallowed the half-chewed bite, a fireball of chili sliding down my throat. I cleared my throat. "It was therapy."

"Chick or dude therapist?"

"Female."

"So, hot, then?" Gage grinned around a mouthful of chili.

Her image flashed before my eyes, as it had done a million times since I'd acted like an idiot in her office. I took another bite of chili, her body materializing in my thoughts like smoke, until I realized I'd forgotten Gage's question.

"Yo, bro. She's hot, isn't she?"

"Who said anything about her being hot?"

"You called her a *female.* Not *chick."*

"Do I need to remind you how many times you've been slapped in the face by calling a woman a *chick*?"

"No, because I always remember the handprints on my ass from them later in the night."

I shook my head.

He continued, "And you're deflecting."

"You don't even know what deflecting means."

"I know for a fact she's hot, and I know you just failed that test miserably."

"How do you know *for a fact* she's hot?"

"I had Jagg look into her."

Jagg, a former Navy SEAL turned homicide detective was as close of a brother to me as my real brothers, and apparently, willing to go behind my back for something that Gage had promised was in my "best interest."

"How did you know I was going to see her?"

"The receptionist of Kline and Associates, Zoey, I think, called to confirm your appointment."

"And then you had Rose Floris researched to make sure I was in good hands."

"Yes, sir."

I shoveled in the chili. I didn't want to ask what he'd dug up about the woman. I didn't want to know. So, I said—

"Tell me everything."

"According to Jagg, Miss—I mean *doctor*—Floris graduated top of her class and even won some awards while she was in college. Definitely smart."

Well, she sure as hell made sure I knew that part.

"Get's better," he continued. "In college, she started a podcast called *Roseology*—clever, huh?—where she talked about psychology, studies, books, you know, boring stuff. Anyway, she gained a huge following and her little hobby exploded. She started doing interviews, conducting her own volunteer-based psychology experiments. Her podcast gained sponsorships. Companies, authors, doctors, paid her to talk about their stuff. According to Jagg, Dr. Floris made six figures doing her podcast alone."

My brows arched. That, I definitely did *not* know. So Rose Floris was a rich, domineering brain-analyzer. Pretty much my worst nightmare in a woman. Those lips be damned.

"You surprised?" He asked.

I shrugged and popped a cracker into my mouth. When I looked up, Gage's face was inches from my own.

I jerked my head back. "What? Dude, back up."

"Dude. She is hot as hell."

I washed the crackers down with a gulp of beer, wishing it was pure grain alcohol.

"I saw a picture." He sat back and continued, "She's got that classy hotness. That book-smart librarian sexy thing."

"She's also as uptight and snotty as a librarian."

He shrugged. "Still hot. And you dodging that fact makes me know you noticed."

I ignored, kept eating.

Gage took a swig of my beer. "She's also an upstanding citizen by the way—no criminal record. *But...*"

I stopped chewing mid-bite.

"She did call the cops twice in the last six months."

"For what?"

"Two separate male clients of hers. One would sit in his car after his appointment and watch her for hours through the window. Got so bad she called the cops to escort her home."

"Who was it?"

"Crazy Carl."

"No shit?"

"No shit."

Crazy Carl was the name given to a former drug addict turned carpenter who'd made quite a name for himself walking the streets at two in the morning singing the national anthem. Every. Single. Night.

"Who was the other guy?"

"Some tourist who saw her at the park. Found out her name, where she worked, started driving two hours every week just to ask her out face to face."

"Desperate, much?"

"No shit. She called the cops when he wouldn't leave the waiting room one day."

"What's his name?"

"Bennie Anderson, currently in jail for—"

"Let me guess. Stalking."

"Nope. Third DWI. Anyway no charges were filed; looks like the responding officer just had a chat with both guys and that was that. Jagg talked to the officer that handled both calls, said he laughed it off."

A twinge of anger popped. Why? I shoved it away... until he said—

"You know, your doctor is a hot commodity around town. Single. The town's most eligible bachelorette. Anyway. All in all, I think you're in good hands. Very sexy hands." Gage sipped his beer. "So tell me about the appointment."

"It was therapy. What do you want me to say?"

"I got that. I mean how did it *go*?"

I chomped on a pickle and washed it down with a beer. Winning combination, by the way.

"She threw me out."

"She what?"

"Something wrong with your hearing, bro?"

"Relax." Gage picked up his beer. "I'm going to need a bit more, *bro*. What do you mean *threw you out?*"

I stirred my chili, beginning to lose my appetite. And that was something. If anything, this new body of mine needed twice as much food as before. Three times, even.

"Feen—"

I huffed out a breath. "We had a little disagreement and she asked me to leave. That was it."

"This disagreement didn't involve the cops, did it?"

My gaze shot up. "No. Jesus, what the hell do you think I am?"

The question went unanswered.

"You have to go back." He said.

The snort that came out of me rolled into a full-blown laugh.

"Seriously, Feen."

"You go back."

"Nice comeback. Phoenix—"

"Gage." I set down my spoon, missing the edge of the table and sending it clamoring on the wooden slats.

Spirit snorted from her stall below.

I grit my teeth. "I don't know what everyone thinks I'm supposed to get out of therapy. I don't need it."

"Yeah, and I didn't need it every time the military mandated that I talk to someone after killing a dozen tangos. Just like you didn't then, either. Because that was our job, we understood that. We were doing what we were supposed to do, and the military was doing what it was supposed to do by giving us a little couch time. We played the game. Damn well, too. But this is different, Feen. What happened to you..." My brother's voice trailed off.

I focused on a knick on the table that needed smoothing out.

Gage continued. "... This is different, Feen. This isn't just you and us shoving emotions aside like we've done all our life. This is physical. You need—"

"Gage—"

"No. *Feen.*" His voice raised, echoing off the walls. "Shut the hell up and listen to what I have to say. What you went through—what your body went through—shit, Feen, you were an inch from death. Dr. Buckley tells us it's a miracle that you pulled through; that most men wouldn't have. But you're not just any man, brother. No man walking this earth would have survived what you did. But there were consequences. Physical ones that need to be addressed... mental ones that need to be addressed."

I scratched my chin, my skin suddenly feeling like it was covered in ants.

Gage continued. "I know it's not fun, man, but in order to get you back to one-hundred, you've got to do this shit."

"I am doing this shit."

"No you're not. You're getting kicked out."

I shifted in my seat, wanting to jump out of the loft door. Not the first time that thought had occurred to me.

"Why won't you even give therapy a shot?"

I grunted, leaned back. "She's... Dr. Floris is one of those... really smart, woman-empowered kind of women."

Gage wrinkled his nose.

"And..." I exhaled, not proud of what I was about to say. "I might have bribed her..."

His brows popped.

"... With sex."

The boisterous laughter that barreled out of him sent the horses shifting in their stalls below.

"You *bribed* your head doctor with sex? And how'd that turn out for you, hot rod?"

"She threatened to choke me with my own balls." The corner of my lip curved.

Snorting, Gage wiped the tears from his eyes. "Gloria Steinem or not, I'm liking this chick already." He picked up his spoon and began eating again. "Well, hate to break it to you, bro, but Rose Floris *does* have you by the balls. Because if you don't go apologize to her and continue with your therapy, she'll ensure you never see your freedom again."

Sighing, my gaze shifted to the rain falling outside.

Gage was right. My fate was now in the hands of a five-foot-three brick balled stunner whose name was Rose *Flower*. The thought of apologizing to her—to anyone—sent my gut clenching, so I did what I always did...

"What's the score?" I dug into my chili.

"Six to zip." Gage swiped the string of melted cheese from the scruff on his chin.

Then, we seamlessly switched the conversation to sports, both needing a moment of reprieve. And while the old Phoenix would have been fully engaged with anything that involved a bat and ball, this one was thinking about my balls squeezed in between Rose's fists.

It hadn't been the first time I'd made an ass out of myself in front of a woman, but in the past, it never mattered. I never cared. We'd settle the score in the bedroom where I always won, and she did too—twice, usually. Then, I'd never see her again, or if I did, I'd implement every tactic I'd learned in SERE training.

Couldn't do that with Rose Flower.

There was no doubt the woman despised me at this point—something else that I wasn't used to with a woman—and that she did, in fact, have me by the balls.

And these facts sent two thoughts spinning in my head: One, apologizing to her would not only feel like destroying the last bit of pride I had, but also like a submission. To her, to my injuries. To this new me.

And two...

What if she didn't take me back?

8

ROSE

*a*t the *click* of the clock, I ripped off the afghan. A waft of frigid air swept over my body.

5:01 a.m.

Three shoddy hours of sleep—on my couch nonetheless —was going to make for one heck of a day. I fixed on the windows that overlooked the back deck, drawn with curtains. Then, I twisted my neck, yelping at the twinge of pain from the crick I already had, and looked at the front door—still locked.

Safe.

I sat up, goosebumps running over my body. My gaze paused on the fireplace I'd never used. No. Now was not the time to try something new.

I swung my legs over the couch and slipped into my fuzzy slippers that read *"Shhh..."* on one, and *"I'm reading,"* on the other. Then, I darted on my tiptoes into my bedroom and grabbed the flannel robe from the door. My stomach dropped as I looked at the bed, where not eight hours earlier I'd found a mysterious stuffed animal sitting on it. Shuddering, I spun around and beelined it to the thermostat, cranking it to a respectable seventy-four degrees. The pipes groaned and kicked as I made my way into the kitchen. After clicking on a dim light above the stove, I set the coffee to brew.

I blew out a breath and rubbed my neck.

What a night. What a *freaking* night.

I pulled open the curtains above the kitchen sink. Black, black, black, but no rain. Silver lining, I guessed.

As the coffee began to spit and gurgle, I crossed my arms over my chest and leaned against the counter where I replayed every scenario I'd drummed up over the course of the night as to who delivered the stuffed animal to my house, and most disturbingly, how they'd gotten inside. The most plausible scenario was that I'd accidently left my door unlocked. But even then, who had left it? My former fiancé was the only person that made sense, but why would he leave flowers on my doorstep, but put a teddy bear on my bed?

That *didn't* make sense.

Chewing on my lower lip, my gaze skimmed the woods, which was one black mass in the darkness of the early morning.

There had to be a logical explanation to Creepy-Ted— that's what I'd named him. A and B always equaled C. Right?

Huffing out a breath, I yanked down a mug from the cabinet, squeezed two teaspoons of honey into the bottom, followed two measured tablespoons of creamer, then filled it to the rim before the coffee had finished brewing. Normally, I'd curl up on the couch and watch The Weather Channel while I checked emails waiting for the caffeine to do its magic, but not that morning.

I was too restless.

I stepped into the living room, unlocked the back door and poked my head outside. Sure enough, Creepy-Ted lay on his side in the exact spot I'd tossed him the night before. You know, removing the bad energy from the house.

I shut the door and shuddered again, this time not from the cold. I hated that bear. And after I implemented the plan I'd devised overnight, I'd push the stuffed animal out of my head and into the past where he belonged. Right into the dumpster.

No... into a bonfire.

Yes.

With that happy thought, I padded to the bathroom and flicked on the light. I scowled at my reflection. Dark circles shaded puffy eyes, my hair a matted mess from tossing and turning all night.

Wouldn't be the first time I had to get creative with makeup.

I squared my shoulders and clicked on the radio.

"... a significant weather pattern beginning to take shape over the next few days. This includes severe thunderstorms with strong winds and hail, and flash floods are to be expected. We're also keeping an eye on the potential of tornadoes developing with these storms. Expect power outages, downed tree limbs, and flooded road conditions. Please ensure you have an emergency plan in place..."

I began mentally checking off my pre-storm grocery list—you know, wine, wine, good book, more wine—and started my morning routine that involved a shower, blow out, strategic makeup to mask the fatigue, a suit steam, and one cup of sugar-free yogurt topped with seven walnuts and six blueberries. Seven because that was the number it took to encircle the rim of the bowl I used every morning, and six because... well, you can't have an odd number without an even one. That just throws everything off.

I chose a grey cashmere sweater with black, wide legged slacks and black pumps. Hearing Mr. Jenkins' voice in my head, I dug out my rain jacket I hadn't used in a year.

The woods were beginning to lighten as I grabbed my keys, my briefcase, Creepy-Ted, and stepped outside. A cool breeze sweetened with rain and budding flowers whipped around me as I locked each deadbolt with strong deliberate movements. I crossed the deck, checking the tree line every few seconds.

After a short drive down the mountain, I turned onto Main Street where Donny's Diner was already packed and a trio of cowboys passed by on horseback, probably five hours already into their workday. That was the thing about Berry Springs. In a world that ran on technology, Berry Springs still celebrated old-town living. Why fix something that ain't broke?

Grayness clung to the sky like a heavy blanket, blocking out the rising sun and keeping in the cool air.

It was 7:37 a.m. by the time I rolled to a stop next to a sign that read *County Morgue*. A Tahoe and dented Subaru sat at the end of the small lot. I had fifty-three minutes until my first client meeting of the day, but had several things on my plate to clear before then. Which meant this impromptu meeting needed to be quick.

With a coffee carrier in one hand and paper bag in the other, I carefully made my way up the sidewalk to a long, unassuming brick building that resembled a library more than a place that housed dozens of dead bodies. While most bushes were beginning to flower, the ones that lined this building were as dead as doornails. Fitting. Steeling myself,

I pressed the faded button on the intercom next to the thick metal door.

Nothing.

I pressed the button again, this time, followed by a not-so-patient knock with my elbow. Finally, the door opened to a mess of red, curly hair and curse words.

"Oh. Sorry. Dr. Floris, come on in. Sorry about that. Thought you were Tabby-talks-a-lot."

With a mane of hair as fiery as her attitude, Jessica Heathrow was the county's medical examiner and was known as much for her infallible instincts while dissecting a dead body, as her ability to out-cuss and out-drink any man in town. Intimidating, but not unworkable, as I'd learned through the years.

Tabby-talks-a-lot was the nickname given to Tabitha Raines, the young, eager new journalist who, if you believed the gossip, carried a set of balls as big as her blonde, teased hair. She was tenacious and unrelenting when it came to chasing a story, and was Jessica's worst nightmare.

No room for two alpha females in that town.

Jessica and I had become friends after she rear-ended me during an icy early morning, months earlier. We were both on our way to work and while waiting for the wreckers, we bonded over our dedication to our jobs and our interest in the inner workings of the human brain.

I raised one of the coffees as Jessica closed the door behind me. Eyes lit like a child's on Christmas morning, she snatched the coffee from my hand, revealing a bevy of new tattoos under her lab coat.

"White chocolate mocha, with extra sprinkles," I said.

She sipped, smiled, then cocked a brow. "Hang on just a minute. Coffee means you stopped by with one, *maybe* two, questions about something. White chocolate mocha means you need a favor. And sprinkles say you need it ASAP."

"True. On all counts, but not from you. From Andrew."

"Ah. Phew."

Her shoulders relaxed and she took another sip. Being the only coroner in a county with as many meth labs as churches, Jessica was overworked. Not that she would ever admit to it.

"In that case, thanks for the coffee. Come on. Andrew's in the lab. You can leave your purse and bag there." She led me through the front office, where the lights remained off to deter the prying media. "He's been here since six, believe it or not."

"You're training him well."

She snorted. "Threatening is probably more accurate."

I sucked in a breath as Jessica pulled open the lab door. I'd been inside a morgue twice in my life, once for a college course, and once to identify a client who'd committed suicide, who had no next of kin. It was a moment I wouldn't wish on my greatest enemy, and one I wished I'd never have to repeat.

My stomach rolled as the smell of formaldehyde, with just a touch of methanol, seeped through my held breath. There was no blocking that scent, or the memories that came with it.

Like any normal lab, the spacious room had walls of cabinets, counters with sinks, silver tables filled with knives and tools that rivaled any torture chamber in any horror movie. Not that I watched many horror movies. In my line of work, I found that the human brain could conjure up things far scarier than a Hollywood studio could create.

Yep, it was a normal lab except for the refrigerated back wall that housed dead bodies in each storage block. A shiver caught me and not because of the sixty-five degree temperature.

The room was dimly lit, with two fluorescent lights spot-lighting two separate tables, both topped with a dead body. At least the body on Jessica's table was covered with a sheet.

For a minute, I thought I might vomit. Too early for dissecting dead bodies. *Way* too early.

Andrew glanced up, a flash of blue irises over wide-rimmed hipster glasses that had slipped to the tip of his nose. A white mask covered the bottom half of his face. He wore a dingy lab coat, loosely buttoned over a vintage Beatles T-shirt, and if I had to guess, jeans, and a pair of slip-on loafers. No socks.

A recent college graduate, Andrew had accepted an internship working side by side with Jessica—an education worthy of its own degree. It was rumored that he was some sort of a math whiz who spent his evenings playing the latest gaming craze with a bottle of fancy imported beer and exotic cheeses. I knew the second half to be true because we frequented the same liquor store and were loyal farmers market attendees. After weeks of running into each other, we'd moved beyond the polite nod to small-talk, all the way to him asking me out on a date. Despite every inch of me wanting to say no, I'd accepted his invitation to coffee, and true to form, I'd talked about work the entire time, then made an excuse to leave. When he'd asked me out again, I'd turned him down. A move I was regretting at that moment because I needed a favor from him. Well, not him, but his brother who was the head of the forensics department at the state crime lab.

He set down his scalpel and pushed up his glasses as we crossed the room.

"Lost, Doctor?"

Okey-dokey, then. Apparently, Andrew was a cheese-loving gamer who didn't handle rejection well. Dammit all to hell.

As Jessica led me to his silver table, I forced my eyes to stay *up*, and not drift down to the grey, waxy body that had a y-incision sliced into the torso.

What a day it was already turning out to be.

"Dr. Floris needs something from you."

Andrew straightened, his focus narrowing on me.

"Does she now?"

"Yep."

He grinned. "Mad that I took the last bottle of Bordeaux from Banshee's Brew?"

"No, I'm mad that you're not covering up the body on your table. I only need five minutes." I raised the coffee I'd brought for him. "And I have something better than Bordeaux."

"Nothing is better than Bordeaux."

"True, but this probably pairs better with wielding a knife sharper than your boss's eye at seven-thirty in the morning."

Jessica grinned at my side. "She's right. No drinking in the lab.... until after noon." She winked. "I'll leave you two to it, then."

Andrew popped off his gloves and took the coffee as Jessica disappeared to her own dead body.

"Butterscotch caramel with whipped cream."

His brows raised. "You know my drink."

"I know that bag of truffles you buy every Sunday at the farmers market."

"Best salted caramel in the state."

"Pastor Paul has a knack for baking."

"And whiskey." He winked.

"But I didn't hear that from you, right?"

"Of course not." He eyed me over the rim as he sipped again, then set the coffee dangerously close to a pair of tweezers with a flap of skin dangling off the end. After pulling on a new pair of gloves, he repositioned his mask, picked up a scalpel and leaned over the body.

All I could think was thank *God* I hadn't had breakfast.

"You'll have to talk while I work. Jessica cracks the whip around here."

"Wouldn't have to if you'd stay past five o'clock in the evening every now and then," Jessica hollered from across the room. Selective hearing or eavesdropping, I wasn't sure which.

His eyes crinkled with a grin under the mask. Then, he positioned the blade and dove into the body on the table.

My mouth pooled with saliva with a wave of nausea. And that was exactly his point. I had a feeling this little flex of his ball sac didn't only have to do with my rejection, but because I wasn't the first person to ask for a favor from him. Cops and detectives were notorious for badgering medical examiners for information, and it was obvious Andrew knew he held the cards, but knew also how to work the system in his favor.

Well, no one worked the system better than I did.

I squared my shoulders.

"Ol' Crazy Carl here sure liked his Bordeaux. Didn't know a liver could turn that shade of green."

"Who?"

"Crazy Carl Higgins."

I frowned as I stared at the grey face on the table.

"Oh my..." My eyes rounded. "I know him. He was a client. I actually called the cops on the guy a few weeks ago."

Andrew's brow cocked. "Yeah? For what?"

"Oh, nothing, it was stupid. I regret it."

"What'd he do?"

"He'd linger around for hours after our appointments. I'd catch him watching me through the windows."

"You must have that effect on men."

I ignored the hint of attitude in his voice and asked, "How'd he die?"

"To be determined, but..." He nodded to Carl's legs. "I'm guessing it wasn't pretty."

I followed Andrew's gaze to the flakey, blackened, rotted circles of skin that dotted the man's legs and arms. My stomach did another nose dive.

"What are those?"

"Burns."

My mouth dropped. "You mean, someone *burned* him?"

Andrew nodded and focused back on the man's gaping chest.

I stared down at the burns on Carl's arms. "The circles are too big to be cigarette or lighter burns."

"That's because they aren't."

"What, then? What was he burned with?" I was grotesquely interested all of the sudden.

"I found electrode gel on his skin."

It took a second, but when it sunk in, I gasped.

"Yep. Crazy Carl was electrocuted. Some sick bastard tortured the guy. Think 'death-row-inmate' electrocuted."

A solid minute ticked by as I stood there in disbelief. I looked across the room to Jessica, who was flickering a glance in our direction.

Andrew switched out his scalpel for a pair of tweezers. "Maybe our local chicken snatcher started to get bored."

"Chicken snatcher?"

He glanced up. "You really don't watch the news, do you?"

"Not unless I have to."

"You should. It's important to know what's going on in our little town."

"Like someone stealing chickens?"

"Yep."

"Live ones?"

"No, cut and trimmed breasts." He rolled his eyes. "Yes, live ones. Been going on a month. Hank the Tank even said one of his calves was stolen right off his farm. I can't believe you don't know this. Over a dozen chickens have been found washed up on Otter Lake or at the bottom of Devil's Cove over the last month."

"What does this have to do with craz—I mean, Carl?"

He looked up again. "Again, the news—"

"I know, I know. I'll start watching tonight. Tell me."

"All the chickens were grossly disfigured. Body parts chopped off, organs missing."

"You're kidding."

"Nope."

I scanned Carl from limb to limb. "Well, he looks intact."

Andrew's gaze narrowed. "All of the chickens found— every single one—had been electrocuted... just as ol' Carl here. All of them had remnants of the same gel used to stick the electric pads on their skin."

I blinked. "Who the hell would do that?"

"A mad man."

I stared at the burns that speckled Carl's legs, my stomach twisting. A mad man, indeed.

"Is that how he died?"

"No. Unfortunately. Like I said, he was tortured before

he officially died. The TOD, or estimated time of death, was about seventy-two hours ago."

"Three days."

"That's correct, Rain Man. The burns happened at least twenty-four hours before he was murdered."

Twenty-four *hours* of torture.

"He also had gel in his head, although no burns."

"Gel? In his hair?"

"Yep. Ever seen an EEG helmet? My guess is something like that."

I shook my head. "That is just creepy."

"We certainly agree there. I've seen some sick things in my life, but this is up there."

"How'd he officially die?"

"The cause of death is myocardial infarction, or, a heart attack. His body couldn't take any more electrical shock."

I shook my head, gaping down at the man who, a few weeks earlier, had spent hours watching me from his car. We'd had four appointments to discuss his anxiety and panic attacks. What had Carl gotten himself into?

"Where was he found?"

"A shallow grave in the woods. As naked as a newborn baby. Dr. Buckley found him two mornings ago while checking his deer cams on his property. Called the cops. Record says the rain had washed out most of the sand and his foot was sticking out of the ground. Can you imagine walking up on that? Heck of a way to start his day."

The horror story continued.

"Yep," Andrew moved up to the head. "Looks like we've got a murderer on the loose in Berry Springs."

"A psychotic murderer," I muttered.

Andrew frowned looking at Carl's head, then pulled off

his glasses and slid on a Dr. Evil-looking pair with layers of magnifying rounds.

My interest piqued, drifting from the sliced-open torso to Carl's head where I hadn't noticed the gaping stab wound at the temple. I covered my mouth and leaned-in. Or, wounds, I should say.

"Was he stabbed? In the head?"

Ignoring me, Andrew cocked his head to get a better angle.

"There's two," I said.

"Two what?"

"Lacerations."

"You're incorrect. Not lacerations. Puncture wounds."

"Puncture wounds on the side of his head?"

"Directly in his temple. The softest and most lethal part of the head, yes."

"His killer cut his head open?"

"I said, *puncture* not laceration. Big difference."

A sick fascination began to replace my uneasy stomach. "But you said he was stabbed."

"He was stabbed, but not with a knife. Try to keep up."

"What's the difference between a puncture wound and a laceration?"

"There's a huge difference. A laceration is a tear in the soft tissue, usually jagged and uneven and open in a V-like shape. Kind of like his chest here. There's significant loss of blood with lacerations. These are most typical with knife wounds. A puncture wound, on the other hand, closes back up and doesn't bleed excessively. Big difference, and very important to be able to tell the difference."

"Because this difference can help you determine how the victim was killed?"

"Not only that, it helps us to determine the murder weapon that was used. Huge in a homicide investigation."

"But you said Carl died of a heart attack?"

"That's right, but this was done moments after he died. He wouldn't have survived this wound. It punctured his brain."

"Oh." I bit my lip. The thought—the image—was terrifying.

"Yeah, like I said, a mad man."

"That's so sick. And you don't think it was done with a knife?"

He shook his head. "Like you noticed, there are two, very similar wounds less than a half-inch apart. Both penetrating into the skin at almost identical lengths."

"So he was stabbed with something twice. By someone with good aim."

"That could be one theory. But with what, *Detective* Floris? That is the question." He winked.

I leaned-in closer. The body was no longer a 'gross, dead man,' but someone with a story to tell. Someone who had been brutally tortured and murdered. Someone who deserved justice. It was like my own little CSI case. Perhaps it was my personal connection to Crazy Carl but I felt an immediate need to help solve his case. I squinted in deep thought, my brain flooding with theories of what could have happened to the man in his final moments of life.

"Ice pick?" I asked. "Maybe he was stabbed with an ice pick?"

"No, the wounds aren't wide enough."

"Letter opener?"

"What is this? The eighteen hundreds? Who uses a letter opener anymore?"

I rolled my eyes, then watched him work for a minute, fascinated, and forgetting why I was there in the first place.

"That's all you got, Detective?" He asked. "An icepick or a letter opener?"

"I'm thinking, I'm thinking..."

Another minute slid by.

"Andrew."

He quickly looked up, an excited outburst apparently being foreign to the room.

"You said *two* puncture wounds, close together, both blades the same length?"

"That's right." He refocused on his work.

I spun on my heel, jogged to the long counter that lined the side of the room and began pulling open drawers. Once I found what I was looking for, I jogged back and raised my hand, excitement pitching my voice. "Scissors." I wagged the shiny pair of small, silver scissors in my hand. "Carl was stabbed with a pair of scissors." My nose wrinkled in disgust. "Stabbed *in the head* with a pair of scissors."

Andrew didn't look up, didn't move, his concentration remained on the hole in the man's head where he was poking around. Finally, he appeared to pull something out of Carl's head. He straightened his back and raised the tweezers. Clamped into the end was a tiny, blue speck.

"You're right, Doctor Floris. Scissors. But scissors with a *blue,* plastic handle."

My jaw dropped, a zing of excitement shooting through me. "That's an actual piece of the scissors used?"

Andrew nodded, staring at the tiny object. "Takes a lot of force to penetrate the brain. A piece of the handle must've broken off."

The image of a man brutally stabbing someone else's head sent my stomach swirling again.

Andrew continued. "We now have a piece of one of the tools used to torture this poor guy. Pull on some gloves and hand me an evidence baggie."

Elated, I did as I was told. He slid the object into a plastic bag, then pulled his mask down. "Nice work, Floris."

I grinned. "All in a day's work."

"Okay, big shot, you get your five minutes now." He pulled off his gloves and grabbed his coffee. "Let's head to the office."

I took another glance at Carl, at the story waiting to be told by what remained of him, and said a little prayer that questions would be answered soon.

As mine would be, hopefully.

I followed Andrew into the front office. He bypassed the light switch and hitched a hip onto the desk, knocking a few pieces of paper marked *confidential* to the floor. He either didn't notice, or didn't care.

"Okay, what do you need from me, Dr. Floris?"

I picked up the paper bag I'd set on the desk before going into the lab.

"Please tell me that's not a head." He said. "Animal or human."

"Worse." I handed it to him. "A teddy bear."

Curiosity wrinkled his forehead. He opened the bag with the caution of a bomb tech. His frown faded into a laugh as he lifted Creepy-Ted from the bag.

"Oh *no,* not a *teddy bear.*" His sarcastic tone innate to millennial hipsters.

"Sure, laugh now, but if you came home to it *sitting on your bed,* you'd be singing a different tune."

His laugh dried up. "Seriously?"

"Seriously."

"Who sent it?"

"No clue."

"No card or anything?"

"Nope."

"So one of your secret admirers left you a little love memento?"

"After breaking into my house."

He examined it, turning the little monster over in his hands. "Okay, well, that's creepy and all, but what's this got to do with me?"

"It doesn't. It has to do with your brother who heads up the forensics department at the state crime lab. I'm hoping he can scan it for fingerprints or something? I'll pay whatever I need to. Under the table, of course."

"Hold the phone." Andrew dropped the bear back into the sack and rolled the top. "First, how many people have touched this thing since you've had it?"

"Only me."

"Okay, that's good. Did you put him into the sack immediately?"

"No. I threw him outside. You know... bad juju in the house."

Andrew sighed and rolled his eyes—millennial, again.

"It's a good thing you don't work in forensics, Dr. Floris, because the first rule in collecting evidence is to handle it as little as possible and store it in an uncontaminated container that shields it from the elements, *including* rain, dirt, mud. You pretty much danced all over it. The odds of finding traceable prints on it..." He laughed.

My patience was waning. "So you're telling me there's nothing you can do?"

"I'm not saying that. I'm just saying you might not get the results you want."

I fisted my hands on my hips. "I know that it's possible to

pull prints from fabric regardless of the fact that it was exposed to the elements."

"From all the news you watch?"

I clicked my tongue. "Come on, Andrew, this is serious."

"Fine. Yes, it's possible, but that fabric usually isn't in the form of long-pile fabrics, like this stuffed animal. Even with non-porous fabrics like leather, fingerprints only last as long as its environment will allow, whether it be inside, *or* outside in the rain. It also depends on how the print was transferred —with oil, sweat, blood. Even then, there are no promises that a full print would have been transferred."

"What about the red bow around its neck? That's not a long-pile fabric."

Andrew studied the bow, then seemed to decide something.

"Okay, you win, Dr. Floris. I'll send my brother a text but can't promise anything."

"That's all I ask."

"And I'll ask for another Butterscotch Caramel coffee. Tomorrow. ... And every morning for the rest of the week."

I rolled my eyes. "Done."

"And—"

Just then, a jacked-up Chevy skidded to a stop a few feet from the front door. Saved by the erratic driver.

"Dammit. That'll be Detective Jagger. Guy's a dog with a bone."

I looked out the window at the beast of a man unfolding himself from the cab of his truck. Tall, dark, handsome. Check, check, check, but this one carried that hostile, bad-boy edge that was like sexual napalm to most women. Menacing, on all counts—and that was before I noticed the tattoos.

"Crazy Carl's his case. Been hounding me from hour

one. Guy's ruthless when it comes to getting his cases solved."

I watched the detective step onto the sidewalk and check his watch, revealing a swath of colorful tattoos under the cuff of his brown leather jacket. The man was everything opposite of what you'd expect from a clean-cut detective. He looked more like a former inmate turned MMA fighter.

Andrew continued, "At least today, I have news for him."

"Thanks to me."

"Don't get too cocky."

"Don't forget to call your brother." I nodded to the paper bag on the desk as the front door opened behind me. "Let me know if you hear something."

"I'll see what we can do."

He shifted his attention to the detective and dismissed me.

9

ROSE

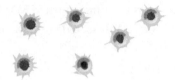

I blew out a breath and leaned back in my office chair, willing the headache between my temples to go away. It had been a day of back to back appointments, playing catch-up in-between, and ending with a brutal monthly staff meeting to recap our current cases, and all on three hours of sleep. And to top it off, Theo still hadn't graced me with his decision about my Equine Assisted Therapy program proposal.

Not surprisingly, word had gotten out about the gruesome murder of Carl Higgins. The town was in an uproar, feeding gossip, demanding answers. Everyone was on edge, excluding Mr. Jenkins. His bakeshop had gone through twenty dozen donut holes in the morning alone. It had been another bleak, grey day, as if the weather knew someone in our small town had been brutally murdered. The temperature had climbed to sixty-five, the heat wave before another string of storms, according to the weatherman. The rain had held off though, the only positive to a day filled with images of Carl's rotted, grey foot sticking out of the mud. No doubt I was going to see that in my nightmares that night.

I opened one eye and glanced at the clock on the wall—4:47 p.m.—and considered packing up. It would have been the first time I'd left before five, ever.

I hadn't heard from Andrew since I'd visited that morning, adding restlessness and anxiety to my fatigued state. Had his brother agreed to scan Creepy-Ted for fingerprints? Or, had Andrew forgotten about the favor? Or maybe Detective Jagger had a gun to his head demanding that he finish his autopsy on Crazy Carl. On second thought, Jagger wouldn't use a gun—it would have been a shank.

I was pondering how to make a shank when someone knocked on my door.

"Come in..."

The door handle jangled, then jangled again. Frowning, I stood and crossed the room just as the door swung open and Zoey stumbled in, balancing two large boxes in her hands. At the doorway, sat two more.

I took one from her hand. "What's this?"

"A lot."

"Yeah, but what?"

"Sorry, my X-Ray vision is on the fritz. A delivery dude—hot, by the way—just delivered them for you."

"From where?"

She shrugged and kicked another box inside.

"He didn't say where they came from?"

"Girl." Zoey heaved out a breath as she shoved in the last box. "I don't—"

"You don't know. Right. Sorry."

"Well, Merry Christmas." Zoey smoothed her cheetah-print blouse and wiped her hands on her pleather spanks. "Cameron and I are going to head to Frank's for a few beers after this. Wanna come?"

"You and Cameron are heading to Frank's for karaoke night."

She flashed an innocent smile. "I can't help it that I have the voice of an angel."

A beer sounded great. Howling coyotes did not.

Frank's Bar was a good ol' southern honky-tonk bar with ninety-nine cent taps and the best barbecue in the tristate area. A favorite with the locals, the bar was tucked away in the outskirts of town, away from the prying eyes of the tourists that flooded the town half the year.

I shook my head. "This angel is calling it a night early. I didn't get much sleep last night."

"Or maybe your ex is waiting at home for you wearing nothing but a G-string and a purple orchid between his teeth?"

I wrinkled my nose at the image, reminding me I had zero sexual attraction to my former fiancé. Zoey, on the other hand, apparently did.

I'd told Zoey about the orchid, but not about Creepy-Ted. I wasn't sure why, exactly, other than I didn't want to have to dissect it more than I already had and bring more "energy" to it. Bad juju and all that.

"I won't say it again," Zoey continued, "but I really think you should give the guy another chance, Rose. I mean, he's..."

"*Marriage material. I know.* You've reminded me a million times."

"He's handsome, educated, comes from money..."

"Nice to know your checklist."

"Oh no, dear. The top of my checklist is how fast the guy can make it out of my house after a throw down."

I laughed.

She continued. "Your checklist is much different... much more conservative. White picket fence, homemade dinners, two point two children and a Labrador retriever."

"Where's the other eight percent of the third kid?"

"Lassie's mouth."

"Lassie was a collie, not a Labrador retriever."

"Fine, whatever. You get the point. You're the marrying kind, Rose."

I smiled and looked down. Good to know that the carefully orchestrated life I'd built around myself wasn't going unnoticed. Thing was, Zoey had no idea it was all a facade. Zoey had no idea about my past.

No one did.

"What about any of those hot doctors you interviewed on your Roseology podcast? Are any of those eligible bachelors?"

"Are you asking for a *friend?*" I winked.

"No, just trying to find you a good man. Why'd you close that down, anyway?"

"Men or my podcast?"

She laughed. "Podcast."

I shifted my weight. "I wanted to put my full focus on this new job." It was a truthful answer, but one that I still questioned every day. I missed doing my podcast, more than I could have ever imagined when I'd canceled it. It had been my little baby, something I'd started from nothing, worked my butt off to grow, and turned it into a success that had stacked my savings account and birthed my love for designer duds. It wasn't the money, though, it was the feeling of accomplishment. Like one step closer to my dream of running my own business.

Yeah, I missed it terribly. But I knew that if Theo would

approve my Equine Therapy Center, it would fill that void. And help potentially thousands of people in the process. Talk about a win, win.

"Anyway," Zoey continued. "Word around Frank's is that your ex is still pining after you. I think you should give him another chance. There's my two cents."

I felt my shoulders begin to tighten. The usual reaction to anyone bringing up my former fiancé and any time I thought about my past.

I swooped down and picked up a box in an effort to drop both the subject, and the anger creeping up.

"Okay, I'll shut up," Zoey said, picking up on my sudden hostility. "I'm just saying, you're not getting any younger is all."

Not getting any *younger*? I dropped the box from my arms, missing my heels by an inch.

"I'm *twenty-eight* years old, Zoey."

"Geez." Her palms lifted to surrender. "Sorry. I'll leave you alone, then." As she made her way across my office, she said, "Don't work too late. More storms are comin', you know."

As the door clicked closed, I glanced out the window where sure enough, a bellow of black clouds sat on the horizon. A few sprinkles began to dot the window, a warning of the storm to come. There was an electricity in the air. Something... like an impending doom deep in my stomach. I inhaled, feeling like the walls were caving in on me. What the heck was wrong with me?

I mentally counted the days from my last period, wondering if I was having an epic bout of PMS, as I sliced through the packing tape.

My jaw dropped as the flaps of the first box opened.

It was a brand-*spanking*-new Apple monitor, in all its gorgeous, sleek, silver glory.

What?

Who?

I moved onto the next box.

Another monitor. Dual Apple monitors.

The third box held a new computer tower and docking station, and the forth, a new keyboard, and a matching mouse and mousepad painted with red roses.

Red roses?

"So your name is Rose Flower."

His voice materialized in my head, pulling me back to the moment I'd first seen him, the moment he'd spun around in my desk chair—the first time Phoenix Steele had given me butterflies. That vision quickly faded, though, to him destroying my desk in a fit of rage.

I blinked, staring at the thousands of dollars of computer equipment on the floor.

No freaking way had he done this.

No. *Freaking.* Way.

I searched for a card, a receipt, or any indication of who had sent it, but there was nothing.

My question was answered by a knock at the door.

"Come in."

Zoey poked her head in with a demure, polite smile that suggested she wasn't alone.

"Ah... There's someone here to see you, Dr. Floris."

"Who—"

She pushed open the door. As if he'd materialized from my thoughts, the man, the myth, the legend, Phoenix Steele, loomed in the doorway. He was wearing the same black leather jacket from the day before, but this time it hung over a *Steele Shadows Security* T-shirt. A worn pair of jeans and scuffed cowboy boots completed the look. His hair was extra mussed, his five o'clock shadow thicker than the day before. His eyes, as blue as a spring's sky, and loaded with as much turbulence.

"I'll, uh, leave you two alone," Zoey said, giving me a questionable look, before shutting the door. So much for my request to give me a heads up if Phoenix came into the office. Thanks, Zoey.

I scrambled off the floor.

His gaze flickered to my sweater.

I cleared my throat.

"Mr. Steele."

"Phoenix," his tone reminding me of when he'd bribed me with sex and money.

"It's Phoenix now? Yesterday, you asked that I call you—"

"It's Phoenix today."

We stared at each other for a moment.

"… Did we have an appointment, Phoenix?"

"No." He shifted his focus to the monitors on the floor, then crossed the room and kneeled by the boxes. I watched him as he began unpacking each box, quickly, efficiently with smooth movements as someone who'd handled tech equipment countless times before.

I was… speechless.

Well, almost.

"Is this… all this, from you?"

He grunted—a yes, apparently—and carried one of the monitors to my desk.

"You sent this here?"

He began clicking buttons and unplugging cords.

I lunged over. *"Wait...* wait… I—"

"I saved it. Don't worry."

"Wait. Phoenix. *Stop.* What are you doing? You can't just replace all my stuff."

"This is a hundred times better than what you have now. Trust me."

Maybe so, but what the hell?

I yanked the monitor from his hands. The quick anger I'd seen the day before flashed across his face, but *this* time, instead of flipping out, his gaze just as quickly went lax, as if something had clicked in his brain—control, restraint. *Effort.* He clasped his hands behind his back and took a step back.

Whoa.

I blinked. "Did you really do this?"

He dipped his chin.

"I can't accept this, Phoenix."

"Why not?"

"It's... too much."

"It's fine." He pulled the monitor from my hands and got back to work.

I stepped back, still struggling with how to handle this odd situation unfolding around me. This unpredictable man unfolding in front of me.

He skirted past me, grabbed the next piece of fancy equipment and began setting it up.

"Is this your way of apologizing, Phoenix?"

"Does that condescending tone come naturally to you?"

"Does your ability to deflect anything involving real emotions come naturally to you?"

"Yes."

"Then, yes."

He kneeled below my desk, my neck automatically

craning to get a look at that backside. Yep. Levi's perfection. His thighs were the size of tree trunks.

I felt the heat begin to rise up my neck. His gaze slid to me as he stood. I tore mine away and began restacking the papers he'd pushed to the side.

"I want you to know you didn't need to do this," I said.

"Yes I did. I damaged your equipment, so I replaced it."

Black and white, simple as that.

"Well." I repositioned the tissue box and fluffed one from the top. "Thank you."

And that was that. Within minutes, my janky old computer system had been replaced with a shiny robot that made me want to do backflips.

He pressed the power button and the system beeped to life. A tingle of excitement flew through me. It was a command center, right there on my desk. Beautiful. Stunning.

Phoenix's massive, calloused, tanned hand covered the dainty mouse as he clicked through a few screens.

"Need your password."

I stepped beside him and bent over. He didn't move an inch. My hand brushed his as I reached for the keyboard.

I glanced over my shoulder. "Do you mind?"

"Not at all." His focus was fixed on my hips.

I nudged him out of the way and typed in my ridiculously long password. He nudged me, took back control, and after a few more clicks, he stepped back.

"There you go."

"Wow. It's amazing." I looked at him. "Thank you, again. You didn't have to do this."

"Yes I did."

I turned my focus back on the computer.

"So. ... How do we do this?" He asked behind me.

"Do what?"

"Do I need to set up another appointment or something?"

My brows popped. "You've decided to move forward with therapy?"

"My doctors decided that for me."

"Perhaps I should rephrase that. You're ready to continue? Now?"

A slight nod.

"With me?" I asked before I could catch myself, then quickly continued that up with, "I know a lot of other great therapists, male. Perhaps I could send a referral—"

"Here's fine."

Well that wasn't a *you're* fine, but whatever.

"Okay... well, for your information, another option would be to put it off a few more weeks, although—"

"Now's fine."

I was shocked. I can honestly say that I never expected to see the guy again. I was also surprised at my pleasure in his desire to schedule another appointment. That he was seeking help. Because the man needed it, in one form or another, he needed therapy. He was a walking time bomb.

I nodded. "Well. ... Okay, then."

"When is your next open spot?"

I narrowed my eyes, testing him. "Let's start now."

Although I'd only had one experience with Phoenix, I knew he was in rare form that day. He was in a submissive state, perhaps from a bruised ego, or perhaps he'd finally come to terms with the fact that I was an important part to getting his life back. Regardless, I needed to capitalize on that moment of openness, of willingness to concede. Moments that I had no doubt were few and far between with Phoenix Steele.

"Right now?" He asked.

"Unless you have something else you need to get to?"

His gaze shifted to the couch, the muscles beginning to work in his jaw.

I was already losing him.

"Let's start now," I repeated quickly.

*L*et's start now.

Well. *Shit.*

Hadn't planned on that. I'd scheduled my trip to Kline and Associates to as close to five o'clock as possible, ensuring a quick, smooth exit. No time to "accidentally" destroy her office again. Honestly, I assumed the woman was going to tell me to take a hike, to never come back, maybe even slap me across the face—okay, fine, that last one might have been a fantasy. Regardless, even in the best case scenario of her agreeing to another appointment with me, I assumed she'd schedule it for later that week. But I couldn't back out, couldn't back down, because I already felt like the woman had me by the balls—and not like she did in my dreams the night before. During that glorious hour of sleep Rose Flower had done things to me that would have most people labeling us clinically insane.

The woman was throwing me off. Just being in a *therapist's* office was throwing me off. Why are those rooms always so small, anyway? As if talking about *feelings* weren't constrictive enough.

I reminded myself that continuing with therapy was the sole reason I'd come back to the office. I guess I just wished I had a second to prepare. Maybe have a drink before.

Maybe three.

But prepare for what? What the hell was there to prepare for? Why couldn't I suck it up and do what I told myself I'd do, which was to appear *not* intellectually or emotionally deficient. I would appear cool, calm, and collected so that she'd sign that little paper that said I could have my freedom back.

God, I *hated* that room.

"Let's begin," Rose repeated, pulling me out of my racing thoughts. She nodded to the couch, those big, almond eyes alert, ready. Not wary like she'd been the day before. Or, scared like she'd been after I flipped out.

No, Rose Floris was ready to stand toe to toe with me.

To take me on.

Let's begin.

I admired that. There was strength behind her eyes, the kind that came from picking yourself up over and over again.

A strength I knew very well.

A strength that, in all honesty, I didn't know that I had anymore.

"Please, sit."

I did as I was told and sat on the edge of the couch.

"Can I get you some coffee?"

"No."

"Okay," She settled behind her desk. "Yesterday we spoke about why you're here—"

"Because the doctors demanded it."

She shifted. "Okay. To get a bit more detailed, the fact of the matter is that certain parts of your life have been restricted until you complete your therapy." The tone of her voice was sharp, clipped, letting me know I wasn't her favorite person. Got it. "Therefore," she continued, "sessions with either myself, or someone else, needs to be completed to give you those restricted items back."

"My freedom."

"Your driver's license and concealed carry license. And, by all intents and purposes, your pride."

My jaw clenched.

"Are we in agreement here?"

"Yes." The answer came out in more of a growl than I intended. Not off to a good start so far.

"Great," she said, pleased with this response. "Now, I want to start by asking, what is it exactly that *you* would like to get out of this therapy?"

"My driver's license and concealed carry license."

"Is that it?"

I flopped open my right palm. Did she not hear the last ten seconds of our conversation?

"Your *only* goal out of hours and hours of therapy is to regain your licenses?"

"My freedom."

"Really? To you, freedom equals *only* your drivers and gun licen—"

"Concealed—"

"*Stop,* Phoenix." She gave me a sharp look. "Do you think that freedom is going to be the same as it was before your injury? You get your licenses back, and all of a sudden your life is going to go right back to the way it was?"

I looked away, because honestly, that hit home. Hard.

Like a fucking Mack truck.

"How about this?" Rose pushed away from her desk and crossed the room to a large dry erase board on the wall. I straightened, watching her walk, the long, confident strides, the scent of something flowery following a moment later. Her weird, wide-legged pants flowed against her legs like silk, brief moments of outlining long, toned legs, and a popping ass. And, side note, that ass *could* pop—just ask my dream.

Focus, Phoenix.

After removing the top from a red marker, she scribbled *#1* at the top of the board.

"Let's set three goals."

She turned to me, a marker in her hand and a gleam in her eye, sending me into some naughty teacher insta-fantasy. The woman turned me into a horny pubescent boy in seconds flat. It was humiliating, and I immediately chocked it up to a side effect from my injury... because that had to be it, right? Because Phoenix responded to no woman like this.

"Yesterday I told you that the type of therapy I do centers around CBT, or Cognitive Behavior Therapy. Are you familiar?"

"I'm familiar with CBD."

"Right." Apparently not her first time to hear that joke. "This isn't that. CBT focuses on changing problematic patterns of thinking. It centers on the idea that over the years our brains develop automatic think patterns that are either productive or destructive. These thought patterns affect our feelings and behaviors, thereby affecting our entire life. What we do, how we do it, our choices, how we feel about ourselves, who we hang out with, etcetera. CBT focuses on breaking down the destructive thought patterns and re-training our brains how to react to situations in a more positive, productive way. What I think you'll like about this, Phoenix, is that we step outside of ourselves—so to speak—and look at our thoughts as a separate entity that we can *control.* Just as we *control* situations, we can *control* our thoughts. You are powerful enough to do it. You just have... to do it."

The passion in her voice was palpable.

She turned back to the board. "So, we start with three goals. Only three. Every time I see you, our torturous discussions," she winked over her shoulder, "will be geared toward these three goals, only. Everything we do, talk about, *everything* will focus on these three goals. That way, when you *draaag* yourself in here, you'll know what to expect and what the conversations will be focused around."

I straightened. Goals. Three. Clear expectations set. I could do that.

"What do you want the first one to be?"

"Driver's license."

She rolled her eyes then pretended to write on the board, "Improve Phoenix's sense of humor, okay."

A grin tugged at my lips.

She winked. Again.

"How about goal number one will be to *not* destroy my office again?"

"Done."

"Good." She began scribbling, squeaks on the board adding to the hot-teacher thing. "Goal number one will be to work on your impulsive aggression."

Nice little spin she did there, but okay. Sneaky cat.

"Alright, onto goal number two. What would you like it to be, aside from your concealed carry license?"

"For you to not shove my balls down my throat. Like you threatened to yesterday."

She grinned, thought for a moment, then drew a little

box in the corner of the board. "Okay, fine, we'll make three goals for me, too. Number one, no ball shoving—"

"Number two can be—"

"Oh, no, no, no. This isn't a one way street, Mr. Steele. You're up next."

It was the first time ever that I liked the way *Mr. Steele* sounded rolling off someone's tongue.

"Number two... let's see..." she tapped the bottom of the marker on her chin. My gaze slid down that long, lean neck the color of porcelain, then to her—

"Ah, I know," she said. "You went to great lengths to let me know you were sorry for destroying my desk. Above and beyond. Over the top. This leads me to believe you're struggling with a heavy dose of guilt, and aren't sure how to contain it. So, goal number two will be for you to release the guilt you carry."

Guilt. My stomach clenched. The woman had no idea. My hands started to do that damn fidgety thing. I picked up one of her vesuvianite stones and began flipping it through my fingertips.

She continued. "Whether the guilt be from a perceived failure from letting your family down, or from having to be on the receiving end of care. You don't like it. You don't know how to handle it." She nodded enthusiastically. "Yes, number two—release guilt."

I watched her scribble the second goal on the board and found myself already wondering what my third goal would be. Rose Flower was calculated, no doubt about that. She was using my military background to get to me. Lay out clear goals, one by one, black and white, no fluff, no *'tell me how that made you feel'* bullshit. Sneaky, sneaky, sneaky. But regardless of her tactics, I liked it. It resonated with me. Reminded me of when my team and I would gather in a situation room listening to our orders before a mission. Felt good.

It felt *doable.*

Speaking of doable…

"You're turn," I said.

"Fine." She moved to her box. "Okay, goal number two for me should be…"

"Work on that annoying, condescending tone that comes so easily to you."

Her brows raised. Nerve, hit.

Her lips twisted as she seemed to search for words. I'd made Rose Flower uncomfortable. Not pissed, but uncomfortable. Am I an ass for enjoying it? Enjoying the fact that I was able to knock her off her pedate a bit? Maybe it was because the seemingly perfect woman became human to me all of the sudden; I don't know.

She turned back to the board and began writing. "Fine. Work on my tone—"

"Condescending tone."

"Thanks for the example," she muttered as she wrote.

I couldn't fight the grin that time. She wrote the word bigger than the rest, a subtle touch of sarcasm to let me know Dr. Fancy-Pants had her own way of deflection—Wit.

"Okay, number three for you?" She turned and stared at me.

The silence dragged out while she strategically waited for me to come up with my own goal. I stared back. A stare-off. A good ol' pissing match. Who would get so uncomfortable that they'd look away first? The internal laughter rang so loudly in my head I wondered if she'd heard it. The woman had no idea what she was up against.

I crossed my arms over my chest, leaned back against the couch, and kicked my cowboy boots onto her table, edging the box of tissues to the very edge. *Dangerously* close to teetering off.

She heaved a sigh with a roll of her eyes that was so dramatic I was surprised they didn't roll right onto the floor.

"Fine..." she said as she stomped over and replaced the tissues to the perfect ninety-degree angle that they had been, then stomped back to the board.

I won.

"Goal number three." Her eyes narrowed with a mischievous warning. "You destroyed my office, then you replaced everything with equipment five times its value, then showed up exactly two minutes after it was delivered—just enough time for me to see what was inside each box. This tells me you personally arranged the delivery and worked it into your schedule, oh, and, you had to arrange some sort of transportation to get it all set up for me—and just in time to sneak out at exactly five o'clock. Yet, after all this effort, you never actually *verbalized* your apology. You never—not once —said the words, 'I'm sorry.'"

I squeezed my arms tighter around my chest.

"This tells me you have trouble with communication—"

My feet hit the floor. "I do *not*—"

She held up her hand. "I don't mean that you physically have trouble forming words and sentences. I mean, emotionally. You have trouble expressing your emotions. Talking things out. Addressing anything that might involve the slightest feeling. So, Phoenix, goal number three is going to be your biggest challenge. Number three is going to be for you to open up to me. This is very important. You can't go through life—"

I leaned forward and slid my forearms onto my knees. "I've got your number three, Dr. Flower..."

She stopped mid-sentence.

"... To relax."

Her chin jerked back. *"Relax?"*

"Yep. Loosen up." I nodded to her desk. "To not have to have everything on your desk at perfect, ninety degree angles. Not to have the pictures that line your walls exactly six inches apart. Six because it's an even number that you can split down the middle. Because five is odd—three on one side and two on the other—and well, that just doesn't sit well with you does it?"

Her gaze shifted to her wall of accolades, then back to me. She blinked.

I continued. "Some people might think your desk is placed at an odd angle. No, not to you. Your desk has been set up where neither the morning sun, or late afternoon sun would reflect in your monitors. That plant you have in the corner? Pruned to perfection with exactly ten elephant ears. Ten, because five and five. Your books? At first I was going to say alphabetized, but nope, you've got them lined up according to ISBN number. Now *that's* impressive. Your post-its, color-coordinated and spaced exactly an inch apart. The floor, top of your file cabinet, desk, windowsills, not a speck of dirt. You, Rose, are what some might call a total control freak, and if I had to guess, you've got a hefty dose of OCD. There's your diagnosis, Doc... but the question is, why? What's the root of all this?"

She stood frozen, staring at me.

I grinned. "So, Miss Flower..."

The twitch of her jaw told me she didn't like that.

"... Goal number three for you is to *relinquish* control. To recognize that it's okay not to be perfect. To loosen up."

Her eyelids fluttered as if coming back to life after a stun gun. She squared her shoulders, lifted her chin and looked down at me from the tip of her nose. After a quick spin on her heel that had more attitude in it than her tone, she began writing on the board. "Goal number three for me: Accept chaos," the sarcasm as thick as the strokes of her marker.

I pushed off the couch, crossed the room and pulled the marker from her hands.

Loosen up, I wrote next to #3 after erasing 'Accept chaos.' Then, I added a number four to her list, and to mine. Beside both, I wrote the words, 'Don't deflect.'

We stood there, together, staring at our weakness spelled out right there on the board in front of us.

She exhaled, looked at me, and I'll be damned if a smile didn't cross her face.

"Okay, then. It looks like we both have a few things to work on. *Together.*"

11

ROSE

*T*he guy had read me like a freaking book. I mean a Freaking. *Book.*

Phoenix Steele had single-handedly stripped me naked, raw, ripped me open, right there in my own office. Assessing me with that gaze that knocked me off balance, no matter the length of my heels. And they were all six inches, by the way, no more, no less, because well, three and three.

Dammit.

Side note: Even in the six inch heels, I was still a good foot shorter than the man standing next to me.

Phoenix had been right on all counts of his assessment of me, and this told me several things about him. One, his cognitive reasoning and judgment weren't as impaired as the reports suggested, which also made me wonder how many other tests he'd manipulated. I had to remind myself that Phoenix had spent decades running special ops in the deepest depths of hell. He knew how to handle—manipulate—a situation, how to read a situation, and how to turn it around to his advantage.

I couldn't help but wonder if his sudden openness to accept his three goals wasn't just a ruse. A stepping stone to his goal, which was to do anything to get his freedom back.

Was it all a game to him?

Was I a pawn?

Was he willing to say or do anything to get what he wanted?

How far would he go?

And perhaps a more unnerving question... how far would I let him go?

He knew he was knocking me off my game. He knew he was turning the tables by reminding me that I was not perfect, therefore, stripping my confidence, and *therefore* stripping my authority.

Yeah, the man knew exactly what he was doing.

As I settled in behind my desk, trying to regain the position of authority in the room, I watched him, watching me. Two screwed up humans seeing right through each other, but neither willing to concede.

I see you, Phoenix.

I see that you are going to be my most difficult case to date.

And I'm up for that freaking challenge.

I'd just picked up my pen when my cell phone rang. My heart skipped a beat as the caller ID blinked.

"Excuse me." I grabbed the phone and pushed out of the chair. "I need to take this."

He nodded to the door, as if granting me the approval to exit. After stepping into the hallway, I checked the front desk to make sure Zoey was gone, then I answered.

"Hello, Rose Floris here."

"Hey Doc, it's Andrew at the morgue. Man," he chuckled. "I never get tired of that opening."

"Did you get ahold of your brother?"

"Well, no, but I definitely have something you're going to want to see."

See?

"Tell me you found prints on Creepy-Ted?"

"No prints. Something much more interesting, though."

"What?"

"A mini video recorder."

My heart dropped to my feet. "I'm sorry, there's no way I heard you—"

"Yep. There was a small spy cam secured in the middle of Ted's bow."

My jaw slacked, my eyes fixed on the window where the sprinkles had turned to rain. A shiver ripped up my spine sending my already clenched fist into a death-grip around the phone.

"Are you sure?"

"As sure as the fact that Dr. Rose Floris has a stalker."

A *stalker.* The words grabbed my throat, choking the air from my windpipe.

A stalker who'd broken into my house.

My pulse started to race.

"Was the recorder on?"

"Yep, 24/7 streaming if I had to guess."

"Streaming? How?"

"It's a wireless recorder. Once your stalker—"

"Please stop saying that."

"Okay, once the *dude who secretly wanted to video you* got into your house, he used your own Wi-Fi to connect to the internet."

"And then what?"

"Probably went home and popped a boner and a bottle of Bordeaux."

"You're sick, you know that?"

"Hey, I've never spied on a woman."

"I can't believe this." I muttered, shaking my head.

Andrew continued. "Hey, at least we know it wasn't Crazy Carl, right?"

Carl's tortured body flashed before my eyes, giving me a dose of nausea along with my racing heart.

"Anyway, I assume the guy set up the camera to stream through one of those live streaming apps, then went home, logged in, and voila."

"Using my own internet connection."

"Yep. If I were you, first thing I'd do when I got home was cut the internet. Or, have fun with it. There's this new lingerie shop down Main Street—"

"This isn't funny."

"It could be. All I'm sayin'."

"Is there a way to trace the computer that the recorder is connected to? Maybe we could find out who it is that way?"

"Well, technically yes, *but* if this guy knows *anything* about technology, or if he's done this before, or if he's even a bit intelligent, he's probably got it routed to a fake IP address. Super easy to do."

"Dammit."

"Yeah. Anyway, I've got the recorder. Wanna see it?"

"Yes, of course." My head started to spin. "Can you have your brother check it for prints?"

"If I were you, I'd call the cops and let them handle it."

"Yeah *right,* Andrew, this will rank right below last week-end's liquor store thief."

Andrew laughed. "No, gerbils were stolen last weekend. And I don't want to know what someone is going to do with twenty gerbils from the pet shop. Maybe we could ask your stalker."

"Stop. *Ugh.*" I slapped my hand on my forehead. "Okay, text me your address. I'll be right there."

"With a bottle of Bordeaux?"

"With a pair of blue-handled scissors."

He laughed again. At least someone thought this was funny.

"Okay, I'll text you the address, but I'm meeting the boys for poker night in forty-five minutes, so make it quick."

"I'll be there before forty-five minutes."

"See you soon."

My pulse raced as I clicked off the phone.

A *stalker.*

Everything I had done the night before ran like a list through my head... Oh my God, I'd changed my clothes. Had the perv seen me undress? Had the whole world seen me naked? Was my naked body broadcasted somewhere on the internet?

My stomach clenched, and for a second I thought I might throw up.

"You okay?"

I spun around, the phone slipping from my grip and clamoring onto the floor. Phoenix picked it up.

"Sorry," I said breathlessly. I took the phone from his hands. "Slippery... uh, cell phone..."

His steely expression told me he didn't buy that.

"I've... I've got to take care of something real quick. I'm sorry."

I breezed past him, but he followed me into my office. I felt his eyes burning into me as I slid behind my computer and began closing out the screens. My hand trembled over the keyboard.

"Are you sure you're alright?"

"Yes. Fine." The cartoon-sounding pitched tone that

came out of me did nothing to convince him. I cleared my throat. "I'm fine. Uh, how about you call tomorrow morning and we'll get our next appointment set up? I'm sorry about this."

Another minute passed. He was watching me, assessing yet again, but I didn't care. My focus was on the ten open emails I needed to finish before I could leave for Andrew's.

When I looked up, Phoenix was gone. Like a ghost. I blinked, stared at the doorway a minute, then pushed Mr. Steele aside and focused on my emails.

It was thirty minutes before I was able to walk away from work. Two phone calls and eight urgent emails—two, I'd left in draft mode. I needed to get to Andrew's, then home and immediately turn off my internet.

I gathered my briefcase and purse and jogged through the lobby, locking the office after slipping outside. The early evening was chilly and as black as coal thanks to the relentless rain. I jogged to my car and plugged Andrew's address into my GPS. According to the directions and aerial map, he lived on fifteen acres outside of town. A drive that would take at least twenty minutes in the rain. The street lights flickered as I pulled onto Main Street and sped through the town's square. The locals had gathered at Donny's Diner for an early dinner. Tad's Tool Shop was bustling with cowboys, probably getting extra supplies to prepare for the severe storms we were supposed to get over the next few days. Banshee's Brew liquor store was packed to the gills, as always.

I took a left at the only stoplight in Berry Springs and followed the curvy road out of town. I was a mile down the road when I saw a large silhouette walking down the shoulder. I flicked on my high beams, squinted through the downpour, and leaned over the steering wheel. My foot slowly pressed the brakes.

No way.

No *freaking* way.

I slowed to four miles an hour and rolled down my window, rain and cold wind swirling inside.

"What the heck are you doing?"

Keeping his stride, Phoenix glanced over his shoulder. "Going home."

My mouth gaped. I pressed the gas and edged next to him. For someone who was in physical therapy, the guy had some speed. Seriously, his walking gait equaled my jog.

Rain poured off his hair, the tip of his nose, his chin. He was soaked to the bone.

"I thought someone was giving you a ride?"

"Rather walk." He kept his eyes ahead.

"You'd rather walk in a rainstorm, in the dark?"

No response.

"Or you didn't want to burden your brothers with a call?"

Nothing.

"Well." I glanced in the rearview mirror and blew out a breath. "You can't walk home."

"Then why don't you sign a waiver that says I'm fine to drive."

"Nice guilt trip."

"Nice organization caddy in your console."

I glanced at the "Happy car" car organizer I'd had secured to my console. Everything in its place, divvied up between adjustable binders and multi-sized pockets. Life changer, those things are.

How had he even seen it?

I looked at the dark road ahead, blurred by sheets of rain. Goosebumps from the chill prickled my arm. I knew he and his brothers lived on a massive compound at the top of Shadow Mountain, but wasn't sure where it was—or where I was for that matter.

"How far away do you live?"

"Not far."

"Define not far."

"Not far."

I shook my head. "Get in."

...

"Get *in.*"

This. Guy.

"Phoenix, *accept help* and get into my damn car. *Now.* I don't have time for your macho male bullcrap right now."

When he still didn't stop, I gassed it, yanked the wheel and drove into the ditch, cutting him off. The SUV bottomed out in a muddy ditch.

That stopped him.

"What the *hell* are you doing, woman?" He asked. "You just got yourself stuck."

"Well if you weren't so bull-headed—"

He opened my door. "Scoot over."

"You scoot over."

We both frowned at each other.

With a huff, I squeezed myself over my *organization caddy* and settled into the passenger seat. After kicking something behind the tires, Phoenix slid behind the wheel, taking up every inch of the seat—heck, the entire left side of the vehicle. The man looked like a giant in the driver's seat. He slammed the car into reverse and with no trouble at all, reversed and, within seconds, we were back on the road.

"What did you put under the tires?"

"Your car mat."

"My *what?*"

"I'll get you another."

"Those were special-made."

"I don't doubt that."

I rolled my eyes.

"Where're we going?" He glanced at the GPS.

"We aren't going anywhere. You drive yourself home, and then I need to get somewhere. Fast."

"You're not going to make it."

"How do you know I'm not going to make it?"

"Forty-five minutes. It's been forty since you hung up with whoever called you."

It was the first time I'd considered that Phoenix had heard my end of the conversation with Andrew. I looked at the clock. He was right. Andrew would leave for his poker night in five minutes.

I was in a pickle.

Following the Italian female voice directing him through the speakers, Phoenix hung a left.

"She sounds hot."

"It's a computer generated voice, you perv."

"Doesn't mean it's not hot. Can you speak in an Italian accent, doctor?"

"Seriously..." I muttered under my breath, shaking my head.

A moment passed.

"What exactly did you hear while I was on the phone?"

"We're here."

He turned next to a red-brick mailbox that matched a small, brick home a few yards from the road. Manicured shrubbery hugged the house, matching the green shutters and garage door. It was the quintessential "newlywed's beginner house," if not for the tie-dye curtains that were pulled tightly against the front window, and the two mismatched folding chairs encircled by empty beer bottles on the front porch. A bachelor pad, by all counts. No cars were parked outside and the house was dark except for a dim light outlining the curtains. Phoenix parked in front of the garage.

I set my purse in the back seat. "Stay here, I'll be right—"

The driver's side door slammed shut.

"You've got to be kidding..." I muttered as I jumped out, my heels stabbing into the wet earth. "Hey." I tip-toe-jogged around the hood. "I said, *hey*."

Ignoring me, Phoenix walked up the porch steps.

"Listen, you don't even know whose house this is, or why we're here. Go sit in the car and wait. I'll be five minutes." Gripping the handrail, I jumped up the steps and fisted the back of his wet coat. "Phoenix. *Go back* to the car."

He finally graced me with his attention and turned, blocking my access to the front door.

"No."

"No?"

"No. Whoever called you, didn't just upset you, they scared you."

"Not true."

"Yeah? Maybe we should add 'do not lie' to your list of goals. Your cagey eyes and trembling hands after you hung up told a different story. Not to mention the blush on your cheeks. Your neck was as red as the bottom of your heels. Why is that, anyway?"

"Why is what?"

"Why is only the sole of your shoe red?"

"It's the brand. The trademark of the brand."

"Of what?"

"Christian Louboutin."

"Lou who?"

"The CEO of a multi-million-dollar company doesn't know about Louboutins?"

"I don't wear heels."

"It's not *just* heels...sheesh," I clicked my tongue. "Are we seriously talking about this right now?"

"Seems odd is all. I mean, make the whole thing red, you know? Anyway, whatever was said on that phone call scared you and I'll be damned if I'm going to let you go into that house alone."

"This isn't any of your business."

"I just made it my business. Together, or not at all. Isn't that right?"

I threw my hands up and pushed past him. "You're impossible."

"This coming from my therapist," he said under his breath as we turned toward the door. I rang the doorbell, waited a few beats, then rang it again. My gaze shifted to the front window, looking for movement, or anything to indicate Andrew was still home.

I bypassed the doorbell and knocked.

"He was expecting you, right?"

"Yes. He might've left already, but..." I glanced back at the car where I'd left my phone. "Surely he would have called or texted me first."

Phoenix nudged me out of the way and grabbed the knob.

"Wait. What are you doing?"

The door slowly opened, a pitched *creak* echoing through the air.

"Stay behind me," Phoenix said in a tone that sent me on alert.

I watched his hand slide to the gun I didn't realize he carried on his belt—regardless that his concealed carry license had been pulled. I wasn't surprised. If I knew anything about Phoenix Steele already it was that he didn't do what he was told. Funny; a car, he didn't need. A gun, he couldn't live without it. It was interesting insight to the man, and made me wonder how much of his life was shaped by his time in the military.

The house smelled of cheap air fresheners, tacos, and the lingering scent of something herbal that suggested Andrew had his own license of sorts—a medical license.

The first thing I noticed was that it was dead silent. No TV noise, hum of a heater, whine of a dishwasher, no video game on loop, nothing.

The house was small with a living room beyond the entryway, bedrooms to the side, and kitchen at the end of the house. The living room had the bare essentials, a massive flat screen TV streaming a baseball game on mute, a pair of mismatched, hand-me-down love seats, and in the corner, a lazy-boy complete with cup holders and an adjustable leg rest. On the coffee table, a half-eaten plate of tacos and a longneck.

"Andrew?" I called out and stepped beside Phoenix.

"I said stay behind me."

Nerves tickled my stomach.

Phoenix kept his hand on his holster as we stepped down the hallway. The room to the left appeared to be an office of sorts—vacant, and lights off—and next to that, a spare room, which was also vacant.

Tap, tap, tap...

I frowned.

Tap, tap, tap...

"You hear that?" I whispered.

Phoenix's eyes were laser-focused on the entryway to the kitchen, where the tapping noise appeared to be coming from. A blast of cool air had the hair on the back of my neck prickling. Phoenix drew his gun in such a smooth, routine manner I might not have noticed if I wasn't looking for it. My heart began to pound as we stepped into the kitchen.

And that's when I saw it. My second dead body of the day.

I gasped. My body froze mid-stride as I stared at the motionless pair of legs just beyond the screen door that was flapping against the wind. The rest of the body was out of view.

Andrew.

Was it Andrew?

Phoenix grabbed my arm and yanked me to the corner of the room.

"Get down. *Now.*" His voice was strong, but calm.

I nodded incessantly, sinking into the corner of the kitchen.

An old, familiar place.

The corner of the kitchen... rain against the windows... my purple nightgown. Flashbacks of that night raced as I huddled in the corner and hugged my knees to my chest. My entire body began to tremble.

I watched Phoenix sweep the room, then step outside, onto the deck, as I sat there like a useless idiot.

Do something, Rose.

911.

I felt around in my pocket, then remembered I left my phone in the car. Screw this, I thought as I pushed to a stance. Thunder rumbled as I stepped outside, into the pouring rain, and my own nightmare.

"Get inside." Phoenix yelled, but the words didn't register.

Lightning streaked the sky as I stumbled backwards, gripping the door frame for balance as I stared down at the body on the deck. Wearing the same vintage T-shirt as earlier, Andrew's dead, rain-soaked body lay face-down on the wooden slats. One arm was tucked under his body, the other splayed to the side as if he were hailing a cab. His knees were bent awkwardly, with bare feet at the bottom of dark denim jeans. It was funny, my first thought was that his feet must be cold and that I should get a blanket for him. But that thought evaporated when Phoenix kneeled and slowly lifted the side of Andrew's body.

I'll never forget it. The way his arm drug with the pull, the limpness of his torso swaying against Phoenix's grip.

And the blood. My God, the blood. The pool of shiny, dark red pooling beneath his body. His shirt was saturated, the colorful swirls of what was once a Beatles T-shirt faded into a solid red stain of blood.

So much *blood.*

But that wasn't the worst of it.

As if in slow motion, Andrew's head lobbed to the side, his glazed-over eyes staring blankly into the rain, his jaw slack as if he were in mid-scream. The left side of his head was matted in blood and as gravity took its final movement, a flap of skin separated from his face, showcasing a laceration that sliced all the way to his ear, leaving it dangling by strings of skin.

Bile rose to my throat and I propelled myself backward, stumbling into the kitchen and falling to the ground inches from a brown, paper bag.

My eyes widened as I grabbed it and ripped it open.

Empty.

I frantically searched the room. But there was no bear, no video camera, anywhere.

Nothing.

I looked back at Andrew on the deck, his ear dangling in the wind.

Then, I turned and vomited all over my Louboutins.

12

ROSE

I watched from the passenger seat of my SUV as the chaos unfolded around me. Blue and red lights sparkled in the rain, bouncing off the trees, the cars, the brick house in front of me. Andrew's front yard was scattered with Berry Springs' finest, both uniformed and plain clothes. And then there was Phoenix, towering over all of them by at least four inches, somehow looking more menacing than those with guns and cuffs at their hips. I watched his movements, the squared shoulders, tight jaw, steely look in his eye as he addressed the other men. The guy had a confidence—an authority—that seemed as innate to him as breathing. It was a side to him I hadn't seen. Yet another layer to the complexity that was Phoenix Steele.

I watched as his gaze flickered again to mine, as it had done countless times since he'd held me while I'd vomited all over his cowboy boots, then carried me to the car, wrapped me in his leather jacket, and turned the heater full blast. He'd found a bottle of water somewhere, and then after making me promise I was okay, he called 911 and took care of business.

The man I watched was strong, efficient, capable. The opposite of what his medical file read. Even then, the sidelong glances from the officers, the whispers when he turned his back, were obvious. It was apparent everyone knew each other, as was common with most small towns, and it was also apparent that Phoenix didn't give a crap about their continued glances at him. But I knew he'd noticed.

He'd tucked his gun into his boot before the first cop car had arrived. I was worried that they'd frisk him, but they didn't, and I couldn't help but wonder if it was because they didn't want to face his wrath once they placed their hands on him. Or, if they were simply scared of him, as so many people seemed to be.

Phoenix was a presence, there was no doubt about that. Someone known, whispered about, wondered about. Someone who commanded the room simply by walking into it.

Our eyes met again, and this time his gaze lingered.

My stomach tickled.

A line of worry drew across his brows and he dipped his chin—*are you still okay?*

Yes. I nodded back. *Thanks to you.*

Two uniforms lingered outside my door, unaware of my presence in the vehicle. I cracked the window and strained to listen.

"... *fresh scratches on the back door lock indicate a break-in. Looks like something sharp did it. Probably a knife.*"

"*No deadbolt?*"

"*Nope, just a handle lock.*"

"*Guy probably used a credit card to pop it. Tracks?*"

"*A few faded boot prints in the mud, but for the most part, the rain washed everything away.*"

"*Anything missing from the house?*"

"*Loose power cords in the bedroom suggest a laptop was plugged in, possibly taken. Dresser doors were open, as if someone was looking for jewelry. We're working on the assumption that the homeowner confronted the intruder and that's when things got ugly.*"

"*Stabbed to death I heard?*"

"*Yep. Pretty messy.*"

"*Any sign of the knife?*"

"*That's the weird thing... the wound doesn't appear to be from a knife. More like puncture wounds...*"

A pair of knuckles rapped at my door, scaring the daylights out of me. I looked for Phoenix—my bodyguard—but he was gone. I rolled down the window.

"Miss Floris, can you please—"

"She already gave her statement." Phoenix's deep voice boomed from the shadows.

"Mr. Steele." In full uniform, the officer turned toward Phoenix. He was young, a rookie I guessed, and at least a foot shorter than Phoenix. "Good. I wanted to have a word with you, too."

"I've already given my statement as well, Willard."

"Who did you speak with?"

"Chief McCord."

"And you?" Willard leaned down to my window.

In a move that was as shocking as awkward, Phoenix nudged Willard out of the way and positioned himself in front of my window.

Protective, much? Uh, *yeah.*

"Alright, guys..." Another voice joined the pissing-match beside me. "Let's break it up."

"Detective Jagger." Officer Willard grumbled, not pleased with Phoenix.

"Willard," the detective replied. "I believe the press has

already gotten wind about an incident on the mountain. Might want to sync up the team."

Another second ticked by and I was steeling myself for a fist fight. Finally, the young officer mumbled something and walked away.

Phoenix turned and leaned into the window. "Don't roll down this window for anyone else. Do you understand me?"

I frowned. "But—"

"For *no one*. I'll be right back."

I rolled up the window and watched him step to the side with Detective Jagger. They fell into conversation, and although Phoenix kept glancing over at me, his demeanor appeared to relax with the detective. This told me the two men were acquaintances, friendly even. Good to know.

Just then, all heads turned to the end of the driveway where a white media van pulled up and a petite, blonde, impeccably-dressed spitfire hopped out of the passenger door and began shouting something to her cameraman who was struggling to catch up.

Then, my driver's side door opened and Phoenix slid behind the wheel. The engine fired up.

"Wait," I hissed in a whisper as if everyone could hear us. "You're not supposed to be driving. You're going to get arrested."

He slammed the car into reverse as Detective Jagger, in all his wide-shouldered massiveness, positioned in front of the windshield, blocking the crowd's view of Phoenix behind the wheel.

Definitely friends.

Phoenix shoved the SUV into reverse and gassed it out of the driveway. We rode down the muddy dirt road in silence as everything faded behind us. Then—

"Talk."

"What? About what?" I snapped back unintentionally, but I was frazzled.

"I want you to tell me everything you told the cops."

"You were standing right there."

"I want to hear it again," his voice was actually shaking with anger. "From the bear found on your bed, to the recorder Andrew said he found in it. Everything, just you and me."

"I don't want to repeat everything right now. I'm—"

The vehicle stopped with such force that my body flung forward. We slid a good twelve-inches on mud before stopping.

"Someone broke into your goddamn house and was *recording you,* Rose!" His eyes were wide, wild. A look I'd seen moments before he'd destroyed my desk. My body tensed from head to toe.

"Calm down, Phoenix."

"I will not calm down until you tell me everything again, and if you leave one single detail out, so help me..."

"Fine."

We sat on the side of the road as I told the story again. He listened, motionless, with white knuckles on the steering wheel and a jaw clenched so tight I was surprised his teeth didn't fall out. His eyes remained fixed on the road, as if that was the only way he wouldn't interrupt. When I finished, he said—

"And you have no idea who could have done it? Who broke into your house and implanted a secret freaking camera?"

"No."

He heaved out a breath. "You told the cops no one has the keys to your home. Was that a lie?"

"No."

"*No one* has keys to your place?"

"No. No one."

He stared at me for a minute as if he didn't believe me. Then—

"Were you fucking Andrew?"

"*What?*" My neck whipped toward him.

He stared back.

"Not that it's any of your business, but no. Andrew and I weren't *having sex*. What would that have to do with anything, anyway? What would it matter if we were?"

"Just gathering the facts, sweetheart."

'Wild Phoenix' had switched to weirdly-possessive 'Jerk Phoenix' in seconds flat. And I didn't like it.

"One, don't call me sweetheart, two, if you slam the brakes like that again, I'll have Chief McCord take you away in a patrol car."

"Wouldn't be the first time."

"I don't doubt that."

"What? Does that scare you? Does it scare you that I've spent time in jail?"

My gaze leveled his. "*You* don't scare me."

"I'll have to work on that then." He pressed the gas with just enough force to show me he didn't give a damn about my threat.

A moment passed.

"Did the cops find the recorder at the scene?"

"No."

"The bear?"

"No."

I laughed a humorless laugh. "They don't believe me. You saw how they looked at me as I told them what happened. Like I was freaking crazy. And even if they did believe me, they have a homicide to deal with and the last thing they're going to worry about is some sicko watching me."

"Jagg is going to personally search Andrew's house before he leaves. If anything is there, he'll find it."

I laughed again, feeling like I was sliding off the rails. "Then, what? The bear and recorder are going to get buried in some evidence box somewhere and I'll never hear about it again. I know how this stuff goes. I know how things slip through the system, trust me on that." The words seethed from my lips. He looked over at me, but I kept my eyes ahead. The guy didn't know a thing about me. About my past.

"They wouldn't be buried in an evidence room, Rose, if they have something to do with a homicide."

"What... what?"

He impatiently shook his head. "Rose, someone broke into your house and implanted a secret video camera. You take the thing to Andrew, and eight hours later, the recorder is gone and the kid is stabbed to death."

"Stop, Phoenix."

"*Think* about it, Rose. I believe you, and I don't think this is some ironic home burglary. I think whoever is stalking you didn't want that recorder to be found. They broke into Andrew's to get it back, Andrew confronted him, and he killed Andrew and took the evidence, then staged it to look like a good ol' fashioned break-in."

"No." I shook my head like a crazy woman. "No. You're wrong. Who... how would anyone even know that I took it to Andrew? Even if the guy was watching me through the camera feed, it would have clicked off when I left the house and broke the internet connection."

"Someone is obsessed with you, Rose. Stalking you.

They know where you live, where you work." He glanced in the rearview mirror.

"You think I was followed to the morgue this morning? No. I would have noticed."

"Would you have?"

"Yes," I snapped.

"Okay. Fine. How many cars were in Andrew's driveway when we left?"

"Uh..."

"Five. Two squad cars, an ambulance, and two trucks. Six, if you count the media van that had just pulled up." He paused. "What was the color of the truck that parked directly in front of yours? The one that you stared at for an hour waiting for me?"

I blinked.

"You don't know because you weren't paying attention to your surroundings."

"Yes, I—"

"No you weren't, Rose. Most people don't, especially under duress. When you were driving to the morgue this morning, you were stressed out. From the rain, the bear, separating your breakfast out by color, height, and weight, whatever. I'm one hundred percent confident a herd of wild buffalo could have been following you and you wouldn't have noticed."

Everything was getting way too real, including the headache pounding between my ears.

He passed the turn that led to Shadow Mountain, where he lived.

"Where are you going?" I asked.

"Your house."

"My house? No. No way."

"Rose, I hate to have to spell this out for you, but it's a

good bet that last night wasn't the first time the sicko broke into your house."

My stomach dropped to my feet. The thought that someone had been watching me even before the bear made my pulse skyrocket. I scrubbed my hands over my face, then held up my palms. It was too much. Everything was too much.

"No. I don't need you to come over. I'm fine. I can call Officer Willard—"

"*I'll* handle it." He snapped like a child.

"Handle *what,* exactly?"

"Someone needs to check your locks, the windows, the property."

"The property? You're crazy—"

"That's right sweetheart, I am crazy. And you *will* deal with this, and you'll deal with me. Period."

I gaped at him. Then, blame it on the two dead bodies I'd seen that day, but I gave up. Surrendered. There was no questioning Phoenix Steele when he had his mind set—and his mind was set on accompanying me home. The man was taking personal responsibility for my safety.

And I found myself wondering... was it like that with every woman... or just me?

13

ROSE

*N*erves tickled my stomach as we topped the driveway to my house. The rain had turned into a deluge, making the steep drive up the mountain hair-raising at best. The cabin looked dark, haunting against the moonless night, and it was the first time that I didn't smile seeing it. My house was my baby. The house I'd renovated from the top down and loved so much. Now it was cold and unwelcoming, forever tainted with the visions of a faceless man breaking in and stealing the one thing most sacred to me, my sense of safety. My privacy. My life.

The bastard who quite possibly also killed Andrew.

A wave of nausea washed over me as the image of his bloody body flashed through my head. I squeezed my eyes shut and shifted in my seat. I wanted it to go away. Everything. I wanted to go to sleep and forget everything that had happened.

Well, that wasn't in the cards.

Phoenix parked under the carport and was out the door before I could even gather my things. I watched him bypass the front porch and head toward the back yard. The headlights silhouetted his tall, thick frame as he disappeared into the rain.

I grabbed my raincoat from the back, pulled it on and pushed out the door. "Hey." I wobbled on my heels as I jogged to catch up. "Where're you going?"

"Perimeter check."

"It's raining. And I don't have a fence." I pulled the strings to the hood around my neck, securing it tightly around my face. I probably looked ridiculous.

He kept walking as if I didn't exist.

"*Hey,* I said I don't have a fence."

"A perimeter is the continuous line that encloses the boundary of something."

"I *just said* I don't have a fence." I yelled over the rain.

"Are you familiar with property lines, Miss Flower?"

"Don't call me that, and I thought we agreed to be less condescending."

"You. You agreed to be less condescending." He slid out of his jacket and draped it over my shoulders.

"And you agreed to work on your communication. So communicate. What are you checking for?"

"Tracks."

The headlights clicked off behind us and everything went dark. I grabbed for him. He paused for a split-second to allow me to grip ahold of his T-shirt. I had no idea how Phoenix could see where he was going, let alone check for tracks.

"I want you to pull together a list of everyone who knows where you live."

"Okay."

"And anyone or any business that has access to your address."

"That's going to take some time."

"Get it done. And spend some more time thinking of anyone who could have an obsession with you. Think beyond the obvious. Any fan mail, messages on social media?"

"Fan mail?"

He didn't say anything.

"You know about my podcast?"

A grunt.

I hadn't considered the fact that he knew about that. But it wasn't a secret, so it made sense. I stumbled on a tree limb and fell directly into Phoenix's strong hold.

"Slow down." I said, embarrassment coloring my tone as I pushed out of his arms.

"Answer the question."

"No, I haven't gotten any creepy mail or messages." We started walking again, this time at a slower pace.

"I want access to your social media."

"What?"

"You heard me."

"*No.* Listen, this is my life—"

"Yeah, and someone is obsessed with it, Rose."

"It's ridiculous."

"It's serious. I know about stalkers. I'd say half the female cases at Steele Shadows Security involve some sort of stalking, and let me tell you, it's more than a weird obsession."

"OLD."

"Old what?"

"No, O-L-D. It's an actual disorder. Obsessive Love Disorder. It's an attachment disorder that's commonly associated with another mental illness, like Borderline Personality Disorder."

"Didn't Jeffery Dahmer have Borderline Personality Disorder?"

"Yes. It's actually common with a lot of serial killers."

"What else causes OLD, specifically?"

"Low self-esteem is most common. Neglect, abuse. Usually there's some tipping point to the obsession. A trigger. Something happens in the person's life, whether it be monumental or something small like a birthday or something, and it sets them off."

"Something that makes them go off the rails, so to speak?"

"Right. A trigger."

We walked a moment in silence.

"You got a boyfriend, Rose?"

The question caught me off guard. "No."

"When was your last relationship?"

"Months ago."

"Before that?"

"Uh, a long time. I'm kind of married to my work."

"How serious were you and your last boyfriend?"

"Decently serious."

"Meaning?"

"We were engaged." I looked down, surprised by my embarrassment.

His stride broke as he looked over at me. He quickly recovered, though, and picked up his pace.

"We'd only dated a few months when he'd asked. I said yes and our relationship was over a month later."

"Why?"

I shrugged and looked away. My ex fiancé was pretty much the last thing I wanted to talk about at that moment.

"What's his name?" His tone was sharp, possessive, and sent me on edge. I didn't like it.

"This isn't really any of your business, okay?"

"You and him still talk?"

I looked at him, his face barely visible through the darkness, but there was no mistaking the heat in his eyes. Why? And why did I feel like these questions had nothing to do with my personal security? And even that—my safety— wasn't his business. He was my *patient* for Christ's sake.

I needed to turn the tables.

"Do you have a girlfriend, Mister Twenty Questions?"

"Oh yeah, the girls are lined up for a mentally deficient unemployed former jarhead without a driver's license."

"You forgot concealed carry."

"Thanks."

"Can we drop this please? I don't want to talk about my ex."

We walked another few minutes in silence as he surveyed the edge of my property that faded into the woods. Him, soaked to the bone in nothing more than a T-shirt, and me, looking like a cartoon character with an oversized rain coat and his leather jacket draped over my shoulders. I still wasn't sure how the heck the guy could see through the darkness, but I assumed it was some superhuman skill he'd developed during his days in the military.

A shiver caught me and I wrapped his jacked tighter.

"So, you're looking for footprints?"

"Footprints, boot prints, broken twigs, breaks in pathway, any sign that someone has passed by here recently. Would be a lot easier if your motion-activated flood lights weren't out."

"I don't have a motion-activated floodlight."

"Exactly."

I rolled my eyes. "Message received. What else?"

He slowed. "Your backyard is small, which is a good

thing, but it backs up to miles of woods, which is not a good thing. You need to get a security fence, and get all the under-brush trimmed and cleared." He stopped mid-stride, clicked on his cell phone light and kneeled down.

I squatted next to him. "What's that? Dog tracks?"

"Coyote."

"Coyote? Out here?"

He gave me a *you're-kidding-me* look.

I cleared my throat. "I meant, a coyote in my yard?"

"Not uncommon. Especially with the rain and cooler temperatures. They're hunting for food."

"How are you sure it's not a dog? I saw this cute little stray on the road a few weeks ago. Tried to grab him but he ran off."

"You shouldn't pick up strays by yourself."

"It was a dog. Not a human."

"They could be rabid." He cut me a glance. "Dog, or human, for that matter."

"Fine. I'll ask for their veterinary records first... the dog's, not the human's." I smirked. "Anyway, how do you know this isn't a dog?"

He picked up a twig and pointed to the tracks. "Coyote tracks are narrower and more oval than a dog's, but even then, it's hard for the untrained eye to tell."

"Train me, then."

He handed me the light. "See here? The gait?" He trailed the stick along the prints in the mud. "This is called the overstep trot, distinctive to coyotes. See how the front and hind feet are on the same side of the body? And see how they land close together? Almost in a straight line?"

I leaned closer, our faces inches apart.

Butterflies... despite everything going on... butterflies. Just being that close to him.

He took back his cell phone and stood. "They're coyote tracks."

"I guess I need to keep a tighter lid on my trash then." I stood.

"No, you want them around."

"Why?"

"More wild animals, less wild people. And if a coyote has been here recently, it's a good chance a human hasn't."

He shined the light into the trees. "This pine is dying."

"Dying? Really?"

"Yep. I'll get it taken care of."

"What do you mean? Cut it down?"

"You've got a better idea?"

"Yeah. Uh, *not* cut it down."

He turned to me. "How tall do you think this tree is?"

"Fifty feet?"

"Close to a hundred, Stevie Wonder."

I slapped his arm.

"And how deep is your backyard?"

"At the risk of being chastised, I'll say thirty feet."

"Exactly. If that tree falls, it's demolishing your cabin and everything inside it."

"How do you know it's sick?"

He picked up a handful of needles from the ground. "See how these aren't only brown, but have thin, black stripes in them? And look at the pine cones. See the black spots? This tree is infected with a fungus called Diplodia. It's a bitch, 'scuse my language."

"Can you save it?"

"Nope. Too far gone."

"Are you sure?"

"Yes."

"I'm sure it will survive the spring."

"No. It will make good firewood for you for the rest of this cold snap."

"I don't do fires."

He turned fully to me and blinked as if I'd told him whiskey and scotch were the same thing.

"You do now." He replied simply.

"You sure are good at telling people what to do, you know that?"

"Yes." He shifted his focus from the dying tree to my cabin. "You got a trimmer?"

"Trimmer for what?"

"The shrubs that line your house need to be either removed or cut back. All of them."

"No way. They just flowered. I don't know what they are, but I love them."

"Forsythias. You can plant them somewhere else."

"I'm leaving them."

"Then you're leaving a perfect place for someone to hide before breaking into your house again. The tree by your carport also needs to be removed. Same reason. Come on. Walk behind me. There's a mud puddle here." I kept ahold of the back of his shirt as he walked and continued, "You'll need motion-activated lights on all four corners of your house. I'll order them from Tad."

"Who's Tad?"

"Tad's Tool Shop."

"I'll get them."

"I'll get them cheaper. What's that?"

I squinted. "Oh, that's an old shed."

"What's in it?"

"Nothing."

He shook his head.

I cocked mine. "I have a feeling your dream woman wears a tool belt and carries an M16."

"I have a feeling your dream man eats Kale and smells like patchouli."

"Oh because all therapists are beatnik hippies?"

"How does it feel to be labeled?"

Touché.

"When was your last girlfriend, Phoenix?"

No response.

"Ah, the Lone Ranger can't remember. Let me guess, the moment a woman tries to get too close, you bolt. Why? Because the playing field becomes blurry. You have to be in control at all times and the only way to do that is to keep a relationship at arm's length."

"Who says I'd have to give up control in a relationship?"

"Uh, every woman on the planet."

"Wrong. Every woman who's never had a real man take care of them."

"I thought we established that you need to accept that you can't control *everything*—"

"Wrong, again." He turned on his heel, stopping inches from my face. I barreled into his chest. Strong hands gripped my hips, rooting me to the ground. He looked down at me with an intensity that had my heart slamming against my ribcage.

"If you were mine, it would be my job to control you, Rose Flower. To keep tabs on you, know where you're at, where you're going. It would be my job to keep you safe, to keep you happy. To keep you comfortable, content. Satisfied. It's my job, as your man, to control all that. It's my job to keep you mine."

My eyes rounded, goosebumps racing over my arms. I searched for words, for any coherent sentence, but came up short as he stared down at me with piercing blue eyes that dared me to question him.

In nothing but a breathy whisper, I finally said, *"If* I was yours."

"... Of course."

He turned and walked away, leaving my pulse racing, jaw slacked, and a rush of heat between my legs that had me trying to remember the last time I'd bought triple-A batteries.

Holy *shit,* was all I could think.

"You coming?"

Oh dear God, yes.

Thorn. That perv.

I snapped out of it and chased after him. In my six inch heels, in the rain, I literally chased after the man.

He was checking the shed when I caught up to him, and to no one's surprise, he'd popped the chintzy lock I'd attached to the rickety double doors.

"There really is nothing in here." He said almost in disbelief.

"Yeah. I don't have tools."

"Who mows your lawn?"

"I have a lawn service."

"I'll need their names, too."

"Of course you will."

"I'd rather you handle your yard yourself, or have me or my brother do it." He surveyed the yard. "You could plant clover this season. Stays green all summer, requires less mowing, less water. And it'll attract deer, good insects."

"And maybe bring me some luck?"

"How about you make your own luck and let me install those flood lights ASAP?"

"Yes, sir."

His brow cocked and a grin tugged his lips.

I smiled wanting those lips on mine. STAT.

A moment passed as he checked the inside of the shed. For what? Who knew.

I ducked inside, out of the rain. "How do you know so much about nature and animals?"

"Grew up in the woods."

"When you weren't busy raising your brothers?"

No response.

"I'm right, aren't I? I have to admit I know a bit about your family. Everyone around here does. And it makes sense, then, the guilt. You're the oldest son and you've always been the leader of the pack. Right? Your brothers idolize you. The unbreakable Phoenix Steele. And now, you're the one needing help, and you can't stand it."

"Am I going to get a bill for this later, Doctor?"

"No. I'm just trying to crack open that shell a bit."

He turned toward me, a black outline against the darkness.

"Might want to get a jackhammer, Miss Flower."

14

PHOENIX

*A*fter shutting down that impending psychoanalysis, I followed Rose Flower up her sloping backyard, and while I kept one eye surveying the woods, the other kept drifting to the curves of her ass and the hypnotic sway that was no match for anything with a pair of balls. Who would've thought I'd think wide-legged slacks were sexy? Or any stuffy, boring office suit for that matter? Most of the women I'd dated considered a cutoff denim skirt as black tie.

There had been an immediate, visceral reaction the first moment I saw Dr. Rose Floris. A normal reaction considering the woman was smokin' hot, but what wasn't normal was the dip in my stomach the second our eyes met. Nerves, but something deeper. Something that I was certain I hadn't felt with another woman. But that was nothing— *nothing*—compared to the moment she told me she was being stalked. The fire that had ignited inside me was so intense, it reminded me of being in a war zone. A protectiveness that rivaled what I felt for my own brothers. A possessiveness that flicked a switch in me, a dangerous desperation to keep her both safe and to eliminate anyone who challenged that.

Anyone who challenged me.

Who challenged what was mine.

Mine.

My Rose Flower.

I didn't like what this woman was doing to me. I knew I was stubborn and short-tempered. Always had been. But after waking up from the coma, that temper was on steroids —like my feelings for her. It unnerved me in a way I hadn't felt before, and my logical side was screaming that this weird tangle of emotions was the *last* thing I needed.

Logical? Or maybe it was that commitment-phobe she'd so quickly pinned.

The woman had me swinging on a pendulum ranging between lust, annoyance, disdain, respect, admiration, and whatever the heck my stomach did when she looked at me.

It was unsafe. *I* was unsafe. Unpredictable... and she made me so much more unpredictable.

I didn't like it.

I needed to control it.

I needed to tuck it away on a shelf, because, above all else someone needed to keep the independent, stubborn, annoying Rose Floris safe.

And that man was going to be me.

I took a note of the single lock on her front door, then followed her inside the cabin.

I wasn't sure what I'd expected but it wasn't what I got. Based on Rose's designer clothes, luxury handbags, and BMW—that looked like a tennis shoe, by the way—I'd expected modern, sleek furniture, pink pillows, bejeweled knick knacks and a stack of rom-coms that stretched to the ceiling. What I got was an earthy, masculine color palette and minimal furniture. Each piece was arranged in ninety-degree angles and identical inches apart. The place was spotless. I'm talking not a speck of dirt anywhere.

A plaid loveseat sat across from a brown leather couch covered with monochrome pillows and a red afghan blanket. Over a beige, woven rug was a cherry oak coffee table, gleaming with what surely took an entire bottle of Pledge. A stack of coasters sat in the middle, of course. The fireplace was the centerpiece of the home, with long-stemmed candles at the ends—burned only to the tips. It was warm, cozy. Surprising. But not nearly as surprising as the fact that there wasn't a single photograph anywhere in sight. No family pictures, no "girls' night" photos. Nothing.

She was eyeing me from the kitchen as she clicked on the overhead light. Again, minimal and spotless. I inwardly laughed to myself. The woman would have a coronary if she knew I slept on hay next to horses.

As I lifted my leg to step past the entryway, she said—

"Wipe your shoes."

I froze, recoiled, wiped.

"May I come in now?"

"Yes."

I crossed the living room, noting the heels she'd kicked off into the corner just below a painting on the wall of a white horse that looked identical to Spirit.

"You like horses?" I asked, surprised, again.

She tossed me a towel. I caught it midair and began wiping myself down as she did the same.

"Do you want something else to put on? I think I have some large t-shirts somewhere, and maybe some sweat pants that might fit."

"I'm good."

"Okay. And, yes. I've always loved horses. Magical creatures, they are. You?"

"Same here."

She slipped out of my leather jacket and her oversized rain coat and began wiping my jacket down.

I took the towel from her, nudged her out of the way and picked up where she left off.

She watched me for a moment before saying, "Horses can be very therapeutic, you know."

I thought of all the times I'd felt a connection to Spirit. Riding her through the woods seemed to be the only moments of contentment, of peace, I'd felt since waking up from the coma.

I glanced over my shoulder where Rose was reaching on her tiptoes for a bottle of wine above the fridge. I pulled it down for her, our bodies brushing against each other.

"Thank you."

Her demeanor had shifted. The fight was gone, the adrenaline rush from seeing a dead body was beginning to take its toll. Her hand shook as she grabbed the corkscrew.

"Here." I took the wine, opened it, and poured her a glass.

She leaned against the countertop, sipped.

I leaned next to her.

A heavy silence settled over the room. I'd seen plenty of dead men in my life, but assumed she hadn't. The first were always jarring. The images tend to replay on a loop in your head. But it fades. Like everything around us, it fades.

Keeping her gaze ahead, her hand drifted to my side and lightly grabbed my T-shirt, the touch like fire through the cotton. We didn't look at each other, simply stood motionless, with her gripping the end of my shirt like a child.

A terrified little girl.

My hand drifted over hers. I willed my brain to say what any normal man would say in that moment. Something sweet, something profound, something right.

You're going to be okay.

But the words remained on the tip of my tongue, locked in some caveman-brain that was incapable of rising to an emotional moment of a woman in need.

She dropped her hand.

Dammit.

Goddammit.

I failed. I was officially incapable of consoling a woman.

My teeth ground as I pushed off the counter. Growing up in a family of Marines, "consoling" involved a bottle of whiskey, or a swift slap in the jaw. Neither would suit this woman. The old Phoenix could easily sidestep an emotional conversation and hypnotize a woman with a couple of tequila shots and the words "special ops." Over the years, I'd found that women were predictable, if nothing else.

But not this one.

This one had a way of turning me into a blubbering Neanderthal.

"Oh." She seemed to snap out of her daze. "I'm so sorry. I didn't even offer you—would you like some wine?"

Yeah, the entire bottle.

"No, thanks, I'm good."

She nodded, then shifted her focus again to the rain outside. Her hands trembled as she took another sip, her expression glazed over. The woman was a mess and I was standing there like a fucking idiot. Two hot messes not knowing how to deal with the situations laid before them. I'd never felt like less of a man as I did in that moment.

I felt that anger begin to simmer in my gut, the frustration of my failure as a man. The beginning of a tornado I knew I couldn't control.

Dr. Rose Floris was too good for a guy like me. That much was obvious. It was also obvious I needed to get out before I made even more of a fool of myself.

As if on cue, she looked at me and said—

"You can check the house. I'm fine. Do your perimeter check, or whatever you call it."

Thank *God.*

"Okay. First, where's your internet modem?"

"Laundry room."

I shifted my focus away from the disappointment in myself to something I could do, I could control, and began a security scan of her house.

I disconnected the internet, ensuring that any more hidden cameras were now useless to her sick stalker.

"Don't turn the internet on again until I've confirmed there are no more cameras in the house. In fact, leave it off for a while."

I expected an argument, but didn't get one. I felt her eyes burning into me as I checked each window.

"Where are you staying tonight?"

"Here."

I stopped, looked over my shoulder. "No you're not."

"Yes, I am." Defiance flickered across her face.

"You will not stay here until I secure your house."

"Fine. After I take you home, I'll run by the store and get some more locks."

"You aren't taking me home. My brother is already on his way." He wasn't, but would be the second I texted him. I didn't like Rose chauffeuring me around. Call it macho male. Whatever.

"Well, you're not staying here. Period."

"Oh, okay, *King* Steele."

"Had that one bottled up for a while, didn't you."

"I don't like you demanding me around."

I went back to the windows, biting back the words, *get used to it, woman.* "What about the girl you work with? The one with red hair and a nose ring. Can you stay with her?"

"I can't get ahold of her."

I narrowed my eyes. "Did you really try to?"

"Yes. I called her from Andrew's while I was waiting in the car. No dice."

"You'll stay with me, then."

"Thank you but, no, I like my job."

"What's that got to do with anything?"

"Staying with a patient would get me fired in an instant. I'm not risking that."

"But you'll risk your life?"

"You're being over the top, Phoenix."

"I'll book you a hotel room, then."

"No."

My jaw clenched. This woman. "What about other friends, family?"

She shook her head.

I felt my patience slipping away. A fearless woman.

A sitting duck.

"How're the windows looking?" She asked from the kitchen, in a feeble attempt to change the subject. I went with it though, while my brain tried to come up with a plan so that I didn't have to physically remove her later.

"Windows 2 and 5 need new locks. I'll get those ordered. And we'll need to drill peep holes in your front and back door." I rattled off more security measures, slipping back into my comfort zone... until I walked into her bedroom.

"Who sent you those flowers?" I snapped.

The question was met with silence, and that answered my question. I spun on my heel, ignoring the warning bell going off in my head telling me to cool it.

"I thought you said you didn't have a boyfriend."

"I don't."

"Who the hell are these orchids from?"

Her eyes slitted with fire, a venom meeting my own. She set her—now empty—wine glass on the counter.

"An old friend."

I don't know which pissed me off more. The fact that she'd slipped into her condescending *I'm-better-than-you* demeanor, or the fact that she thought she could get away with any answer like that. Like I was too stupid to know they were from another man.

Another *man.*

My fists clenched at my side. "Hand delivered?"

"No."

"When? When were they sent?"

"Yesterday."

"The same day you found the bear?"

"Yes."

"Well, Sherlock, there's your prime fucking suspect right there."

"Don't talk to me like I'm a child—"

"Don't talk to me like I'm an idiot."

Her lips curled to a snarl as she crossed the room. "The person who delivered the flowers did not plant the video recorder."

"How do you know that?"

"Because the person who sent the flowers doesn't have a key to my house."

"He broke in."

"The flowers were left on the *doorstep.*" Her voice pitched in the first explosion of emotion I'd seen from her. "Why would he leave flowers on my door, then break into my house?"

"*He.*"

"That's right, Phoenix. *He.*"

"*Who's* he?"

"My ex fiancé."

My insides started vibrating. "Give me a name."

"None of your business."

"Name, Rose."

"You don't know him."

"*Rose.*"

She crossed her arms over her chest, lips pressed in a thin line. Finally, she said, "Josh Davis."

There have been few times in my life that I'd been genuinely shocked. This one, though, took the cake. And that's saying something. My jaw literally slacked open—wasn't proud of that, but that was the least of my worries. Her eyes rounded, too, perhaps realizing, for the first time, that it was a good bet that two former Marines did know each other. Yeah, I knew Josh Davis. My arch-fucking-nemesis and the asshole who was responsible for spreading my medical information all over fucking town.

I couldn't even repeat his name. "Are you *kidding* me?"

"No, I'm not *kidding* you."

I'd stepped into my own twilight zone.

"Where is he?" My gaze darted around the cabin as if I'd expected him to materialize out of thin dust. Trust me, I wished he would have.

She threw up her arms. "What does it matter?"

"He's an entitled, spoiled, cock-sucking, douchebag. Who, by the way, is more than capable of breaking into your house and setting up his own personal peep show." My pulse roared in my ears. "Where is he? I want to talk to him. *Now.*"

"You're not going to talk to him. You need to calm down."

"What did the card say?"

"That's none of your business, Phoenix."

I jabbed my fingers through my hair and began pacing.

"Why do you hate him?"

"We served together in Afghanistan," I snarled.

"And?"

"And what? Captain needle-dick is the poorest excuse for a soldier and deserves to rot in hell." Flashbacks popped in my head like little explosions, along with shooting pains against my temples. I blinked, willing the lightning to subside.

"I can't believe you dated that asshat. What the hell were you thinking, *doctor?*"

"How *dare* you talk to me like that?"

"How dare you date someone like that? You're too good for that piece of shit. And why are you so sure he didn't plant a camera in your bedroom? Are you pussy-whipped by his bank account like everyone else?" *Stop, Phoenix, stop,* the little voice in my head said. But I didn't. In fact, I followed that little doozy up with, "I figured someone who considers themselves a *doctor* would have more sense than that."

Her little nostrils flared with anger, her jaw twitching as her hands curled to fists.

Rose had fight in her.

She stepped toe-to-toe with me. And dammit, I respected that.

"Because, Phoenix..." The sneer in her tone was as cold as ice. "Josh doesn't need to put a camera in my bedroom. He's already seen every inch of my naked body."

The fury that rose through me actually wavered my vision.

With that final bomb, she spun on her heel, stormed past me and yanked open the front door. Rain whipped inside, spinning her hair around an expression that told me I'd just sealed the deal on making sure Dr. Floris saw me as nothing more than a total asshole.

My time was up. I was being kicked out of her house, her life.

Well, at least I was going out with a bang.

I breezed past the woman, the slamming door missing my ass by a half-inch.

Wind whipped over my heated skin as I stepped off the deck.

Josh. Fucking. Davis.

Josh Davis and Rose Floris.

Engaged.

The rage released in a guttural scream as my fist connected with a tree. Again, again, again, the bark flying into the air with speckles of my own blood.

Josh Davis and Rose Floris.

Another knuckle split open.

Josh Davis and Rose Floris.

When the third knuckle split, I stopped, gripped the trunk and rested my forehead against the cold, wet bark.

I hated myself.

My heart was still racing when I looked over my shoulder and saw Rose's silhouette in the window. Then, the curtains were yanked closed, and she disappeared.

Good. *Go,* I thought, because you're too good for me.

Because I am crazy.

I am fucking crazy.

15

PHOENIX

I'd just stepped off the bottom of Rose's driveway when two headlights cut through the darkness. I glanced up the hill where her house was barely visible through the rain, then back at the lights.

The truck slowed, the window rolled down. Not one to miss much, my younger brother, Gunner narrowed his eyes.

"What'd you do to your hand?"

I glanced at the blood dripping off my fingertips.

"Fell into a tree."

He propped his tattooed elbow on the windowsill. He didn't ask if I was okay. That wasn't his style. Gunner was the wallflower of the family, the black sheep. Soft-spoken, although you'd lose a tooth for comparing him to anything soft. He was never the life of the party, never the leader of the pack, but he was the type of guy that when he spoke, the world stopped and everyone listened. Not a single person challenged Gunner Steele and got away with it. While I was in the hospital, Gunner had taken my place at the helm and ran the family business and took care of our younger brothers. He did it, did it well, even though I knew he'd hated every second of it. Gunner was the guy you could count on.

Like I was then.

He grabbed a bag from the backseat, thrust it out the window. "Your ride's in the back."

I glanced at the small trailer attached to the truck. A black snout and black hair to match poked out the side.

"Got a blanket on her?"

"Yep."

I flung the backpack over my shoulder. "Everything in there?"

"Everything you just texted me. Plus tacos and a fifth of Jack."

The corner of my lip curled up. Yep, you could always count on Gunner Steele.

"Heard about Andrew from the morgue." He said.

"Word's out already, huh?"

"Oh yeah. It was all the talk at the liquor store. Bad?"

"Bad."

He nodded and looked away. We'd seen some bad shit in our day, most of which still visited us in our deepest, darkest sleep. When we allowed ourselves to sleep, anyway.

"I need a favor."

"Besides this?"

"Yep."

"I need you to determine Josh Davis's whereabouts last night."

His eyes narrowed, but true to form, he didn't ask. "Will do."

"Also, have Wolf pull a list of current clients at Kline and Associates and then compare that list to criminal records."

Wolf Blackwood, our head of security at Steele Shadows

was known as much for his genius-level IQ as his ability to hack into secure systems. My personal favorite thing about him.

"Also, have him compile another list of every retailer in the area that sells mini spy cams. Give that list to Jagg and have him talk to the owners. Try to get the names of everyone in the area who purchased one recently."

"Done."

"One more thing. Tell Jagg to stay close to Andrew's case and to keep me up to date."

"Will do. Need anything else?"

"Not right now."

"Alright, bro." His gaze flickered to the cabin on the hill. He didn't ask what I was doing there, or who she was. Not because he didn't care, but because I had no doubt he already knew. He'd probably had Wolf pull everything on the homeowner as soon as I texted him the address. Gunner very likely knew more about Rose than I did at that point.

We were protective of each other. Always had been.

Gunner helped me pull Spirit from the trailer then hopped back in the truck. He looked up at the sky. "Gonna get cold."

"I'll be alright."

"Talkin' about the tacos."

I grinned, pulling Spirit away from the truck. "Night, bro."

With a nod, the window rolled up and the truck disappeared down the dirt road.

The wind whistled through the trees as I stroked Spirit's mane.

"Thanks for coming."

She snorted.

Gripping her reins, we made our way back up the hill, although this time, I took the woods to avoid being seen. Spirit walked slowly, smoothly beside me. A content partner. Happy to just be.

Taking note of every rock, tree, log, twig, I took mental inventory of Rose's property, then, journeyed deeper into the woods to do one more perimeter check.

An hour later, I perched myself between two boulders, with Spirit next to a thicket of pines that blocked the wind. The rain had stopped, but the temperatures had dropped. I settled in, my eyes locked on Rose's cabin just past the tree line. From the spot I'd chosen, I could see her entire house and most of the back yard.

No one was getting into that house tonight.

No one was getting past me.

I fixated on the bedroom window and found myself wishing she'd walk by. Maybe look outside. I wanted to see her. Just see her face once again.

Minutes ticked on, the silence of night settling into the woods.

I pulled the whiskey from the bag and took a swig.

I checked the time; almost ten o'clock.

Another minute slid by, then, like a click of an alarm, my focus shifted behind me. A finely tuned instinct that told me I wasn't alone.

Seconds faded to minutes as I mentally tracked the person who had set up shop behind a thicket of bushes six yards to my east.

I waited, listening.

A few more minutes passed.

Finally, I sighed, shook my head, and looked down.

Gunner might not have known the full reasons of why I was doing what I was doing, but between Andrew's murder, the odd request to send me my horse and a bag, and my bloody knuckles, he'd taken it upon himself to be my spot for the evening. My *uninvited* spot. I'm sure he knew that I knew he was there. I'm sure he wasn't announcing his presence on purpose because he knew I'd drag his ass home.

The Steele brothers were loyal and always had each other's backs. But I couldn't help but wonder if it weren't for my "injury," if Gunner would've been back home. Instead, he was there, in the damn cold, in case I needed something.

In case I couldn't handle the situation I'd placed myself into.

That cut me deeper than any guilt I'd felt before.

I'd become the burden of all burdens. I was failing my family, my business, myself.

I took a gulp, the amber liquid sliding down my throat with that familiar burn.

What had I turned into?

Who was I?

I was someone who needed to walk away from Dr. Floris. She didn't need my baggage, and I didn't need whatever the hell the woman was doing to me.

I decided that after that night, I'd find another therapist, and that would be that.

After I made sure Rose made it through the night untouched.

With that plan in place, I grabbed my bag and ripped it open. I pulled the camouflage tarp, thermal blanket, and pocket warmers from the bag, set them aside. Pulled out the box of tacos, set them aside. Then, I grabbed the night vision scope and scanned the windows, then the woods around the cabin as I would do a hundred more times over the course of the night.

Seconds passed and I imagined her sliding into bed.

Wondering what she was thinking.

Wondering if she was thinking about me.

Wondering if she felt like I failed her, too.

16

PHOENIX

*T*wo hours later, headlights suddenly flooded the woods. I tossed the tacos aside and jumped up. Puffs of exhaust rolled from Rose's SUV. I looked at my watch—12:14 a.m.

Where the hell was Rose going at midnight?

My first thought went to Josh. Perhaps she was seeking comfort in her former fiancé's arms... because Lord knew I wasn't able to provide that.

Rose's silhouette slid into the vehicle.

"Want me to track her?" Gunner said behind me, magically appearing like a ghost.

"No. I'll do it. Go home, Gunner. I've got this."

"Take my truck. It's at the bottom of the ridge."

"I'll lose her by then. Spirit and I can cut down the middle of the mountain as she takes the roads."

"Alright, I'll stay and watch the house."

I jumped onto Spirit and looked down at my younger brother. "I owe you."

"I'm eating the rest of your tacos."

I flapped the reins. "Let's go, girl."

Spirit and I followed the taillights down the driveway. We followed Rose through the backroads, taking shortcuts through the woods that wrapped the mountain. Even though it had been months since Spirit and I had ridden that side of the mountain, it was as if she knew where we were going. Who we were following, and why. Rose's words drifted through my head.

Horses can be very therapeutic, you know.

I stroked Spirit's mane as she picked up a hiking trail and pushed into a trot.

Rose and Spirit, two intelligent, strong-willed, bull-headed women as strong as an ox and as beautiful as the rising sun. The two women who saw me for who I truly was.

One I'd tamed, and one, I was scared to death could tame me.

One I'd let in, the other I'd pushed away with an iron fist.

I was a piece of work.

We followed the BMW out of the woods and onto acres of pasture that led to a small ranch house nestled against the tree line, only a few miles from Rose's house.

Definitely not Josh Davis's house.

So, who's was it?

Spirit and I slipped into the trees and watched as Rose parked alongside the house. The front door opened, a dark silhouette stepping outside. I couldn't tell if it was a man or woman. Rose stepped inside, and the door was shut.

Shit.

I pulled the gun from my belt and clicked my heels. "Come on, girl."

Spirit and I slinked through the trees, getting as close to the house as possible without being seen. Pastures, and thirty acres of forest—give or take—surrounded the home.

An old, blue seventy-nine Ford was sitting out in the driveway.

A light inside flicked on, then another, then another. Movement caught my eye and I watched as two silhouettes sat in front of a large window at the front of the house. Rose dropped her head into her hands and the other silhouette wrapped an arm around her.

I frowned, my mind racing.

Rose had no family, that was apparent. She also appeared to have no friends.

Who was Rose visiting?

I guided Spirit behind a tree and sat back in the saddle, watching the silhouette through the windows.

Rose Floris had secrets.

And just like that, just when I thought I could walk away, I was sucked back in.

17

ROSE

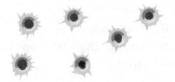

*I*f there was an image next to "ticking time-bomb" in the dictionary, I was it. My insides felt like they were about to jump out of my skin by the time I parked in front of Kline and Associates. I've never been good on little sleep, but when you add a dead body and a fight with a jealous, stubborn, short-sided control freak to my already exhausted state, I was the one in need of some therapy. Or a valium—which wouldn't pair well with the gallon of coffee I'd drunk that morning, by the way.

I was a hot mess.

The positive was that it was the first morning without rain in days, the calm before the storms to come the next day, the weatherman had warned.

My hand trembled as I pushed through the door of the office.

Zoey jumped up from the front desk, the little braids she was wearing that day bouncing on her shoulders. I think a few even had bells.

"Rose, are you *okay?*"

Well that answered my question if the word had gotten

out that I'd been the one to find Andrew's body. Damn gossips.

She took the briefcase and coffee from my hands. I hung onto my purse.

"I'm okay," I lied. "Thanks." I frowned as I looked back at her. Dark circles accompanied puffy, bloodshot eyes. Instead of her usual trend-setting attire, she wore a simple sweater over faded skinny jeans.

"Are *you* okay?" I asked.

She waved her hand in the air. "Yes. Irish car bombs."

"Irish car bombs? You spend the night at a frat house or something?"

She rolled her eyes. "Pretty much. Anyway, I can't believe you're here. You should have called in sick or something."

Truth was, I'd considered it, but nothing was going to ease my anxiety and I might as well put it toward something productive. I was hoping work would take my mind off things, as it had done so many times before.

"Anyway, seriously, are you okay?" Her hands brushed over my back like one might stroke a cat.

"Yeah, I'm okay."

"Did you really see it? Him?"

I wrinkled my nose as the image flashed through my head.

"Sorry. Okay. Geez... *Andrew.* I mean, I can't believe it. Do they have any idea who did it?"

"I don't know."

"I heard it was a random break-in. What were you doing over there, anyway?"

"Picking something up. Can we not talk about this?"

"I'm sorry. Okay. I just can't believe it. And after that poor guy was found in the woods. What was his name again?"

"Carl."

"Crazy Carl. That's right. Gosh, two back-to-back murders in our sleepy little town." She waved her hands in the air. "Anyway, I'm sorry I didn't answer when you called last night. I was kinda on..." she leaned in. "A date."

My eyebrows popped. "A date? With who?"

Just then, Cameron breezed through the front door wearing a smile bigger than the hoops that hung from Zoey's ear. There were a few things about Cameron I knew to be true. One was that he hated mornings, and two was that the only thing he got excited for was fifty cent shots at Frank's... and perhaps a willing woman.

My brow cocked.

Zoey's cheeks flushed.

And that answered my question about who her date was with.

"What a beautiful day, huh?"

Zoey and I glanced out the window at the bleak, overcast morning.

Cameron sipped his coffee, oblivious to my frazzled state.

"Someone was murdered last night, Cameron." Zoey said.

"Doesn't mean it can't be a pretty morning." He raised his coffee.

"Actually, it does." I said. "And side note, I'm pretty sure a travel mug that reads *Thunder Cunt* is mildly inappropriate for an office."

"Hey. My Dad got this for me."

"Explains a lot." Zoey muttered.

Cameron balled an empty fast food wrapper and tossed it into the overflowing trash can. "Gross. Who's week is it to take out the trash?"

Zoey pointed to me. I pointed to her.

"Fine." She said. "It's my week. Sorry, kind of got distracted this morning hearing about another murder. I'll take it out tonight."

Theo poked his head out of his office, the concern on his bearded face telling me he'd also heard the news. His gaze skirted between the three of us as he crossed the lobby wearing his usual brown, three-piece wool suit.

"You okay?" He asked.

My patience cashed out. "I'm okay. How does everyone know?"

"I ran into Tabitha after leaving Frank's last night." Zoey said. "Told me everything."

"Good to know Tabby-talks-a-lot is living up to her name."

"She asked me if I knew Andrew, or knew what you were doing over there. Fishing for facts, I guess. But if you ask me, she was fishing for a heck of a lot more than that with those boobs she had on display."

"Anything for a story." Theo said, then turned to me. "Seriously, are you okay?"

"I'm fine. Really."

"Well, I sent you an email earlier. You're more than welcome to take the day off. I can cover the appointments you can't reschedule."

"It's okay."

"Really, Rose."

"I can handle it. I want to be here." And that was the honest truth. The last place I wanted to be was my home, where according to Phoenix, I was a sitting duck, and also where I'd kept envisioning him freaking out on me in a childish, jealous rage. I didn't want to see the guy ever again. And so, on the drive into work, I'd decided to refer Phoenix to another therapist and cut ties with the man. It would be the first time I'd ever released a patient.

Phoenix would be the first patient I couldn't handle.

It was a lot.

A lot.

I took my briefcase and coffee back from Zoey's hands. "I've got a busy morning."

"Let me know if you need anything, girl."

"Thanks."

As Zoey and Cameron stepped away, I turned to Theo.

"Have you made a decision about my Equine Assisted Therapy proposal?"

"I'll have an answer for you by tomorrow night."

I bit back my irritation and nodded. "Thank you."

With that, I turned and slipped into my office. I'd settled behind my computer when Cameron knocked at the door.

"Yes?"

He sauntered in and dropped a stack of envelopes on my desk.

"Mail."

"Thanks."

"You really doing okay?"

"Please stop asking. Hey, you know Theo will send you packing if you and Zoey keep hooking up."

He snorted. "Maybe you should say that in the mirror."

"What?"

"Miss Talks-a-lot mentioned a certain billionaire playboy was at the scene last night. With *you.*"

I rolled my eyes and shook my head.

"Ah, so it's true."

"He needed a ride."

"Don't we all?"

"Real mature. And by the way, Zoey's my friend so you can't talk like that if you're going to start dating her."

"Date her? Who said anything about dating? Kinda hard to hook up when the woman ditches the date before happy hour is even over. Zoey's all talk when it comes to handling her liquor."

"Irish car bombs'll do that to the best of us."

"Not all of us. Anyway, it was probably a good thing she left early because it wasn't long after that the news broke about Andrew." He narrowed his eyes. "What were you doing over there anyway?"

I looked away. "Picking something up."

"What?"

"My privacy."

"Okay, message received."

The front door chimed.

Cameron glanced over his shoulder. "That's my nine o'clock. Anyway, be careful with Mr. Steele. That guy's no good. See ya."

His words lingered like a lead weight as he walked out of the room.

No good.

Four hours and back to back appointments later, I was beat. I pulled off my glasses and rubbed my temples, willing the headache I'd had for twenty-four hours to magically go away. No luck. I needed ibuprofen. Coffee. Something. Anything.

I blew out a breath and pushed away from my desk.

1:27 p.m.

As if on cue, my stomach grumbled. With vending machine tunnel vision, I grabbed a handful of quarters, yanked open my office door, and walked right into a rock-hard chest that smelled like fresh air and leather.

The quarters tumbled to the floor, one landing on the top of Phoenix's scuffed, black combat boots.

I swooped down to pick them up, stealing a glance at the front desk where Zoey was nowhere in sight.

Dammit.

With the quarters clutched in my hands, I took a step back. Phoenix's gaze pinned me with an intensity that knocked my balance off even more.

Every emotion I'd spent the day trying to bury crept back up in the form of a baseball-sized lump in my throat. My heart started to race simply looking at the man. I was angry, hurt, confused.

Scared.

I didn't know what to make of the last twenty-four hours of my life.

Of the man standing in front of me.

"Can I help you?" I asked. If he didn't know I was still upset about the night before, he did then.

"I'm here for my appointment."

"What appointment?"

"The one I booked earlier this morning."

"The one you... you really want to... are you *kidding?*" I stuttered like I'd just licked peanut butter from the spoon. The *nerve* of the guy.

My gaze cut to the front desk—empty. *Zoey.*

"You seriously made another appointment with me?"

"Yes."

I looked at the clock on the wall trying to throw together an exit plan.

"For one-thirty?"

"Yes."

A moment stretched between us.

Theo walked by, glancing in our direction.

Damn, damn, damn...

"Well." The artificial politeness came out of me like burning acid. "I guess if you have an appointment... Come on in, then."

Dammit, dammit, dammit.

My jaw clenched as I walked to my desk. The door clicked closed behind me. I lowered into my chair, my back as stiff as a rod. Phoenix had taken his spot on the couch and was rolling one of my vesuvianite stones between his fingers, per usual.

We stared at each other for what seemed like two lifetimes, the weight in the room suddenly suffocating, closing in on me with a dead body, the argument, the undeniable attraction between us. Pandora's box had been opened, and no matter how much I tried to pretend it wasn't the case, me and Phoenix's professional relationship had morphed into something else. Something that sent me lopsided and scared the crap out of me. The man was unpredictable, a loose cannon. "No good." He was everything I'd spent the last twenty years trying to avoid.

Yet there he was, staring at me with those baby blue eyes, pushing his way into my life, expecting another dog and pony show of me trying to heal what was broken while he fought me every inch of the way.

Lord, the man was sexy.

I inhaled, then launched.

"You can't talk to me like you did last night, Phoenix. Ever again. I won't accept it. I won't put up with it. Do you understand me?"

"Yes. I'm sorry."

I blinked.

I'm sorry.

The words lingered. I expected him to backtrack, or maybe pass out right there on my floor from the admission that he had done something wrong. He didn't, so I continued.

"You should know, too, that I've decided to transfer your case to someone better suited—"

"Transfer my case?"

"That's right. After last night... after everything that happened..."

"It won't happen again."

"It's not enough, Phoenix." I snapped. "This is too important. Lines have been crossed, and I won't jeopardize your treatment. You deserve better than—"

He pushed off the couch. My body tensed as he crossed the room, placed his palms on my desk and leaned in like he had when he'd bribed me with sex and money days earlier.

Instead of doing that again, though, he said, "You deserve better than the way I treated you last night, Rose. You were confused, scared, vulnerable and I took advantage of it. I was wrong to speak to you the way I did, and to react the way I did. I'm sorry. It won't happen again."

I blinked again, forcing the shock of the words away. Words were only words, after all.

"No, Phoenix. *No.* That doesn't make everything okay. How can I know for sure..."

"I just told you it won't happen again, and it won't. I'm a lot of things, Rose, but a liar isn't one of them. I'm true to my word. It won't happen again, and I won't say it again."

"Your therapy is too important. I know a great psychologist, his name is—"

"*No.* Rose, it's you. It's you. You're for me. You're mine." His voice cracked.

My eyes widened.

"Please." There was a desperation in his voice. "You're the only one who can... Please." His eyes shifted away, shamed by his display of emotions. "Please. I need help." His eyes met mine again and I swear he had tears in them. "I need help. Please. Help me."

Tears filled my own eyes as we stared at each other, my heart pounding so loudly I was sure he could hear it.

"Okay," I whispered finally. "Okay."

He released a breath, then straightened. His eyes were wide, bright, like a child who wasn't sure how to react to what had just happened.

I knew that look. That look had shaped my life.

"Take a deep breath," I said.

His gaze locked on mine and I watched his shoulders slowly rise, drop.

"Again."

I breathed with him, the desk between us, although it felt like I could reach out and grab onto the connection between us.

"One more time."

We breathed together.

He nodded—*thank you.*

I dipped my chin.

I watched him turn and cross the room and sink into the couch with the weight of a man that had just loosened the armor around him.

His gaze shifted to the dry erase board. "Let's focus on the goals."

I smiled, suddenly overwhelmed with pride. I was so damn proud of him.

"Alright," I said. "Let's begin."

18

ROSE

"*H*ow would you describe yourself?"

"Now, or before?"

"Both."

Phoenix glanced down at his hands, clasped in his lap.

"Before, unstoppable. Now... Weak."

"Define weak."

"I can't control myself."

"Emotionally, or physically?"

"Both."

"Are you aware of this—we'll call it new—response to situations? That you are acting out of character?"

"Yes."

"And how do you feel when it happens?"

"I get pissed the hell off."

"At yourself?"

"Yes."

"You fight it, then? The emotions?"

"Yes."

"Because that's what you've spent your life doing. Right?"

He glanced down.

"Except, Phoenix, here's the deal with this. This is different. This isn't terrorists or evildoers that you can eliminate with a pull of a trigger. This is science. You are fighting science." I waited a beat to let that sink in, however it may. "Can I explain further?"

I took his lack of response as concession.

"The bullet penetrated your head on the upper, right side, above your eyebrow. In your prefrontal cortex, to be exact. This part of the brain is closely linked with the limbic system, which is the area of the brain that controls our behavioral and emotional responses. The root of your issues, so to speak."

He was watching me now, a hint of interest in his eyes. We were off *feelings* now and into *facts,* which he responded to. Just as I would have. So I took it further.

"The limbic system is made up of four main parts. First is the amygdala, a very powerful part of the brain that evaluates your emotional response to situations; think, happy, sad, etcetera. This is where your fight or flight sensory is housed, something that most combat veterans are very familiar with."

He dipped his chin in acknowledgment.

"The hippocampus is located in the temporal lobe and is associated with how we form new memories based on past experiences. The thalamus and hypothalamus are associated with pleasure like arousal and rage, and controlling those emotions. The cingulate gyrus links sight and smell to memories and deciphers how we respond to those, whether it be anger, whatever. Finally, the ventral tegmental is involved in the transmission of dopamine, which affects our moods. All of these parts work together to send messages to the prefrontal cortex, which tells us how to interpret and respond. How to act.

"You see, the bullet damaged the part of your brain that takes all the little messages from the limbic system and processes them into empathy, shame, compassion, guilt, pleasure, fear, anger. The thing is, though, Phoenix, damage to this part of the brain messes with your social emotions— but leaves your logic reasoning intact. You have that now. You still own that. You still control that."

Something flickered in his face. Hope.

"When you are fighting yourself, you are fighting emotions that are a direct result of your injury. You are fighting something you can't control and only making it worse. You're fighting the healing process of your body. These emotions will subside, I promise. You will heal."

He looked down.

"Think of it like a broken arm. The swelling is a side effect you can't control. You have to let your body heal. With a broken arm, you're put in a cast for a few months. This limits your mobility and tests your patience, but you have to allow the bone to heal. You listen to your doctor, take his or her advice, and allow it to heal. Before you know it, your arm is back to normal and your life is back to normal."

He stopped fidgeting with the stone and looked up.

"The brain is a very powerful thing and we're still learning about it every day. Take your ego out of this and try to look at your brain as something separate than you, than your body. Look at it like something that has been damaged and needs to heal. It's not you, it's the organ in your body called your brain. *You* are not damaged. *You* are not weak. *You* are not crazy. Your brain is simply misfiring, and needs to heal." I leaned forward, and emphasized, "Phoenix, you're not only fighting something you can't control, you're worsening its effects."

"But how do I *not* fight it when that's what my body's natural response is to do?"

"That's *exactly* why we're here. That's what therapy is all about. To teach you how to do that. One way is to control your environment. Until you're healed, you should control your environment. I'm sure Dr. Buckley gave you meds, which, I'm guessing you aren't taking. You should consider taking them, at least for the headaches. And he probably advised you to take it easy, stay home, stay off work, lay off the booze, live in as calm of an environment as you can while your brain heals."

"So don't destroy my therapist's desk or walk up on a dead body?"

I grinned. "Exactly." I sighed. "There has to be a level of acceptance here. You have to accept that your physical body is injured, and that only you can take steps to fix it. I can only guide you. You have to put in the work by being open to therapy, both physical and psychological, taking your medicine, resting, changing your environment. You can control that, Phoenix. You can control it. So, control it."

Frustrated, he stood and turned his back to me. He scrubbed his hands over his face and began pacing.

"You're strong, Phoenix." My own voice wavered at his obvious emotions, maybe even tears. "You survived a gunshot wound that most people wouldn't have. You can survive this."

I heard him sniff and forced myself to look away to give him a moment of privacy, and if I'm being honest, to give myself a moment, too.

He ran his fingers through his hair with an inhale, then squared his shoulders and sat back down on the couch.

"Keep going."

"Are you sure?"

"Yes."

"Okay." I took a quick sip of water. "Now that we've established that *you* aren't weak, let's talk about good things. Tell me something you like about yourself."

He stilled, blinked. You'd think I'd just asked him to draw a map of the female reproductive system. I was surprised, shocked, even. A man with an ego the size of Texas was at a loss for words when asked to compliment himself. And then I realized, it wasn't an ego that was driving Phoenix's unruliness, it was his pride. A pride badly injured.

So I switched tactics.

"Okay... then tell me, what's the most important thing in your life?"

"My family." His response was immediate and had nothing to do with his healing, as I'd expected. This concerned me because it suggested not only that his primary focus wasn't on getting better, but also that he didn't see himself as worthy enough to put his full focus on.

"What would they say they like most about you?"

Again, no response to this question. He shifted his weight, avoiding eye contact.

"What would they say about you, then? Anything at all?"

An icy gaze met mine. "That I'm a goddamn burden."

"I doubt that."

"Why?"

"Because they love you. They look up to you. More than that, though, I doubt they'd say that because you don't allow yourself to be a burden. You won't accept help from anyone. Why?"

With a guttural groan, he surged to his feet, plucked a

stress ball from my desk and began squeezing the thing a million miles a minute.

"Because I don't want them to see me like this."

"Why? They're family."

"Because I don't want to let them down, alright? You don't understand, Rose. I'm the oldest brother. I raised my brothers while my dad worked, and I became the head of household when he died. I run a multi-million dollar company, with offices all over the country. Let me rephrase that—I *did* run it before a bullet lodged in my brain."

"It will come back. Everything will come back."

"What if it doesn't?" He raised his voice and spun to face me. "What if it doesn't, Rose? You don't get it. Even if everything does go back to normal... if I heal completely... I'm... I'm afraid they won't look at me the same anymore, alright? That no one will. That everything will be different. People will question my decisions, wondering if I was having a damn relapse or something. *Dammit.*" He began pacing again. "You should see the look in my brothers' eyes when they talk to me. Like I'm a fucking toddler. Or, the looks I get at the grocery store, the diner, the feed store. Sorry. Sorry for the damn language."

"It's fine, please don't worry about it. And the looks you're getting around town aren't new. I think you got looks before. Your ruthless military reputation precedes you. You're a pretty intimidating presence. You have to know that."

"It's not the same. It's different."

"I think people are just as wary of you now as before the incident. Circumstances are different, sure, but I think your perception of yourself is what has changed. Tell me *something* you like about yourself. Please."

"Nothing, Rose. Nothing. I can't stand the person I am

right now." He walked to the window, covered his mouth with his hand and stared at dark clouds in the distance. A minute passed, then in a voice as if he were talking to himself, he said, "I look at myself in the mirror and I don't recognize myself. I look at my hands, my arms, my legs, as if they are separate from my body. Like they aren't even my own." He turned to me, a confused, pained look on his face that broke my heart. "How screwed up is that?"

A moment ticked by as I mustered up the courage to ask the question I'd been wondering since we'd first met.

"Phoenix I want you to think about this next question carefully. I want you to consider your answer before you respond. Be truthful. Alright?"

"I will."

"Do you ever think about hurting yourself?"

"No."

"Ending your life?"

His gaze shifted to the window in an expressionless stare.

"I wouldn't do that to my family." He said finally. "That's not how we do things. We face problems head on and fix it."

"But this is different."

"It is." He nodded.

"Because you can't fix it with your hands."

He nodded.

I stood, walked over to him. "I don't want you to become a statistic, Phoenix."

"Oh, you mean, statistics like, patients with some sort of traumatic brain injury are four times more likely to commit suicide than the general population? And those that are depressed, on top of that, are twenty-one times higher to commit suicide? *Twenty-one* times." He turned to me, a fire behind those blue eyes. "I spent decades in the military,

Rose, don't forget that. I know all about TBI and the effect it has on even the most badass of men. I've lost brothers, not only on the battlefields, but to the very statistics I just rattled off." His jaw clenched as he looked down at me. "I think of those men every day, every night as I go to sleep. See their faces, see their families' faces. I—we, you, our country— owe them the greatest respect and I'll have a word with anyone who judges them for choices they made. They are to be remembered and given the utmost respect. I'll see them again, but not at the cost of my own hand. Not because I'm too good for it. Because they wouldn't want that."

My hand drifted to his arm. When it connected, he flinched. My heart skipped a beat as we stared at each other.

It's weird now, looking back at that moment, it was as if my body knew something bigger than me was happening there. Little paths unfolding around us, about to take us to places we'd never been before... and some I'd never go back to. The universe was in control of that moment, and I knew, without question, we were both exactly where we were supposed to be at that very moment.

He took a deep breath, a small step back. "The one question that I keep having... the one I can't let go of, is wondering if..." His eyes shimmered and he looked away.

"Tell me, Phoenix."

"If I would have rather not come out of it. If I would rather be dead than... whatever I've become."

"You'll become yourself again." I gripped his arm again, pulling him back to me. "But even stronger. This will make you stronger. I can already see it in you. I believe in you. I believe in you so much, Phoenix."

He closed his eyes, pulled out of my grasp and walked away, taking the heat, the emotion, but leaving a moment that I'd never forget.

"Enough of that." He said.

"Okay."

"Thank you. Let's continue." He took his place on the couch.

I nodded, swallowed the lump in my throat and slipped back behind my desk surprised that he wanted to keep going. Ironically, I was the one who'd become an emotional mess. But Phoenix didn't give up once he'd set his mind to something.

"Okay." I sipped my water, and took a deep breath. "Okay. Let's focus on triggers. Emotionally, what sets you off?"

"Anything. Everything."

"Is there anything in particular? Something that you've noticed sets you off more than others?"

"You."

My chin jerked back. The response felt like a shockwave hitting me from across the room.

"What exactly about me sets you off?"

"Your independence. Your fearlessness."

"Some people might think independence and courage is a good trait in another human."

"I said fearlessness. An entirely different animal."

"I disagree."

"Courage is the ability to face a fear head on and take action, despite the threat. Fearlessness is not acknowledging the threat in the first place. Very different."

"And what don't you like about my independence?"

"That I'm not part of it."

He said it so matter-of-factly that it took away the implication of it. Of *us*.

"Rose, let me secure your house, your property. Let me handle all of it."

I dropped my head in my hands and groaned. "I don't know what's happening here, Phoenix. I don't know what's happening between us. I need to figure it out. But one thing I know I can handle is getting my house secured. I don't need you to do all that. I can handle it."

"Like I can handle my recovery by myself?"

Touché.

He slid his elbows onto his knees and leaned forward.

"Someone broke into your house. Someone videoed you without your approval. Andrew was stabbed to death after discovering the camera. I believe you are in danger, Rose. And if you don't accept my help to ensure your safety, I will find someone else to do it."

"It's not your job to protect me, Phoenix."

"I've made it my job."

"It's my job to keep you safe, to keep you happy. To keep you comfortable, content. Satisfied. It's my job, as your man, to control it. It's my job to keep you mine." His words from the evening before echoed in my head.

A moment slid by while we stared at each other.

He'd said his piece, and he was done.

Well, I wasn't.

"Would you feel this way with another psychologist? Would you feel this protective if you were sitting across from Dr. Brecklebaum, the psychologist across town?" It was a loaded question on so many levels. I was practically begging the man to tell me he felt something for me. Something romantic. Something other than seeing me as a ticket to his freedom. Or, a roadblock, perhaps.

"Why are you so independent?" He asked.

"What kind of question is that?"

"One that's as loaded as the one you just asked me."

I shifted in my seat. "There's nothing wrong with a woman being independent."

"There certainly isn't. I didn't say that. But this one wears it like a shield of armor."

A second slid by.

"Tell me about it."

"About what?"

"About what's in your past that's made you think you can't depend on anyone else."

I felt the heat rising up my neck and I wasn't sure if it was from the memories flooding back into my brain or from the intensity of his gaze.

He continued. "There isn't a single personal picture in your office, in your home. No brothers, sisters, friends. Every material thing you possess is placed just so, how, and where you want it. Control. You're gripping onto it with bloody fingertips. My question is why."

The heat reached my cheeks.

"Tell me about your childhood, Rose. Tell me about your family."

"No." I began fumbling with the papers on my desk, because they needed to be re-stacked at that second. "Don't do this. Don't turn the tables. This is about *you*. We're here because of you."

"I'm willing to bet your organization caddy in your fancy BMW that I'm not the only screwed up one in the room."

"Maybe so, but this appointment isn't for me, it's for you."

"The difference is, though, that you know everything about me, down to the size of my underwear. Extra-large, by the way. But I don't know anything about you. I'm an open book. You're locked up tighter than the corners of your bedsheets."

I snorted. "Hardly. And this is how this works, Phoenix. I'm the doctor, you're the patient. Not me. If you can't accept that, there's the door." My back was straight, my hands clenched on my desk. I took a silent deep breath. *You are in control, you are in control, you are the one in control. Focus, focus, focus.*

"Tell me, Rose."

"Tell you *what?*"

"Your childhood."

Then, I lost it.

"I'm a foster kid, alright? A freaking orphan." It blurted out of me like a murder confession. "There. Is that what you want? You freaking feel better now?" Tears threatened to sting my eyes. I pushed them away.

He simply stared back at me.

The dam broke. "My dad, who I never met, left my mom when she was pregnant and died in federal prison where he was locked up for a slew of things including drug trafficking and third degree assault. Nice, huh? My mom died in a car accident after dropping me off at daycare one day. I was put into the system and tossed around from house to house like a freaking hot potato. It was horrific. That's my childhood."

My desk phone buzzed.

We stared at each other, tears welling in my eyes.

It buzzed again.

My hand shook as I clicked the button.

"Yes?"

"I'm sorry to disturb you," Zoey's voice sounded through the speaker, "But you've got a phone call. Also, your two o'clock is here early."

Zoey, finally to the rescue with a fake appointment— although a year too late.

"Thanks." I clicked off, grabbed a tissue and began twisting it around in my fingers.

Phoenix didn't move, and I couldn't take any more. I was so done. Emotionally cashed the hell out.

"I have to go. I mean, you have to go."

Phoenix pushed off the couch and crossed the room, his gaze locked on mine with each step. Butterflies fluttered in my stomach as if my body knew what was about to happen before my head did. With heat in his eyes and determination on his face, he rounded my desk, took my face in his hands and kissed me.

The man kissed me into oblivion.

My body went weak, my thoughts evaporated, tingles bursting over my skin. The passion, the intensity, the pounding heartbeat telling me there was no going back from this.

No... there was no going back after Phoenix Steele.

I was released, left floating on some euphoric cloud, and when I finally opened my eyes, he was gone.

19

PHOENIX

*T*he familiar scent of cedar and stale beer wrapped me like a redneck hug as I pushed through the door of Frank's Bar. A cowbell jangled above the entryway—not that anyone noticed, or heard it even. The watering hole was packed, especially for five o'clock on a weeknight. The crack of a pool stick from somewhere in the back faded into the low melody of a Willie Nelson song.

Frank's Bar was a staple in Berry Springs. Something about it gave the locals deeper accents, a trucker's vocabulary, a pair of steel balls, and superhuman liver. I loved the place. As always, the men were dressed in their dirtiest Carhartts and cowboy hats, the women in skin-tight jeans, low-cut shirts, and bejeweled boots with just enough scuff on the tips to make you cover your balls when you talked to them. It was a small town bar on a small town Friday night.

A bar I used to shut down on a weekly basis.

Used to, being the key words there.

Heads turned as I crossed the room, lingering gazes accompanied by a murmur of whispers.

Rose's voice echoed in my head...

They watched you before the incident, Phoenix. You just didn't notice.

I kept telling myself she was right as I maneuvered through the crowd.

The main room was dimly lit, specked with polished wooden tables and chairs, all made by local craftsmen. The walls, shadowed with just enough privacy for even the shiest cowboy to make a move. The primary decor consisted of road signs, antlers, and flickering beer lights.

Ignoring a few shoutouts, I made my way to the bar and saddled up on the end.

"Mr. Steele. I mean, Phoenix, well, I'll be damned. Evening to ya."

Frank, owner and retired Berry Springs police officer, wiped his hands on his apron as he walked over, his gaze assessing me with both surprise and caution.

"Long time no see." He stretched out his tanned, leather hand. "How you doing?"

"Can't complain. Good to see you."

We shook hands. He stared at me for a moment. Expecting more from a man who'd been shot in the head months earlier?

"Well. Glad all is well. How's the weather outside lookin'?" He grabbed a short glass from the rack and began filling it with ice.

"Cloudy."

"Roads are already washed out and we're supposed to get another round of storms tomorrow. Stan the Weatherman said even a chance of tornados." His head tilted to the side. "You made it down your mountain alright?"

I didn't think you were supposed to be driving, is what he meant. After all, the entire town had heard the details of my medical records thanks to Josh fucking Davis.

"A little water on the roads is no match for Spirit," I replied.

"Ah, yes. That's good. She's a good horse." Seemingly relieved that I wasn't behind a steering wheel, he grabbed a bottle of Johnnie Walker—my usual. He unscrewed the cap and began pouring two fingers—my usual.

I watched as the amber colored liquid filled the glass, and for the second time in a handful of minutes, Rose's voice...

Lay off the booze until you're healed.

My jaw clenched, my fingers curling to fists on the bar. The woman had become my damn mother. Annoying... and disgusting, considering my dreams the night before. But for better or worse, I couldn't get her voice out of my head.

Lay off the booze...

"Just water tonight, Frank."

Frank froze mid-pour. He blinked. "I'm... I'm sorry, I don't think I heard—"

"Water."

Christ.

"Oh. Uh." He looked down at the highball in his hand, then back at me, then again at the glass. "Sorry."

You'd think I asked the man to make me a Shirley fucking Temple. He set the whiskey on the back counter, grabbed a taller glass, scooped the ice, and filled it with water.

"With a lemon." I added. "Two. Two lemons."

This time a grin tugged at his lips. "You got it, Mr. Steele." He slid the water in front of me. "Anything else?"

I shook my head.

"Okay, then. Enjoy." He dipped his chin and moved onto the next patron.

I looked at my water.

My *water.*

My brothers and I had been to Frank's Bar countless times, and never once—not a single time—had any of us ordered something that didn't involve pure grain alcohol. I stared down at the water, my own disbelief of what I'd ordered triggering insecurities in me. And that was one emotion the old Phoenix never experienced. Never. I stared at the two lemon slices as if someone had laid a Rubik's cube in front of me. They were brown, by the way, because who ordered anything with lemons at Frank's? Except this was no puzzle. This water symbolized my new life. The restrictions, the chains, the boundaries.

Water instead of whiskey.

Therapy instead of war.

Chains instead of freedom.

Submission to it all.

Yeah, this water symbolized submission.

Submission to my circumstance, my weakness.

Submission to Rose.

Shit. Fuck. Goddammit.

The woman was pushing so far past my comfort zone I was losing the man I used to be. Before Rose. Before meeting the only woman who seemed to be able to strip me naked and make me look at myself in ways I never thought I would.

The only woman who'd never given up on me. Blind faith.

My Rose Flower.

That *kiss.*

Kissing her had felt like the biggest release I'd had since waking up from the coma, and this coming from a guy who punched a hole through the hospital wall. Kissing Rose was like taking some pill that made you forget everyone and everything around you. Swept you away, to the closest thing to heaven on earth. All of a sudden I was thinking about my future, *our* future, daydreaming about children and a freaking white picket fence. Foreign thoughts for the old Phoenix. Did I want all that... *could* I?

How could a woman I'd only just met make me order water at a bar?

Yep, Rose Floris had me by the balls.

I wrapped my hands around the icy glass.

I did not know this man.

I didn't know a man who got debilitating headaches, who spent half his day in therapy. A man with limits.

A man who submitted to a woman.

I was losing control of whatever life I had left.

Just as I lifted the glass to throw it against the wall—

"Brother."

As if he'd anticipated my next move, Ax's hand clamped down on my shoulder. That deep, ever-calming voice of my younger brother breaking the tornado spinning inside me.

He eyed the water as he slid onto the barstool next to me. He didn't say anything about it, didn't address it. He simply accepted it, filed it away, and assessed this unexpected situation.

As was Ax.

"You're here early."

"Meeting Jagg as soon as he gets off work."

"Ah. Heard you've got the detective pulling some favors."

"We'll see if he delivers."

Ax scanned the crowd, a habit from serving decades in the military.

"Spirit's drawn quite the crowd outside."

My brow raised.

"Don't worry, she's fine." He flagged down Frank and ordered a Shiner. "What's with the axe in the saddle bag?"

"Tree."

He tipped his head to the side. "Woman."

I grunted.

Between Gunner and Jagg, I had no doubt Ax knew about my overnight security watch at Rose's house.

"Missed you at dinner last night," He said as Frank slid his beer down the bar. He sipped. "Celeste made pulled pork sandwiches. Well, not made so much as brought them home after a bad date."

"Another one, huh?"

"Oh yeah."

Celeste, former Marine and full-time badass, had recently been promoted from office manager of Steele Shadows Security to security detail. She'd become like a sister to us, and while the woman could outshoot anyone in town, her luck with men, however, was another story.

"By the way, Gunner asked me to tell you that our best friend, Josh Davis, has spent the last two evenings curled up with a wine cooler and remote control."

"How does he know this?"

"Got friendly with Davis's housekeeper."

"Did she say if he left the house? Even for a bit?"

"Nope. Says he came home from work and was in for the night. Kid doesn't like the rain, apparently." He grinned.

"How is she certain he never left?"

"She's a live-in housekeeper. Said aside from running a few errands at his request, she never left the house."

"What errands?"

"Flower shop."

I stilled, my wheels turning. If Josh's housekeeper delivered the orchids to Rose's front door, then that made him less likely to be the person who broke in. There went prime suspect number one.

Ax narrowed his eyes. "Anything I need to know about here?"

"No."

"Okay then."

We sat in silence for a moment.

"Dr. Buckley dropped by this afternoon."

I frowned. "Everyone okay?"

He nodded. "Doc swung by on his way to his weekend cabin. Said ol' Hoyt got himself a twelve point just off our property yesterday."

Ah, Ax, and his ever clever ways to make his point. Dr. Robby Hoyt was the town's pharmacist—the town's pharmacist that I hadn't seen since leaving the hospital. Which was exactly Ax's point, and, if I had to guess, the purpose of Buckley's visit to the house.

"I'm not taking the pills, Ax."

"I know you aren't. And so does Buckley and Hoyt. You haven't filled a single prescription."

Consider taking your meds, Phoenix, at least for the headaches... Rose's voice, again.

A moment slid by.

"Tell me about her." Ax said.

"About who?"

"The woman you just thought about."

My hand squeezed around the water, the icy condensation sizzling against my heated skin.

"Your therapist, Feen. Tell me about her."

"Rose Floris."

"And?"

"She's... different."

"Smart?" He grinned.

"Controlling."

"Helpful?"

"Determined."

"Compliant?"

"Pain in my ass."

He grinned, sipped his beer, then looked at me.

"Hot?"

"Stunning."

"A smart, attractive, assertive, pain in your ass." He chuckled. "Yep, definitely not the type of woman you're used to." He paused. "Heard you rearranged her desk."

I looked at him. "Where'd you hear that?"

"The whole neighborhood heard it, including old man Jenkins at the bakeshop."

"Didn't know a human with a pair of balls could be such a gossip."

"Gossip, then?"

"Frustration."

"And Dr. Floris accepted you back into her office after?"

"More or less."

I could feel Ax's grin more than I saw it. He knew me. He knew if I wanted something badly enough, nothing would stand in my way, even if I had to spend thousands of dollars on new computer equipment to get through the door.

"I like this one," he said. "Listen to her, Phoenix. You won't listen to us. You won't listen to your doctors. But based on that ice water you've got in front of you, you're listening to someone. Your therapist of all people. ... I'm proud of you."

A moment slid by.

"Having a strong woman in your life isn't all that bad you know."

Just then—

"Especially when they look like Pamela Anderson. Pre-PETA, of course, you know, Baywatch Pamela Anderson." Jagg's gravelly voice sounded behind us. "You've got a smorgasbord of drunk cowgirls stroking your horse like it's their last jug of jungle juice."

Wearing a beanie, black leather jacket, and combat boots, Jagg breezed up to the bar looking more like his former Navy SEAL self than a jacked-up sleuth. New ink peeked out of his collar, connecting to the tattoos that covered his torso and arms. Jagg loved his ink. Gage was behind him, stopping to chat with a couple off-duty cops about a client he'd recently taken who was getting severely bullied at high school. Somehow I didn't think the cops were going to approve Gage's idea, which was to have the kid add a rack of Bushmasters to the back window of his Chevy.

"Private dick." Ax nodded to Jagg as they two shook hands.

"Mister private dick to you." His hand clamped my shoulder. "How you doing?"

I dipped my chin.

The detective settled into the seat next to me and ordered a beer from the blushing bartender.

"Anything new on the chicken case?" Ax asked him.

The 'Chicken Case' was the name given to the string of electrocuted chicken parts being washed up all over town. The citizens were on edge, and rightly so. Spirit and I had ridden up on one of the headless animals earlier in the week. Not pretty.

Jagg released an exhale, a brief, rare display of fatigue in the man's demeanor. Max Jagger was a legendary SEAL in the Navy, a ruthless soldier who led each mission as if it were his last, and when he'd gotten out, he'd carried that resolve to his new job as a homicide detective. Jagg had a wicked—and I do mean *wicked*—intelligence that helped him put together pieces of a puzzle that no one else even noticed were there. The man put his life into his work, and although he'd never admit it, I believed he got too connected to his cases. Took each case personally. A challenge, or perhaps a vigilante need for justice for those who could no longer speak. Maybe it was because the man had never had a serious relationship with anyone in his life. I understood that.

"Well, we now know how the chickens were dismantled." Jagg said.

"Phoenix's axe outside?" Ax quipped.

"Scissors. The sick bastard cut them to pieces before, and after, electrocuting them. Like a mad scientist."

"Are you heading up the case? I thought you only worked homicides."

"The fried chickens potentially link to one of my homicides." His gaze flickered to me. I noticed.

Ax signaled for Frank. "Well, spending the day in chicken guts gets you a free shot."

"Chicken guts were only half my day. The other six hours were spent sitting out in my truck trying to get a bead on the kingpin of a local meth ring."

"I thought your mom moved away."

Ax laughed.

Jagger grinned. "Ah, well, how sweet, Feen. Looks like someone's getting their sense of humor back. Feelin' okay after that one? Need to stretch first next time?"

Gage walked up. "Guy needs more than a good stretching."

A crowd had gathered around the bar, all the five o'clockers stopping in on their way home.

Frank walked up, nodded to Jagg and Gage. "Howdy do, boys. Whiskey?"

"Doubles."

"The usual. Got it. More water, Phoenix?"

Before I could shake my head—

"Ice *Water*? Phoenix Steele drinking *water*? Well, I'll be a son of a—"

Before the drunk cowboy behind us could finish his slurred sentence, Ax, Gage, and Jagg spun around, a chorus of barks at my back.

"You got a fucking problem with that, son?"

"Yeah, ice water; the same temperature of your girlfriend's—"

"Ever had a colonic, Conner? Bend over."

The last one from Gage. Funny how the guy could work an asshole or a nipple into any conversation.

The old Phoenix would have been the first to throw a punch. Not that night. That night...

Create a calm environment for yourself... Rose's voice.

In a simultaneous wave, the crowd took a step back and the boys turned back toward me.

Jagg kicked over the stool next to him, signaling to everyone that no one else was welcome at that side of the bar.

I sipped my water, and for the first time, I felt proud of myself. Rose would have been proud.

I turned my attention to Jagg, the entire reason I was there. "You get the name of the owner of that ranch house on the east side of Shadow Mountain?"

After Rose's secret midnight rendezvous to the mystery house the evening before, I had Wolf and Jagg pull what they could on the homeowner. Wolf's initial pull said that the house belonged to an LLC that hadn't had any deposits or withdrawals in a decade.

"The LLC belonged to a small vet clinic that belonged to a man named George Wallace, a veterinarian who died fifteen years ago."

"Dead?"

"According to the state death records, yep."

I frowned. "Someone *alive* is living there now and I need to know who it is, and if they have any kind of record."

Jagg nodded. "Give me a few hours."

"Thanks."

His dark eyes narrowed. "Does this have anything to do with Rose Floris and the Kline and Associates client list Gunner gave me to run criminal checks on?"

"Anything come up?"

"You're asking if I found any criminal records connected to the clientele of a mental health facility?"

I tilted my head to the side letting him know I wasn't in the mood.

"Short answer, yes." He said. "And it will take some time to filter through them all."

"Any that stood out? Breaking and entering, peeping toms, loitering on private property?"

"A few B&Es at a liquor store and pharmacy. Go figure. There were two harassment charges."

"Stalking?"

He nodded. "Former exes who couldn't let go. One got a restraining order."

"Pull both of their addresses for me."

"Done. One address is the state pen, the other six feet underground. Heroin overdose."

Dammit.

If Josh wasn't Rose's stalker, and none of her clients were, then who? Someone from her past? Or perhaps some hard-up pervert who'd seen her around town. Rose was stunning. Smart. Alluring. Easy to form an attachment to. An obsession.

Jagg continued, "I did find something when I chatted with the owners of a few shops around town that sell electronics."

My back straightened.

He took a drink of his whiskey—always neat—then said, "A mini spy cam was purchased from Tad's Tool Shop last week."

"Tell me you've got a name."

"Nope."

"Security footage?"

He reached in his back pocket and slapped a grainy black and white image on the bar top.

"That's it?"

"You're welcome."

I stared down at one-half of a dark silhouette walking into Tad's Tool Shop—the other half out of camera view. The person was wearing a baseball cap and dark jacket with the collar flipped up. Couldn't even see the bottom-half of the body.

Jagg continued, "Darth Vader here walked into Tad's exactly six minutes before the recorder was purchased last Wednesday."

"There isn't another security camera in the store?"

"One. Broken."

"Why the hell is the angle so off on this picture?"

"Someone drove a backhoe through Tad's front door. Knocked it off center."

"Why didn't Tad fix it?" Because that was more curious than someone driving a loader through his shop.

"Says he never checks the thing. Considers the revolver under the cash register security enough."

Like every other citizen of Berry Springs.

"What about street cams?"

Jagg cocked his head. "Dude, I've kinda got this other job to do. You know, real cases, with real threats, that involve *real* police reports."

"What did the customer pay with? Can we track that?"

"Darth paid with a Visa gift card. Untraceable—with our resources, anyway—and I really don't think the Feds are gonna be willing to do you solid on this one."

Gage, who'd finally joined the conversation, hovered over my shoulder. "Why are you so sure that's a guy?"

I blinked, staring down at the photo.

He continued, "You can't even determine the height or weight from that angle. Can't even tell if there's hair under that collar."

"Are you saying you think it could be a woman video-taping Rose?"

"Rose, huh? Not Doctor Hot-Pants, huh?" Gage chided, chuckling. "Just joking. Seriously, though, why couldn't it be another chick filming her?"

"Because this isn't your bedroom, Gage. Not every woman is as willing to record themselves as your exes."

"Shame."

Jagg took us back to the point. "You know the situation better than any of us. Any idea on the motive? Regardless of a man or a woman?"

"There's only one reason someone hides a camera in a woman's *bedroom.*"

"Is there, Phoenix? Maybe this isn't just some pervert. Maybe she has something he—or she—wants. Maybe someone is keeping tabs on her because Dr. Floris knows something about them that they don't want to get out."

I chewed on that for a moment, my mind drifting to the

bomb she dropped about her childhood spent in foster care, and the mystery late night visit to the ranch house. One thing was for sure, Rose had secrets, and I needed to get to the bottom of them.

Jagg took a sip of my water. "Not bad. Anyway, you gotta step out of your possessive bubble and start thinking like a detective, Feen."

"Who says I'm possessive?"

"The fist your hand curled into when Gage called her Doctor Hot-Pants." He looked at Gage. "Show some respect, will ya?"

"This from the guy who won't let a female drive his truck. How about I show some respect to this fine establishment by ordering another drink. See ya."

I waited until Gage sauntered away before pinning the detective.

"What are you leaving out, Jagg?"

His lack of response told me my instinct was correct.

"Tell me."

"How well do you know this woman that's got you sleeping outside her house and pulling on these strings for?"

I opened my mouth, but paused.

"Exactly. Do you happen to know anything about her relationship with Andrew McGregor? The guy you and her so ironically stumbled onto? The guy who was stabbed to death in the temple?"

I waited, knowing he wasn't done.

"What about the fact that she went on a date with him? A few weeks ago."

My blood ignited. "What?"

"Yep. They went for coffee nine days ago."

"You sure?"

"Yep."

"I'm not done, my friend. Andrew's official cause of death was from the puncture wound to his head. You know who else got stabbed in the side of the dead? The body that Andrew was doing an autopsy on the day he got murdered. Crazy Carl. Andrew's autopsy notes suggest a pair of blue-handled scissors were used."

"Same on the chickens?"

"Hell of coincidence. I'm not done, though. Crazy Carl was one of the guys Rose had called the cops on for sitting outside her office building all day, watching her through the windows."

My eyes rounded as I looked at him.

"Yep. Both Andrew and Carl had a personal, romantic interest in Dr. Floris."

I stilled, my thoughts racing at breakneck speed.

"There are connections here, each leading to Rose. Your therapist is the common thread here, Phoenix."

"Are you saying you think she did it? Went nuts in a chicken coop then killed her client and Andrew? Give me a break."

"Calm down, dude. And it's my job to make those kind of assumptions, and if you can't handle an objective conversation about this, there's the fucking door. I'm just saying you can't ignore the connection."

"She didn't kill Andrew, Jagg. I was with her that afternoon."

"I believe you. But the fact of the matter remains. And if she isn't our killer, then someone appears to be killing the men who take an interest in her."

"An obsessed pervert."

"A madman."

My gut clenched.

He continued, "And I'd watch my back if I were you."

The noise of the bar faded into a low buzz as my brain spun.

Eyeing me, Jagg leaned back and took another sip of whiskey.

I turned fully to him. "If you know something else, tell me now, man. Right now."

His eyes narrowed. "Rose Floris has got a locked file with the department of family and protective services. Something happened when she was a kid. Something big. Someone adopted her, homeschooled her, kept her out of the public, but those details are locked up, too. She left Berry Springs at seventeen for college, came back eight months ago, and all of a sudden, two men who took an interest in her are murdered. The woman has secrets, Phoenix. And if you're not going to find out what they are, then I will."

I pushed away from the bar and stood.

"Where you going?" Jagg leaned forward.

Gage and Ax both stopped mid-conversation and turned toward me.

Ignoring them, I started to cross the room when the front door opened, a gust of wind accompanying a dark silhouette. My eyes narrowed before I even saw the guy, as if I could sense him. A blast of adrenaline shot through my veins as I looked at King Douchebag, the one and only, Josh Davis. Our eyes locked. Everything stopped as we stalked toward each other, the chatter, the music, everything faded into tunnel vision. I felt my brothers behind me as I neared the guy who'd slept with my Rose Flower. Funnily enough, that was my issue at that moment. Not the fact that he'd spread my business all over town.

Control your environment, Rose's voice, louder this time.

"Keep walking, Feen," Ax growled at my back as Gage flanked Josh from the side.

Stop, Phoenix. Don't do it. A new voice slipped into my head. My own.

I barreled my shoulder into Josh's as we passed. He stumbled backward and all hell broke loose. I was grabbed by Ax while Gage and Jagg hung back to deal with the two-hundred pound pussy of excuse for a man. As my brother dragged me outside, the crowd's voices began to register—

"What the hell is wrong with that guy?"

"Haven't you heard? Dude's gone crazy."

And the grand finale of it all, laughter followed by—

"Someone give that guy his damn meds."

Once outside, I jerked my arm from Ax's grip. My pulse roared as I stomped to Spirit, my ride. God, I missed my Harley. It was the first time—*ever*—that I felt embarrassed. And I fucking hated it.

Ax crossed the parking lot a half-step behind me, in case I decided to go back in and finish what I'd started.

Control your environment...

Control your environment...

Control your environment.

... *Screw you Doctor,* is what I thought at that moment. The woman was turning me into a water-drinking pussy who backed down from a fight.

My eyes landed on a brand-new, apple red, spotless Rolls Royce. A *Rolls Royce.* I knew it was Josh's not only because who else would drive a Rolls to a honky tonk bar, but because it was parked in the handicapped spot.

I officially unhinged.

Pulling the Ka-BAR from my boot, I stalked over to the Rolls.

"Phoenix, *no,* don't—"

Before Ax could finish his sentence, I sent a two-inch slash into the wall of the tire.

"Dammit, Feen."

I flipped Spirit's reins back and jumped on.

"Where you going?"

I jerked the reins, but Ax grabbed the horse's bridle.

"You need to go home, brother."

"Let *go*, brother."

We stared at each other a moment.

He released the bridle.

"Go home, Feen. *Home.*"

As I rode out of the parking lot, we both knew I wasn't going home.

20

ROSE

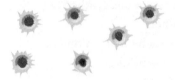

$\mathcal{M}$y stomach knotted as I turned onto my driveway, a feeling that was becoming habit over the last few days. My eyes skirted the darkening woods around me, a sunless dusk that looked more like twilight.

It was 7:04 p.m., and had been another long day at work.

True to Stan the weatherman's prediction, the temperature had reached almost seventy that day, making the atmosphere ideal for severe weather. There was an electricity, an energy in the air that had more to do with the pending thunderstorms. Despite the kiss of all kisses, I was on edge, restless. Or, perhaps because of it. After Phoenix had left my office, I'd spent ten minutes calming my heartbeat and resisting the urge to chase after him and rip his clothes off. It was the best kiss I'd ever had in my life, and that threw me off. Not only because I could lose my job over it, but because of the power behind it. Somehow I knew that it wasn't a casual kiss. Anything but, in fact. It was loaded. Loaded with the intensity that came with Phoenix Steele. Loaded with what was undeniably happening between us. Something serious, something deeper than I'd ever felt before. Something life changing. It scared me, to be honest, and sent a steady buzz of anxiety vibrating through my body the rest of the afternoon.

And going home to an empty house did nothing to help that.

Phoenix was right. I needed better locks—*more* locks—and flood lights. Heck, I even considered getting a gun. Where to begin with all that, though?

I hadn't heard anything from Berry Springs PD about finding the stuffed animal or video recorder in Andrew's house. Shocker. And it made me wonder, even more, if Phoenix was right. If Andrew's death and my stalker *were* connected, despite the cops calling his death a robbery gone wrong.

My faceless stalker was taking my sense of independence. I hated that. I thought of Phoenix, and how he must feel with his independence being ripped away.

I'm not the only screwed up one in this room.

His words had echoed in my head a hundred times since he'd left my office.

No, he wasn't the only screwed up one in the room. In fact, Phoenix had no idea exactly how screwed up I was.

I rolled to a stop under my carport and turned off the engine, hyper aware of any movement around me.

Suddenly, a bright floodlight flicked on above me, then another, then another. The entire perimeter of the carport was illuminated. Not in an offensive, blinding fluorescent way, but in a warm glow that said, 'welcome home, I've got you.'

Phoenix.

A smile crossed my lips as I looked over my shoulder.

Had he done this?

I grabbed my briefcase, purse, and empty coffee mug

and pushed out the door. The fresh smell of spring and something else earthy swept past me in a mild rush of wind. I looked around for any sign of Phoenix, or whoever had installed the lights, but there was nothing. No car, tracks, nothing. Yes, I was looking for *tracks* now, thanks to my new bodyguard.

The house was dark as I stepped inside, the air was still. I flicked on the entry light, set my things on the end table and looked around. No sign of anyone being in my home. The silence buzzed in my ears, a reminder of how alone I was—and how I didn't want to be. I clicked on the TV, then the table lamps as I padded through the living room. The monotone voices from the local news faded behind me as I made my way into the kitchen, beelining it to the liquor cabinet. I'd just poured a man-sized glass of wine when—

Whack!

My body jolted, sloshing wine on my white blouse.

Another *whack*... then another.

My gaze shifted to the windows that looked out to the backyard.

Another *whack*.

What the heck?

Wine in hand, I padded into the living room and peered through curtains I'd drawn before leaving that morning.

My heart fell to my feet.

Standing at the base of my backyard stood Phoenix, as tall and thick as the trees around him, with an axe in his hand and a massive pine tree at his feet. The dead tree that he was worried would fall on my house.

Sweat shimmered off of his tanned forehead and thick arms, his grey T-shirt clinging to his body like paint. And below that, tight-fitting Levi's and combat boots to complete the bad boy outdoorsman fantasy. As if that weren't sexy enough, a magnificent white horse stood on the other side of the tree, saddled, with its reins dropping below its cute little nose.

The man had ridden to my house on his white horse.

White horse.

Knight in shining armor. Check.

I watched him as he raised the axe, his muscles flexing against thin cotton that was stretched to the seams, then swing it down with a speed and control that told me it wasn't the first tree he'd chopped down.

Saliva pooled in my mouth, heat warmed between my legs. It was the sexiest thing I'd ever laid eyes on, kiss or no kiss earlier.

He stilled and somehow I knew he sensed me. It was a weird sixth sense we somehow already had with each other. He straightened, looked over his shoulder, and met my gaze.

Butterflies burst in my stomach.

The corner of his lip curled.

What are you doing, I mouthed through the window.

He jerked his chin to the tree.

I laughed and shook my head. I held up a finger—*one minute*—then darted to my bathroom like a lovesick schoolgirl. After stripping off my work clothes, I searched the closet for longer than I cared to admit, then settled on a fitted T-shirt that said 'I-didn't-try-too-hard-but-check-out-my-curves,' a pair of skinny jeans, and pull-on boots. After smoothing my hair, I dabbed on some lip gloss and a touch of French perfume behind the ear—the good stuff I saved for special occasions.

That's when I knew I had it bad.

I grabbed a bottle of water then jogged down the steps of my back deck.

"What the heck are you doing?" I couldn't fight the smile as I jogged across the yard.

"Supposed to get bad storms tomorrow. Hurricane force winds. This tree would have been in your living room."

His smile reached his eyes as he looked down at me. He was happy to see me, but there was something else in his look that I couldn't quite put my finger on. His gaze lingered, searching my face, searching for something.

I handed him the water. "Sounds like I owe you a thank you then."

"You owe me a new axe."

"Done." I shifted my attention to the gleaming white horse beside us. "Who is this beauty?"

"Her name's Spirit." The pride evident in his voice.

"Hi there, Spirit." I stroked her ink-black mane and she nestled into my shoulder.

"She likes you. She's skittish around people she doesn't know."

"She's beautiful." I held her snout. "You're beautiful, baby girl." I turned to Phoenix. "I think I have some carrots if she's hungry?"

He laughed at this. "She's all filled up on carrots and apples for now."

"What? Horses don't eat carrots and apples?"

"Mainly in the cartoons."

"I bet it's a better dinner than hay."

Spirit snorted.

"See?" I rubbed her snout.

Phoenix smiled, his eyes twinkling in a way I'd never seen before. A real, genuine smile. It was spectacular. Stunning, and it sent my pulse beating a bit faster.

I looked at the half-chopped tree in my backyard.

"Have you been here since after our appointment this afternoon?"

"Made a stop first." That lingering look, again.

I cocked my head. "You okay?"

"Depends."

"On what?"

"On how this evening goes."

"Sounds loaded."

"Could be."

I crossed my arms over my chest. "I'm not in the mood for mind games right now."

"Ironic, considering that's your job." He winked.

I rolled my eyes and turned my focus on the chopped wood because I really *wasn't* in the mood for mind games, or whatever Phoenix had bottled up inside him but wasn't saying.

"You've done too much. Really, thank you. Seriously." I looked back at him. "Thank you."

"You're welcome."

He nodded toward the house where a huge stack of wood leaned against the brick. "It'll take some time to get the rest of this chopped up but you've got enough to last you for the next few cold nights. And, yes, each piece is cut in the exact same dimensions, and stacked in perfect symmetry."

I slapped his arm.

"I noticed there were no logs inside yesterday." He said, because of course he'd noticed that teeny tiny little detail. "Where's your current stack?"

"Current stack of what?"

"Newspapers. *Wood,* Rose, where's your current stack of wood?"

"Oh. Well, I've, ah, never used the fireplace."

He looked at me as if I'd sprouted wings.

"What?" He blinked. "Have you ever built a fire?"

"No."

His eyelids flittered in the closest thing to an eye roll without actually being an eye roll. He turned and took off up the hill.

"Follow me."

My pleasure.

When we reached the wood pile, he stacked two logs in my arms, then filled his own.

"Walk next to me."

We fell in step together up the hill.

I glanced over my shoulder. "What about Spirit?"

"She's fine."

"Did you tie her to a tree?"

"Don't need to."

He ushered me to go ahead of him at the door. The house was all lit up, with the hint of my perfume in the air when we stepped inside. Such a different feeling than when I'd walked in minutes earlier. This time, I felt light on my feet. Happy, even.

Safe.

I started across the living room, and when I noticed he wasn't following me, I turned to see him frozen in the doorway.

"What?"

He glanced down at his muddy boots and pants covered with wood shavings.

I laughed. "Come in. Don't worry about it. It's fine."

And shockingly, it was.

We met at the fireplace. He kneeled next to me, took the logs from my arms, and stacked them into the wood basket on the side.

"Ready for your lesson, Rose Flower?"

Rose Flower. To my utter shock, I was beginning to like the pet name he'd given me. I like the way it sounded when he said it.

"Sure, Davy Crockett. Show me what you've got."

"This is no joking matter, and neither is the King of the Wild Frontier."

"Sheesh, okay, okay."

"You need to know how to start a fire, especially living alone. We're supposed to get severe weather tomorrow, that's going to bring another cold snap. What was your plan if your electricity went out, big shot?"

"I have flashlights."

"And how large an area do your dollar-store flashlights heat?"

I sucked in a breath. "Oh. You meant for heat. Okay. Got it. I understand. Fine. Teach me, Obi Wan Kenobi."

He didn't laugh. He was busy placing kindling in the box. Serious business, apparently.

"First and foremost, every few years you need to have your chimney inspected and cleaned by a professional. Or me." He winked again and it was the first time I was seeing a lighter Phoenix. A relaxed Phoenix. One with less stress, less weight on his shoulders. He was in his element, and I hoped, even for a minute, that he'd forgotten about his troubles.

He continued, "Over time creosote builds up, which can cause a chimney fire. Not good. Very important to have it inspected." He turned to me. "Got it?"

"Yes, sir."

He grinned. "Atta girl. Considering you renovated the place recently, I'm assuming your builder checked the chimney so we're going to cross that off. Next," he reached around me and flicked open a little vent on the side of the box. "Always open the damper so smoke doesn't fill your living room."

"Got it."

"Now to starting the actual fire. Many amateurs do the 'top down' method. Big logs on bottom, smaller on top, bada bing. But considering you're a doctor, I think we can skip over the easy way."

I narrowed my eyes.

Another wink. "I'm going to show you the 'log cabin' method. Grab two of the logs that I've removed the bark from, and put them on the grate about six inches apart."

Apparently, this was a teach-a-man-to-fish-scenario. Okay, then.

"Good, next, grab the twigs, we call them kindling, and place them between." He looked around. "We need..." He reached back and pulled a magazine from my coffee table.

"Hey. That's my Vogue."

"You'll get another next month."

I cringed as he shredded the glossy, perfumed pages, rolling them into tight little wands.

"Add these to the kindling. Then, grab two more logs, and stack those perpendicular on the bottom two. Next, two more on top, the other way."

I did as I was told.

"It looks like a little log cabin."

"Nothing gets past you. Now," he pulled a lighter from his pocket and handed it to me. "Light the kindling."

"You always carry a lighter in your pocket?"

"Yeah."

Five minutes later, the fire was roaring and my confidence was growing. I was actually having *fun*.

"See? Not so hard is it?"

"Not with you helping out."

"Exactly." He sat back on his haunches and focused on me. "Next up, I'll show you how to work the security system I'm going to install."

He brushed off his hands and stood, looking out the window. "Got a bit more light left. I'm going to make another dent in the tree. My brother's dropping off a chainsaw in a minute."

I stood. "Thank you. For everything."

"I'll get the rest of it taken care of this weekend."

"How can I pay you?"

He took a step closer and my heart skipped a beat. "I've got plenty of money, Rose." The twinkle in his eye highlighting the innuendo. You could practically reach out and grab the sexual tension between us.

"What, then?" I whispered as he leaned in, practically begging him to kiss me again.

He leaned down, his lips barely grazing past my lips, blazing a trail against my cheek. Goosebumps rippled as his whisper tickled my ear.

"I want you to never see Josh Davis again."

Warm, soft lips met my ear lobe, not a kiss, but an erotic touch, a hypnotic foreplay to something I realized I wanted more than anything in the world.

"... Done." The soft submissive voice that came out of me was not my own.

Satisfied, he pulled back, leaving me desperate for more. I blinked, cool air replacing the heat between us.

"Be right back."

His lip curved to a smile, a sparkle in his eye that told me he knew exactly what he was doing to me, and my panties, for that matter. Then, he turned and walked out the door taking all the energy, the electricity, the warmth—the comfort—with him.

My protection.

My peace of mind.

My... what?

I plucked the wine glass from the counter and watched him ride down the driveway on his big, white horse, to meet his brother.

Phoenix Steele, my patient.

My knight in shining armor.

My weakness.

The last of the porch light caught his face as he turned and locked eyes with me.

A smile crossed my lips, a desperate need crossed my body.

He winked, then faded into the darkness.

And I knew, at that moment, I was falling in love with Phoenix Steele.

I knew I was in trouble.

I just didn't realize, at the time, exactly how much.

21

PHOENIX

*I*t was past ten o'clock in the evening by the time I finished chopping the tree. The manual labor, along with the drop in temperatures with nightfall, had cooled the anger and adrenaline that had spiked while speaking with Jagg at Frank's Bar. I'd expected to launch into my assault of questions the moment Rose arrived at her house and found me in the backyard, but I'll be damned if seeing her didn't have some immediate calming effect on me. Hell, I'd forgotten why I was there in the first place. When she'd jogged down the hill in her little boots with a smile across those red lips, I didn't want to bring everything up. Didn't want to talk about death, secrets, mystery midnight visits, doubts. I wanted to suspend that brief moment of bliss I got just from seeing her. The woman calmed me. Made me forget everything. Made me happy.

It was hypnotic, almost.

I set down the chainsaw Gunner had dropped off, spent a minute with Spirit, then made my way up to the house contemplating how to address my questions without upsetting her. Because I realized I cared about that. More than anything else.

The low melody of instrumental jazz music floated through the air as I pushed open the front door. My gaze shifted to the blazing fire in the fireplace and pride swelled. Rose had made, and maintained, her first fire, all by herself. It was like a little piece of me had been in there with her. I liked that. I liked that I'd had a hand in that fire; that I'd made my stamp on the place.

The cabin was warm with the savory scent of something Italian lingering in the air. My stomach growled. A candle was lit in the living room. Vanilla, if I had to guess. Not because Rose was boring, but because Rose was a confident simplicity. Classic, gentle, yet commanding with an authority that made you take notice. Timeless, like vanilla.

An almost-empty glass of wine sat on the coffee table next to an open book.

There was a warmth, a coziness to the place that reminded me of my own home growing up when my greatest worry was how to beat my brothers at a game of war that afternoon. When things were happier.

Her head popped around the kitchen wall. "Hi, there. Come in."

She'd changed into a pair of flannel pajama bottoms, a sweatshirt that read 'I get psyched for Psychology,' and fuzzy slippers. Her long, black hair was up in a messy bun, and dammit if she didn't look sexier than she did in her designer suits. In pajamas, Rose Floris was sexier and more tantalizing than the hottest stripper in Vegas. I'd done the leg work there, trust me.

And at that moment, I realized there was no place in the world I'd rather be.

My heart gave a little kick.

When I stepped into the kitchen, she was pulling down a plate from a cabinet filled with matching dinnerware sets, each stacked according to color. She set the plate—only one—on the counter, then uncovered a glass casserole dish. Steam unfurled from a lasagna, cheese bubbling over the sides. She'd cooked for me, and despite the immediate excitement, I felt bad that she'd gone to the trouble.

She scooped a hefty amount onto the plate, then breezed past me and set it on the table in the breakfast nook.

"Sit."

"Oh. No, it's okay. I'm not hungry."

"Yes, you are. Sit."

"I'm good."

"*Sit,* Phoenix."

"Are you going to eat with me?"

"*Sit.*"

I did as I was told. She placed a tall glass of tea—with two lemons—in front of me. Her hand rested on my shoulder. I looked up.

"Eat," she said looking down at me.

"You didn't have to do this."

"I know. But you look like dog crap. No offense. We'll talk about whatever it is that's on your mind later, but you're going to eat first. Based on the circles under your eyes, I'm guessing you haven't eaten dinner today, or lunch."

Or, breakfast, but she didn't need to know that.

My mouth watered as I looked down at the food. Each bubbling layer was distinct and oozing with filling. It was something a New York chef would make.

"You really made this?"

"That's a hefty insult for someone with Italian blood."

"Sorry." I picked up my fork and dug in—and literally groaned in satisfaction.

She smiled. "Good?"

"The best I've ever had," I muttered around a mouthful. And that wasn't a lie. "Aren't you going to eat?"

"Already did. Wasn't sure if you were going to come back inside or sneak off."

"Hefty dish on a whim." I was shoveling the food into my mouth like a hyena. "Not that I'm complaining." A string of cheese dripped off my chin.

She smiled at my vigor, then said, "When I cook, I make big batches to feed myself through the week. Lasagna freezes well."

"You cook often?"

"Mondays, Wednesdays, Fridays, and Sundays." Because of course she had a cooking schedule.

"Mondays, Wednesdays, Fridays, Sundays," I repeated. "I'll mark my calendar."

She looked down at the plate in front of me that was already half-empty. "Might need to add a few days then." She winked.

"What else do you like to cook?"

"Italian food, mostly. It's not all cheese and sauce you know."

"Olives." I wrinkled my nose.

"The man doesn't like olives. Note to self."

I wiped my mouth and sat back. "Italian because... your roots?"

She briefly looked down. "Yes. The only roots I know. I know my grandparents on one side were Italian."

"And you've never been?"

"No. It's on the bucket list though." She waved a hand in the air to dismiss the subject. "Anyway. Eat."

We fell into casual, easy conversation over my second helping. I chugged the rest of the tea—sweetened to perfection; a task that did not go unappreciated in the south—and met a pair of smiling eyes.

"Thank you," I said. "I feel better. Like a million bucks, actually."

"Good." She smiled a big, toothy smile. The cutest thing I'd ever seen. "You're welcome."

I began gathering my plates. She quickly stood and reached for them.

"No." I said.

Her hand dropped, a touch of surprise in her eyes. I felt her gaze on me as I washed my plate and my glass at the sink.

"Thank you for everything you've done around here," she said. "To be honest, I'm not sure that I would have chosen to stay tonight without the outdoor lights."

"Because that's the only thing you need to keep you safe. Lights."

"Hey, you said it would help deter peeping toms."

I set the plate in the cabinet and turned to face her.

"What?"

"I don't think a peeping tom is your biggest worry, Rose."

Something flashed in her eyes. Concern, worry. Fear. "What do you know that I don't?"

"I have some questions for you, Rose, and I need you to be honest. And I need you to answer every one of them."

She stilled. "...Okay."

"What exactly was your relationship with Andrew McGregor?"

"Oh. First, we have not had sex, as I've already told you. We kept running into each other around town, and one day, he asked me on a date. We went to coffee, I felt absolutely nothing, and denied his request for a second date. That's it. No kissing, no sex, nothing."

"Why did you go to him for help with the stuffed animal found on your bed?"

"I remembered him telling me that he had a brother in forensics. So I went to him for a favor. That's it."

"Is that the whole truth?"

"Yes."

"What about Carl Higgins?"

She looked down, a flash of guilt on her face. "I shouldn't have called the cops on him, but I did. He'd wait outside of work for me for hours. It was creepy."

"What was he coming to the clinic for?"

"Anxiety. Panic attacks. He'd recently turned sober and was dealing with the withdrawals."

"Do you know if he had a wife, girlfriend?"

"He said he didn't."

"I want to see his file."

"I can't. Confidentiality."

"I want to see it, Rose."

She stared at me for a moment. A swift nod, then, "Okay. I'll pull it for you. Under the table."

"Thank you."

"You really think the same person that killed Andrew, also killed Carl?"

"Yes."

She shuddered, but her expression told me she'd been thinking about the same thing.

"And I think you're next."

Her fingers trembled as she reached for the glass of wine.

A minute stretched between us.

"It's time, Rose. It's time for you to take this seriously.

Someone has formed a sick obsession with you and we need to consider all angles. Look at everyone. I need you to look into your past. I know it's uncomfortable, but we need to talk about it. We need to figure out who is after you."

Her gaze shifted to the living room. After a moment, she seemed to decide something and said, "Go stoke the fire. I'll be right there."

Five minutes later, she returned with two cups of coffee and a glistening slice of tiramisu.

She set it on the coffee table.

"You keep this up and I might never leave."

"Sorry that there's only one piece. Thought we could share. I've kind of indulged over the last forty-eight hours."

"Stress eater?"

She smiled.

"Someone I know might refer to that as emotional eating."

"Hey, I'm the only one with the license to psychoanalyze in this room." She winked and handed me a cup of coffee. "Decaf."

"Because it's healthier."

"Of course."

I wanted to tell her I hadn't had a drop of alcohol that evening. I wanted her to be proud of me, to know that her efforts were making a difference. That her blind faith in me wasn't for nothing. I wanted to tell her that she was good at her job. But, true to form, I fumbled with the praise.

I sipped—black and strong. Exactly the way I drank it.

"Try it." She nodded to the dessert.

"Don't have to tell me twice."

She was deflecting and that was okay with me. We'd get to it.

She watched me take a bite. As suspected, it was heaven.

The woman could cook. And it was then that I realized Rose enjoyed pleasing people through their stomachs. As if I wasn't attracted to her enough.

A satisfied twinkle in her eye had her sipping her coffee and leaning back in the arm chair.

I took another bite, then set it on the coffee table between us.

"Tell me."

Her hand squeezed around her mug.

I leaned forward, knees on elbows. "Tell me about what happened to you while you were in foster care."

The fire cracked next to us, hissing as if sensing the mood unfolding in the room.

"Please tell me." I repeated.

"Do you know that there are almost a half million children in foster care in the United States?" She said.

My brows popped. I didn't, and that number was staggering.

"When my mom died, I was put into the system because my dad was in jail. He died shortly after, by the way. I had no living grandparents, aunts, uncles, brothers, sisters, nothing. I was told I'd be adopted quickly. Didn't happen. The first seven years of my life were spent being shipped from home to home, stranger to stranger, school to school, waiting to be adopted by someone who thought I was worthy enough. It's funny," she said thoughtfully as she gazed at the fire, "I don't remember too much of most of the homes I was in. Repressed memories, I learned later while in college."

"Unconsciously blocking something that had a high level of stress. That's a lot for a child."

"Yes, it is. But it's not only that. It was the lack of structure, the lack of genuine relationships, role models. The only constant I had was the feeling of abandonment. I spent every day anticipating that knock at the door where my caseworker would take me to my next 'fill-in parents.' I was at the mercy of the system. Instead of a human, a system was in control of my welfare." A sharp gaze cut to me. "That's pretty screwed up."

She slid her coffee on the table with a scowl.

"What about your caseworker?"

She snorted. "I had three, total. The last one I rarely saw, and I found out years later, he was arrested for possessing child pornography, by the way. He had no clue about the conditions I was living in. He didn't care. That's why I got myself out." Her gaze locked on the fire.

I grabbed the wine she'd been drinking earlier that evening and handed it to her.

"Tell me what happened at the last house." Without even hearing the story, my protective streak was raging.

Little did I know then what I was about to hear.

She sipped, took a deep breath, and began.

"I was placed with a man and woman who said they couldn't conceive and wanted to be foster parents to fill the void. Little did everyone know, the cause of the infertility was from a life of excessive drug use. But they hid it well. The man, Earl, worked for a manufacturing company and was gone all the time on sales trips. The woman, Cheryl, was a stay at home wife with nothing to do. The first time I saw him hit her was after she'd tried to serve him a cold dinner a week after I moved in. The first time he hit me was when he tripped over a shoe that I'd left in the hallway."

White hot anger furled through my system. I curled both my fists, and my toes in my boots, in an effort to dispel the rush of adrenaline.

Her steely gaze pinned me. "Yes, I was physically abused, Phoenix. They were two screwed up individuals who had no business being foster parents. But that's *the system,*" she emphasized. "They're desperate for foster homes. Anyway, it didn't take long for me, even at eight years old, to realize Cheryl was not only cheating on her abusive husband, but was a drug addict and also sold drugs on the side." She paused. "Have you ever been to a drug dealer's house?"

It was a rhetorical question, but back in my door-kicking days, I'd been to plenty. And my stomach was rolling.

"It's a revolving door of strangers," she continued. "Day and night, people in and out of the house. One after the other. Lights are always on. No sleeping. It's a madhouse. I'd hide. Every second I wasn't in school, I'd hide under the kitchen table because they never ate there. That was my spot."

She began turning the wine glass around in her hands.

"One day, I was hiding in the kitchen after school, my usual routine. I remember being so hungry that day. Abnormally so. Anyway, in the living room—the next room over..." Her voice cracked. "Cheryl died of a heroin overdose. Right there, twenty feet from me. She died with a purple ligature around her bicep and a needle in her arm. I had no idea." Her voice wavered and tears filled her eyes. She looked at me, a childlike desperation pulling at her face. "I didn't know, Phoenix. I didn't know. I would have tried to save her, I promise. I hated that woman, but I wouldn't have let her die. I would have tried to save her."

I slid off the couch, pried the wine glass from her clutch and set it aside. I kneeled at her feet. She gripped onto my hands as her eyes glazed over in a memory so haunting she was no longer in the present. I swear, her voice even changed when she started again. Softer, scared, a child's voice.

"Earl came home and found her. He screamed my name;

I think he thought I actually did it. Or, he blamed me for it." Tears rolled down her cheeks. "I remember thinking I was going to be taken to jail charged for murder. An eight year old thinking that. Can you imagine that?"

I wiped the tears. "It wasn't your fault, Rose. It wasn't your fault. Release the guilt, just like you've told me to."

"It's tough, isn't it?"

"Yeah. I get it."

She blew out a breath. "I still blame myself. To this day, I blame myself for her death."

"You can't. It wasn't your fault. You didn't put the needle in her arm and pull the trigger, so to speak. It wasn't your fault."

My heart broke for her. And also, in a weird twist of fate, I heard my own words in response to what I was going through, too.

Fate. Funny thing.

"Tell me the rest of the story. Because I know you're not done."

"When he started screaming at me, I ran. I ran up the staircase, grabbed a bag I kept hidden under my bed. I literally had a go-bag for all the times I thought about running away. An eight year old with a go-bag."

Tears streamed down her face. My heart pounded like a drum in my chest.

"As he pounded on my bedroom door, I jumped out the window and ran into the woods. He would have killed me that night. I know it."

The room fell silent.

I held her hand while she took a deep breath, then continued. "After that, after I lived in the woods for three days, alone, until a woman on horseback found me. I was dehydrated, sick, with infections all over my skin from hiking through the terrain." Her eyes met mine. Her chin lifted. "That woman was June Massey."

And the pieces of the puzzle began to slowly click together.

"Let me guess. She lives in a ranch house on the other side of the mountain."

"Yes." A smile touched Rose's lips. "That's why I bought this cabin. To be close to her."

So the midnight mystery visit had been to the woman who had saved her life.

"June not only adopted me, but took it upon herself to homeschool me when I was too scared to go back to school. Believe it or not, I was so embarrassed by my life. By everything that had happened. I remember begging her to keep it a secret from the public. Not many people around here even know she adopted me. I stayed within those four walls for seven years, healing. June saved my life. She's the reason I'm everything that I am."

"I had no idea."

"No, you wouldn't. Like I said, not many do. I didn't go to public school, and let me tell you, that was a blessing for me. I was pretty screwed up for a while, and therapy got me through it."

"Why haven't you stayed with June the last few days? Through everything that's happened?"

"Because I didn't want her to worry about me. The woman has been through enough because of me. I didn't want to burden her, or for her to feel obligated to take care of me *again*. Surely, you of all people, can understand that."

I nodded. "You got me there. The guilt of being a burden. Yeah, I get that."

She sighed. "Anyway, I was homeschooled until I left for

college at seventeen." She grinned. "I had a full semester of advanced classes under my belt at that point."

"I don't doubt that. Is all this why you studied psychology?"

She nodded. "I started studying psychology around age ten, when I realized how beneficial it was. I became obsessed. For the first time in my life, I felt like I understood what was going on in my brain. Why I was the way I was. It was an epiphany of sorts."

I'd had the same epiphany recently, thanks to her. Little did I know the why's of it, or the heavy meaning behind why she explained my injury to me in the way she did. It was because that was how *she* adapted through her pain; and now, me, too.

She continued, "I remember reading an article about how severe trauma to young children can literally change their brain. Their physiology. It's called Adverse Childhood Experiences. Because children have trouble verbalizing their emotions, bad experiences play on loop in their heads over and over. Think about that; the same horror show replaying in your head over and over. That kind of stress releases harmful chemicals into the brain and can result in a lack of growth in the part of their brain that controls impulses and determines good from bad."

"The Prefrontal Cortex."

Her eyes lit up. "Bingo. Sounds familiar, huh?"

"Thanks to you, yes."

Yes, we were much more similar creatures than I'd realized, and that was the first moment that my physical attraction to Rose was second only to my respect for her. She came out of her circumstance.

I could come out of mine.

She squeezed my hand. "You've told me that you feel like

you don't know who you are. I hope you know now that I truly understand that feeling. Because I don't either, Phoenix." Her eyes filled with tears again. "I have no clue who I am. Where I came from. When I fill out medical forms, I know nothing of my past. Only that my grandparents were Italian. That's it."

Still kneeling at her knees, I stroked her palm with my thumb, shockingly, fighting my own tears. I understood this woman. So much.

"Oh, Phoenix," she blurted out, then sunk her head into her hands and began sobbing.

I pulled her into my arms. Her body went limp against mine as she dropped to the floor with me. She settled into my chest as I leaned us against the couch, and she cried and cried, and cried.

I stroked her head, kissing the top, inhaling the scent of the woman I'd do anything to keep safe, to keep happy. Looking back, that's when I knew I was falling in love with Rose Floris.

My beautiful Rose Flower.

After a few minutes, she pulled away, wiped her face and laughed. *"Geez.* I'm supposed to be *your* therapist."

I cupped her face and kissed her forehead. "Don't worry, my bag of crazy still runs circles around yours."

She laughed. "I'll give you that. Well, now you know why I am the way I am." She pulled her coffee from the table and took a sip and leaned back against the couch. I kept my hand on her thigh.

"Through my schooling, I learned that everything 'weird' about me has to do with my childhood. My OCD, my perfectionism, my uptight, condescending nature—as you'd call it." She winked at me, then focused back on the fire. "But the biggest side effect has been my need for control. I never had control growing up, so I grip onto it now like some elusive gift that might escape me one day. I have to have the routine, the mundane. I want the white picket fence, a family. I want *normal*. I've spent my life trying to control everything, keeping everything in its place, trying to make decisions based on facts instead of my heart." She looked up at me. "*That's* why I dated Josh Davis, Phoenix. That's why I said yes to his proposal."

"Because he's perfect on paper. He's your white picket fence."

"Exactly. He had everything. He served his country, had a solid education, solid family, solid future. Turns out he was also a solid jerk."

"Is that why you left him?"

A moment passed.

Her hand drifted to mine, those dark eyes locking onto mine.

"No. I left him, Phoenix, because he didn't give me butterflies."

Butterflies rippled through my own stomach.

I took her face in my hands and kissed her. And this time, I took my time. Two crazy, messed-up people finally finding the one that makes them whole again. I knew her soul, and she knew mine. Everything culminating in that single kiss. We were one. In that moment, we were one.

My Rose Flower.

A bright light flickered behind my closed eyes. I jerked back, scanning the room. More lights, moving across the walls in waves.

Headlights.

She slowly opened her eyes, then froze when they met mine.

"What's wrong?"

"You expecting someone?"

"No."

"You sure about that?"

"I'm sure."

I pulled the SIG from my ankle holster as I stood.

"Stay here."

Skirting the wall, I jogged to the front window, where a red Rolls Royce was pulling up the driveway.

22

PHOENIX

I watched Josh Davis unfold himself from his car, taking note of the spare tire on the front.

Should've slashed all four.

He slammed the door and stumbled on the first step, this telling me he'd closed down the bar. And also, of the two of us, he was the one who shouldn't be allowed to operate a motor vehicle.

I holstered my gun.

"Who is it?" Rose hissed from the living room floor.

"Your ex fiancé."

"My *what?*"

Her mouth dropped—make that unhinged—which answered my question of if she'd been expecting him.

She jumped off the floor and darted to the front window.

"No *way*. Are you sure?"

Knock at the door.

She looked back at me, wide-eyed.

"Any idea why he'd be showing up at your house at ten at night?"

"No. I promise; *no.*"

I reached for the handle. "Well, let's see then, shall we?"

She grabbed my arm. "No. This is my house, Phoenix. Let me handle this."

I didn't move.

"Phoenix. *Please.* I've got this."

I clenched my jaw and took a step back. Damn the woman.

The shitstain knocked again, this time louder. Impatient prick.

I stepped behind Rose as she opened the door.

His eyes immediately locked on mine, and looking back, I wished I could have taken a picture of the shock that crossed his face. I was, without doubt, the absolute last person he expected to see in his former fiancés house. But that shock was quickly replaced by tequila-induced anger— a type of anger that never turned out well.

Good to see you, too, you fucking son of a bitch.

He barged into the house, a flush rising up his neck.

Rose flickered a glance at me as she stepped back.

I stepped forward.

"What's *he* doing here?" Josh demanded.

Rose's eyes darted back and forth between us, sensing the instant tension. Would have been impossible not to. The temperature in the room tripled the moment the door opened. Rose's controlled, calm environment had deteriorated in an instant. Again, that mother fucker.

As I opened my mouth to respond for her, she darted me a glance that reminded me to 'let her handle this.'

Restraint, restraint, restraint...

She turned back to Josh. "Phoenix is here to help me with some things around the house."

Help her with some things *around the house?* Funny, considering she'd just had her tongue in my mouth.

"Why didn't you call me?" He asked.

"Because she called me." I stepped forward. Guess that was all the restraint I had.

He stepped forward, too, blocking me from Rose.

I did *not* like this.

"You slit my tire tonight, Steele?" He sneered, his chest puffing like a high school kid.

"Your throat's next if you don't take a step back."

He inched closer. "I'm going to add that to the bill you're going to get for destroying my company's construction equipment."

"Staple it to my medical bills that you can't seem to keep your fucking nose out of."

"Guys. *Stop.*" Rose stepped between us, her eyes pinning mine—*Do not engage.*

Do not engage.

Do not engage.

Control your environment.

Do not engage.

She spun around to Josh. "What are you doing here, anyway?"

The shithead peeled his eyes away from mine and focused on her. I hated it. I hated when he looked at her.

She. Was. *Mine.*

"I heard about the break-in. Why didn't you call, Rose?"

Her name off his lips was a nuclear bomb going off between my temples.

"Because I handled it, Josh."

"With *this* guy?" He jerked his chin toward me.

She reached around him for the door and yanked it open. "Yes. With him. And I'm fine. You don't need to check up on me anymore."

"The hell I don't. Come on."

"It's time for you to leave, Josh."

He glowered down at her. "You were always so damn stubborn. You're going to take better care of yourself, and it's not going to be here."

"I'm *fine* here."

"With *him?* Seriously, Rose? What the hell? The guy belongs in a padded room. Come. *On.*"

Funny, it wasn't the padded room comment that made me snap, it was the way he grabbed her arm and yanked her to him.

My fist slammed into the side of his face.

And we began.

Two former Marines, one fighting for his pride, the other fighting for his woman. A lethal combination.

Rose's shouts faded as he swung back, missing my chin by an inch. That's when that old familiar adrenaline rush took over, and I slipped into a place I'd been many times before. Uncontrolled, unbridled rage.

It felt damn good.

I tackled the bastard, sending us through the doorway and onto the front porch. The headlock I got him in was answered back by a headbutt to my jaw. It hurt like a son of a bitch, but I actually laughed. Like a madman, I laughed. See, the thing is, our little tussle wasn't two regular rednecks fighting. No, when you get two former spec ops soldiers together, it's about more than hand to hand combat. It's about winning. The main difference between us and others is that we loved the fight. We were trained for it. Something clicks inside us, a sick drive bordering on enjoyment when we take that first punch. Marines are a different breed. We fight different. And if there was ever a moment to prove that, it was then. Two jacked up jarheads, who'd killed more men than they could count, in a fight to the end.

A challenge I was more than ready to face.

We scrambled to our feet and I got him with a right hook.

Then, he got me with a left, followed by a kick to the knee. It wasn't the knee that momentarily stunned me, it was the lightning that shot through the right side of my head from his punch. Something vicious, blinding, raw. Something that sent off an internal alarm.

Something new; something I'd never felt before in a fight.

Rose's screaming came into orbit then, and it wasn't, *"stop fighting you barbarians,"* it was, *"No!* Josh, *don't hit his head."*

Don't hit his head.

My injury.

Fuck.

It was the first time ever, in my entire life, that my focus broke during hand to hand combat.

His gaze flickered to my head, the corner of his lip curled up. He had a new target, and all I could think was—
bring it.

He lunged. Our bodies tumbled off the porch and into the cool mud below.

"How's your head?" Josh chided as we wrestled.

"Better than your balls." I sent my knee into his groin.

Like a caged animal, the guy bucked out of my hold, then, one punch, another, another.

Pain.

Pain.

Pain.

Something snapped in me. I can't explain it, although looking back, I wonder if it was my survival instinct. Our fight was no longer a game, no longer a release of pent up rage. I was going to get myself legitimately hurt, possibly worse.

In a wave of adrenaline, I swung with every bit of strength in my body. I swung to survive.

My fist connected with his eye. Blood sprayed like paint, then streamed down his face, blinding him. He swung back, messy, though. I caught his arm mid-swing, twisted it. He released a bellow of pain as his body followed the flow and his face slammed into the ground. Chest heaving, I pinned the fucker, straddled him, and leaned down into his ear.

Blood pooled in the dirt beneath him.

"You ever come to Rose's house again, I'll make sure you never see out of that eye again."

His grunt told me he was dazed. Down for the count.

I spat the blood from my mouth and pushed off the asshole.

The world around me started to register in a hazy *whomp, whomp, whomp* with my pulse.

Rose.

I turned to see her, standing on the porch with her hand over her mouth and tears streaming down her cheeks.

My heart sank.

A bit unsteady on my feet, I crossed the dirt to the porch and wrapped my hands around her waist.

"I'm sorry. Baby, please, don't cry," I whispered. "Are you okay?"

She fisted my shirt, a desperation in her eyes I'll never forget. "Are *you* okay? Phoenix, are you okay?"

"I'm fine." I gripped the rail and hopped onto the porch. "Come here. I'm so sorry. Come here."

She fell into my chest and sobbed. We rocked back and forth.

The growl of an engine pulled my attention away. Josh's

face looked like a crushed tomato as he paused before shutting the car door.

"She's mine, Davis." I said. "She's mine now."

He scowled, looking at her in my arms, then slammed the door and disappeared down the hill.

At that moment I knew two things. One, I wouldn't have to worry about Josh Davis again.

Two, Josh Davis wasn't Rose's stalker.

23

ROSE

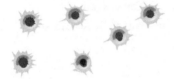

My stomach swirled, that sick, nauseous feeling that comes with watching a brutal fist fight. Tears flowed down my face. I focused on the sound of Phoenix's heartbeat as he held me against his chest. I will never, ever forget that moment for the rest of my life. And that was saying something. I gripped his sweaty T-shirt, pinning him there, close to me, away from harm.

To anchor me.

The sound of rocks crunching under tires told me that Josh was leaving. He'd given up. The fight was over, and I had a feeling I'd never see my former fiancé again.

I lifted my cheek off Phoenix's chest. He'd wiped most of the blood from his face, but spatters still covered his neck and shirt. I didn't know if it was his, or Josh's.

It was so much blood. Watching the two massive, jacked-up men fight had been horrifying. I'd never forget it, including—

"She's mine now."

Phoenix told Josh I was his.

His.

It was too much. My head was spinning faster than my stomach. I didn't know what to think but I knew one thing, at that second, I couldn't handle it. Between the dead bodies, my stalker, and me opening up the past I'd tried so hard to bury, I was done. It was as if the last forty-eight hours had finally taken its toll, crumbling around me with a weight I could no longer bear.

I pushed away from his chest, a tornado of emotions whirling inside me. Anger blazed from me.

"What the *hell* do you think you were doing?"

"I'm sorry." He pulled me to him again. "I'm sorry, Rose. I didn't mean to upset you."

"You could have hurt—you could have gotten yourself *killed!*"

Tears welled in my eyes again and I stormed past him, into the house. A million incoherent thoughts raced through my head as I crossed the living room. I wasn't only pissed; it was *everything*. Phoenix, the kiss—*that kiss*—the feelings, the hypnotic way he stole my thoughts. Then, Josh showing up at my door. Then, the fight, like two vicious dogs. All capped off with Phoenix's words—*she's mine.*

Biting back the tears, I yanked the first aid kit from below the kitchen sink, an ice-pack from the freezer, then stalked back into the living room.

Phoenix was standing in the doorway.

"Come in." I snapped.

The front door shut quietly. I avoided eye contact as I jerked my chin to the couch, where he obediently sat. I ripped open an antiseptic wipe, dropped to my knees and focused on his face—everything but his piercing gaze that would surely send me into another sobbing mess.

"Here." I shoved the ice pack at him. "Put this on your stupid jaw."

I wiped the cut on his cheek and the blood around it. My chin began to quiver as the image of Josh slamming his fist into Phoenix's head flashed through my mind.

"Hey," Phoenix whispered.

"No," I muttered. *"No."*

Hands trembling, I tore open a butterfly stitch and applied it to his cheek, a skill I'd picked up thanks to the dozen times I'd done it to myself growing up.

"Hey," he whispered again.

I clenched my jaw, keeping my focus on his wounds. One look and I'd break. I knew it.

His hands slowly, gently, pulled mine down and away from his face. He kissed a knuckle, then another, then another.

"Rose. Please look at me."

A tear slid down my cheek as I finally looked into his eyes.

"I love you."

My heart froze. Breath, words, escaped me.

"I love you, Rose."

He squeezed my hands, pulled me to him, and kissed me. Softly.

I love you, Rose.

Phoenix Steele loved me.

Tears spilled down my cheeks as I kissed him back. I grabbed at him, at anything, kissing desperately with a voracity that had my pulse skyrocketing.

I love you, I thought, *I love you, too.*

And I did. I was absolutely, totally, one-hundred percent, head-over-heels for the guy.

He dropped to the floor with me, two arms enveloping me in a warm blanket that pulled me away from the swirling chaos and into a safe zone that seemed to melt away every fear, question, irrational thought. The man could simply dissolve me. Strip me naked where there was nowhere else to hide.

Like no one had ever done before.

Wrapped in his arms, I pulled away from the kiss and... let go.

"I love you, Phoenix." I whispered. "I love you, too."

His lips crushed into mine and my muscles went weak, every muscle melting under the weight of the words that I knew had just changed the course of my life. And it was that moment that I surrendered to him, as his woman, *as his*. Because with Phoenix, there was no other way. I was his, or no one's.

And that was just fine with me.

He fisted my hair, tilted my face and devoured me with a possessiveness as if reading my mind. Marking me as his. *Demanding* that I was his.

And that was so damn hot.

I felt a swirl of energy inside me, an almost animalistic need for intimacy with the man who demanded everything from me. The untouchable, untamable bad boy who loved me. I grabbed his shirt, twisted the fabric in my hand in an attempt to rip it from his body. Letting him know I was ready. Ready for him. I was ready to be shown how lucky I was to be his.

I was ready to be *taken*.

He got the message.

My sweatshirt was pulled from my body, his hands blazing a trail over my bare skin, settling onto my breasts. A low groan escaped him as his fingers rolled over the nipples, sending each perching in that beautiful spark of pain. It was the first time, ever, that I wasn't insecure when a man felt my breasts for the first time. Barely a B-cup had a way of making even the most confident woman blush, but not with him. There was no mistaking his attraction to me, his *need* for me. An obsession. Love. Mine. I knew it in his touch, his kiss, his eyes when he looked at me.

I knew my life was changing in that very moment.

He guided me onto the thick rug in front of the crackling fire, a golden glow washing over us. My eyes flickered to the windows, the sprinkles of rain swirling like diamonds against the darkness outside. It was as if we were part of a beautiful, magical energy everywhere around us. His lips slid to my ear, the warm breath sending heat pooling between my legs. Then, his lips slid down my neck, my chest. I wrapped my arms around his taut back as he took my breast into his mouth. He yanked down my pajama bottoms, the heat from the fire washing over my bare skin. I kicked them off.

And... was suddenly completely naked.

A giddy smile tugged at my lips at the freedom of it. That was it. There was literally no more undressing this guy could do to me. To my body or my soul. That was me, buck-ass naked right there in the middle of the living room.

He lifted his head from my chest and I watched him scan me from head to toe. He met my gaze, a small, cocky smile tugging at his own lips.

"You're beautiful, Rose."

I smiled, my heart skipping a beat.

Then a blaze across those blues irises. "And you're mine."

"Take me, then," I whispered. "Show me."

His eyes twinkled before his face disappeared into my skin, lower, lower, lower. My pulse skyrocketed as he grabbed my knees and pushed them up, and forward.

Lips on my thighs, my hips, my inner hips.

I began to throb, the rush of blood pulsing between my legs and the guy hadn't even touched the most intimate part of me.

And then he did.

Warm, wet lips enclosed over me, his tongue sliding between my inner lips.

Breath escaped me as I gripped his head, running my fingers through his mussed hair. My muscles begin to loosen, my weight sinking into the floor as he devoured me like I was the most delicious thing on earth. But that was nothing compared to the electricity that jolted through my veins when his tongue slid over my clit. Warm, slick pressure circled the tiny bud, fingers sliding in and out of me, sending me into a whirling oblivion.

Tingles fired over the delicate skin as my insides squeezed, swelling, readying for the thunderstorm to come.

And then it did, in an uncontrollable force, I came. I tipped my head back and screamed his name as the orgasm ripped through me, wave after wave.

When I opened my eyes, he was kneeling at my feet, watching me come out of my daze with a passion, a hunger, that had my heart kick starting again.

"Are you ready for me to show you?" His voice was low, husky.

My brows lifted. "I thought you just did."

"That's nothing."

"Then... yes." Because it was the only appropriate response.

I was picked up from the floor as if I weighed ten pounds and carried to the bedroom. Not as a new bride so much, but as a caveman would carry his woman. I was tossed onto the bed in such a way that had me fighting to grab for him. I watched him take off his clothes, my naked body writhing over the covers, my hand drifting between my legs in a subconscious desperation for him. He watched me watch him strip.

My fingertips slid between my inner lips, still wet with my orgasm, as I skimmed his body, tanned and rippled to perfection. He wasn't one of those thin, shredded guys. No, Phoenix was a man. A *M-A-N*. Thick as a freaking tank, he had a wide, rock hard body that genetics had taken their time on. The man was a freaking monster, the sexiest beast I'd ever seen. All alpha, every inch.

Then, he slid off his boxers. His erection sprung up, long, thick, veiny perfection.

My jaw slid open.

"It's yours."

I was officially hypnotized.

"Come here," I breathed out.

He crawled on top of me, those massive arms pinning both sides of me.

His eyes locked on mine as he lowered onto me, his tip finding my opening.

"I love you, Rose. I love you." The words were spoken in a way as if he were relieved to say it out loud. As if he needed to say it again, and again.

"I love—"

I squeaked as he pushed inside me, stealing my words and knocking the breath from my lungs.

My head reared back, chin tilting up as a whine escaped my lips.

"That's it." He whispered into my ear. "Take it. It's yours."

My nails dug into his skin. I couldn't speak, couldn't form a sentence. He slid out, then back in, my body stretching around the man that was Phoenix Steele. I shifted my hips and held on for the ride, each thrust reaching deeper depths of me, his head rubbing my g-spot with every thrust, his springy hair tickling my clit.

He cupped my face and kissed me, harder, faster, deeper.

Just as I was on the brink of another orgasm, he pulled out.

I protested.

This was met with me being flipped onto my stomach.

Oh my God, was all I could think. I fisted the comforter as I was pulled by my waist to the edge of the bed, bent at the hips, my toes barely reaching the hardwood floor. His hands caressed my back, my ass, tracing my curves, until settling onto my hips.

"God, you're beautiful. Every inch of you."

His cock teased my opening, I bit my lip, then he pushed into me.

This time, I squealed.

He liked that.

In, out, he rode me, pinning me in place, reminding me I was his. I desperately grasped at the comforter, a feeble attempt to release the sensations coursing through me.

He slid one hand under my stomach, his finger rubbing my clit as he thrust in and out.

My entire body began to vibrate. It was no longer mine. I had no control of what this man was doing to me.

"Phoenix. Oh, *Phoenix.*"

His finger rubbed harder, faster against my clit.

"You're mine, Rose. Mine," the words came out in a pant. "Tell me."

"I'm yours," I whined, my vision beginning to waver. "I'm yours."

With those final words his warmth filled me up as I screamed his name one more time.

24

PHOENIX

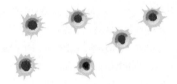

The next morning was spent like the evening before—except, twice. The first round of thunderstorms of the day had woken us up before five, and I can confidently say it was the first time I didn't mind doing physical activity before sunrise. Rose had that way about her. Just when I thought things couldn't get better, they did. It was like I'd walked into my own dream. Rose had opened the door for me and I stepped right in. She had that kind of effect on me. She had a way of sweeping me up and making me forget everyone and everything around me, and I hadn't realized how much I needed that.

Getting a glimpse behind the layers and layers that made up Rose Floris had felt like an honor. That she'd trusted me, that she'd bared her soul to me the same way I had done to her. We were open books with each other now, and there was something so freeing that came with that.

Rose loved me. She didn't need to tell me, but when she did, I'd felt some sort of validation. That I was worthy of her love. And I swear, when those words escaped her lips, something deep down inside me healed. A strength renewed. I had Rose. She loved me. And with her at my side, I could do anything.

We could do anything.

Together.

As she'd fallen asleep in my arms, I made a promise to myself to never, ever let her down again. After that, I'd held her as she slept as if I didn't want the night to end. Gripping onto her in a silent plea, as if I might wake up and realize it had all been a dream. I'd listened to the deep inhales and exhales of her breath, knowing I would never forget that moment. Not only because the sex was that good—holy *shit,* it was—but because it was the first time that I actually relaxed. It was the first time that I felt happy. And not just since I'd awoken from the coma... I'm talking in years.

Sometime after one in the morning, I forced myself out of her bed to do a quick perimeter check and check on Spirit. The horse would wander, but she always came back. After that, I scanned the house for anything out of place, searching the kitchen, living room, the deck. I'd called Jagg —the guy never slept, either—asking for an update on Andrew's homicide, to which there was nothing new. And still no stuffed animal or video recorder had turned up. He'd spent the day driving from store to store inquiring about blue-handled scissors, the presumed murder weapon in both Crazy Carl's and Andrew McGregor's case, and then trying to obtain warrants to pull the credit card data of who'd purchased a pair. As you can imagine, the list of Berry Springers who'd purchased a pair of scissors in the last year was endless. I'd updated him with only as many details of Rose's past to convince him that she wasn't a suspect. Yes, Rose had a past, Rose had secrets, but those secrets did not involve killing someone.

Sometime after that, Rose had risen with the sun—

fitting—and we'd had coffee together in the living room, facing the deck, listening to the thunderstorms roll in and watching the lightning streak in the sky in a comfortable silence. A stillness.

We fit.

We both knew it.

And hell on earth wasn't taking this away from me.

She glanced at the clock then reached over and grabbed my hand.

"I've got to get into the shower."

My brows popped up.

"No." She laughed. "I mean, I have to *actually* take a shower. Get ready for the day."

I looked at the clock—6:47 a.m.

I didn't want that morning to end. I didn't want to face reality. I wanted to stay in our little bubble, day after day, and have sex until we both couldn't walk.

She grinned, reading me like a book. "My first appointment isn't until nine, but I have something I have to do before then."

I lifted my hand.

She laughed. A beautiful, smooth laugh. Relaxed. "Not you. If we have sex again, I'm going to need a pair of crutches to make it through the day."

"I'll carry you."

"All day, huh? Carry me around from room to room, to work, to the grocery store."

"Call in sick to work and I'll run your errands."

"No. Theo's supposed to make a decision on a business proposal I presented to him. I'd like to hear that answer... at least before he fires me when he finds out that I hooked up with one of my clients."

"Hooked up?"

"Okay, fine, mind-blowing, best-in-my-life, soul-shattering *love making*."

"Can I get that tattooed across your back?"

She laughed, then looked out the window, a sudden worry crossing her face.

I laid my hand over hers. "Hey. We'll figure this thing out, okay? I won't be your patient forever. Hope not, anyway." I winked. She laughed. "One day at a time, okay?"

"One day at a time," she repeated and nodded, giving me that smile again. A moment passed as she stared at me, then seemed to decide something.

"Want to come with me?"

"To work?"

"No. To the thing I have to do before work."

"Yes." I said instantly, and it was that moment I realized I'd do anything, whatever, whenever, Rose asked of me. Anything to stay next to the woman. Crazy.

"Good." She pushed off the couch. "We'll leave in thirty minutes."

"Who takes thirty minutes to get ready?"

She stopped on a dime and spun on her heel. A more dramatic reaction than when I suggested a tattoo. "I do. Longer, even. And I always will. Understood?"

I laughed, threw up my hands in surrender. "Okay. Noted. Glad we got that established." I pushed out of the chair and pulled her to me, kissed that nose. "Where are we going?"

"Breakfast."

As if the morning couldn't get any better. Wait... yes it could. I followed her into the bathroom.

"Guess I need a shower too, then."

. . .

An hour later we pulled onto a long driveway that ran between two pastures. Even through the dark haze of the stormy morning, I recognized the ranch house where I'd followed her a few evenings before.

June Massey.

I looked over at the smile on her face.

"I hope you brought your appetite," she said. "Park under the oak tree."

I rolled to a stop and cut the engine. We'd taken her SUV, but I'd insisted on driving. She'd conceded without any fight. That trust, again.

Before I could take the keys out of the ignition, she was out the door and on the front porch, and into the arms of a woman wearing khaki pants, a blue sweater, and hiking boots. While Rose was smiling like a child, June had spotted me like a guard dog through the car. With narrowed eyes, the woman unabashedly assessed me as I stepped out of the car.

A few whispers were exchanged by the women, then both turned and faced me. I have no issues admitting that I never had a confidence problem around women, but something about seeing the woman who'd stripped me naked, both physically and mentally, the night before, next to another woman with slitted eyes, pinched lips, and an assessing gaze, had me stuffing my hands into my pockets.

"June, meet Phoenix Steele."

June's head tilted as she reached out her hand. "Phoenix."

"Pleasure to meet you, Ms. Massey." I sounded like a high school kid meeting his date's parents.

"We'll see about that," June responded cooly.

Make that *very protective* parents.

The women turned and walked into the house. My cue to follow, I guess.

My stomach growled as I crossed the threshold. The scent of hot bacon, pancakes, and fresh coffee filled a house that resembled the front page of *Southern Living* magazine. Brown leather couches, hardwood floors, candles, hand-crafted knick knacks, a fire crackling in the fireplace. Dozens of photographs filled the walls, most of horses.

I stopped to look at a few.

"June is an exceptional photographer," Rose said over my shoulder, the pride evident in her voice.

The home owner laughed at this as she walked into the kitchen. "Come on, now. Show and tell later."

I followed Rose into the kitchen where June was setting another placemat on the table. I watched Rose work alongside June in a seamless, comfortable rhythm. Yes, Rose had a family. Maybe not in the traditional sense, but the love was the same. It was written all over both women's faces.

June pulled down a plate and a glass from the cabinet.

I stepped forward. "Here. Let me—"

"No, sir." June shooed me away. "My kitchen. Sit."

"Yes, ma'am."

Rose grinned and met me at the table. "No one messes in her kitchen."

"Not if they want to get asked back again." June flickered me a glance laced with warning that had me clearing my throat.

"Seriously, sit." Rose grinned as she sat.

I settled in across from Rose. "You do this every day?"

"Only on Friday mornings."

"I like to send her into the weekend with a full stomach and cleared head. My girl needs to work less and relax more."

Rose rolled her eyes.

Moments later, a feast was laid in front of me, plates filled with sausage, bacon, blueberry pancakes, and fresh fruit. A cup of warm maple syrup was set next to a carafe of piping hot coffee. Talk about walking into a dream.

I reached for the carafe. June slapped my hand away, picked it up and filled my cup. "I come from a time when women still serve men," she slid me a look, "as long as they're worthy enough. And I always serve in my own kitchen."

"Yes, ma'am."

And serve me she did. I couldn't see the edge of my plate by the time June took her seat at the head of the table, with a cup of coffee and plate of fruit.

She eyed me as I took my first bite, reminding me of Rose when she'd served me lasagna the evening before. Yes, family. And much like Rose, June was one hell of a cook. Warm, fluffy pancakes with a hint of vanilla against cinnamon blueberry. Best flapjacks I'd ever had.

Mouth full, I looked up and realized Rose was watching me, too.

"It's good," I forced out between the mouthful.

Both women smiled, then, satisfied with my reaction, turned their focus onto their own plates.

"So, Phoenix, how did you and Rose meet?"

The sausage went down my throat like a bowling ball. I wiped my mouth, sipped coffee, and squared my shoulders.

"I'm one of her patients."

"Are you now?"

"Yes, ma'am." I steeled myself for the question of why I was seeking therapy. Instead, I got—

"Gettin' anything out of it?"

I looked at Rose, eyeing me over the rim of her coffee.

"Well, if feeling like I'm standing stark raving naked in the middle of Times Square after leaving her office means I'm getting something out of it, then yes."

June grinned. "Growth and comfort do not coexist. Remember that."

"If that's the truth, I should be healed."

June's head angled to the side. "Rose makes you uncomfortable?"

"Yes. In a good way, though, I'm coming to understand."

"Says a lot for a former Marine."

"War I could handle."

"Being stripped of your armor, you can't."

"Rose is the first to do it."

"She'll be the last."

I met Rose's gaze across the table, where she'd set down her fork. A smile crossed my lips. Yeah. June was right. Rose would be the last.

A moment slid by as Rose and I smiled at each other.

June clapped her hands, grinning now, too. "Alright then, now that we got that out of the way, tell me Rose, anything new on EAT?"

"What's EAT?" I asked.

With that, the conversation slipped seamlessly from the third degree to the business proposal Rose had mentioned earlier that morning, between herself, June, and Kline and Associates. I listened to Rose talk about Equine Assisted Therapy and the healing power of horses, watching the passion as she spoke, her eyes lighting up at how many people the therapy could help. They'd asked my opinion on the proposal, and as I spoke about my business, Steele Shadows Security, I realized how much I missed it. It reminded me not only of the passion I had for my business, but also that I was damn good at it. It felt good, sitting there at the breakfast table, discussing business over a plate of flapjacks. *I* felt good, being able to help and provide insight.

And I realized then, Rose was bringing me back to life.

Rose, single handedly, was healing me.

After breakfast, Rose wanted to show me the stable where she intended to conduct the therapy, to which I agreed because I didn't want to leave the place. It felt like home, in a weird, different way. Like a family.

Like my future wife.

We took off down a rutted road that cut across the fields. The rain was coming down in sheets now.

"So what did you think?"

"Of breakfast, or of June?"

"Both."

"Both could hold their own at any table."

Rose smiled.

"She reminds me of you," I said. "The mannerisms, quick wit, the way she says so much with only a few words."

Rose laughed. "Oh you have no idea. Her mind games are epic. Something always means something deeper. She's hell on wheels."

"Well, the apple doesn't fall too far from the tree there." I winked. "She's also fiercely independent. Like you."

A line of concern ran between Rose's brows. "She's been alone for two decades. I worry about her."

"Where's mister Massey?"

"Died of a heart attack two months before she found me in the woods. We saved each other, she always tells me."

"Does she know about your stalker? Everything that's going on?"

Rose shook her head. "Not really. The night we found Andrew, I went to her house, seeking her comfort, I guess. She knows about me finding his body, but that's it." She paused. "Since taking this new job at Kline, she's pushed that she'd like to see me 'lay roots' here. I think she enjoys me being close by. She wouldn't tell me that, though, because she wouldn't want me to feel obligated. But I know it, and that's why I included her in my business proposal." She looked at me. "Kline and Associates is a stepping stone to opening my own clinic one day."

"With an equine therapy center."

"Exactly. Working side by side with June every day, hopefully repaying her for everything she's done for me. I'd offered to move in with her when I moved back to town, but she wouldn't have it. Wants me to live my own life. Thinks she'd hamper that, I guess."

"Serving breakfasts like that? You'd be the most popular bachelorette in town. Would've been, I should say."

She looked over, smiled. "Would've been, huh?"

"That breakfast sealed the deal. You can thank the blueberry pancakes."

"Note to self that I need to make you my own version of them."

"Do they come with red high heels and matching thong?"

"No thong."

"Dear Lord."

She laughed. "Okay, here we are. Future home of Kline and Associates Equine Therapy Center."

I looked at the red stable through the rain, which had obviously been repainted, but it still needed a lot of work. I'd had to restrain myself from offering to back the project financially, mainly because I liked my balls. Because there was no doubt both women would have kicked them under the table at the insult of being offered a free hand.

After the tour, we loaded up and headed back to the

house where June met us on the front porch with two to-go cups of coffee.

"Make sure my Rose doesn't work too hard, okay?"

"Yes, ma'am." I took the coffee as Rose ran into the house for her purse. "Thank you for breakfast."

"Pleasure's mine." June narrowed her eyes. "Keep her safe, you understand?"

"You don't need to worry about that."

"I have a feeling I don't, but Rose, she's just... special. I'm her only family, and well, she's mine. Never had kids of my own after I adopted her... funny thing is, I found out years later I couldn't have had children even if I tried. Funny thing, life is, isn't it?"

Sure was.

Her strong face softened. "When I found Rose in the woods, I *saw* her. Do you know what I mean? A strong, beautiful, tortured soul." June paused, and I realized I was hanging onto her every word. "I see the same thing in you, Phoenix Steele. You need to accept that things change. We all change. Sure, we fight it, but sometimes we're fighting changes that are good. And we're fighting them simply because they're new. Uncharted territory. You need to allow this new light inside of you to shine. The world's not all bad, you know. It's okay to be happy even when the world tells you that you're not supposed to be. When Rose became mine, she showed me who I really was. She's my daughter. I don't want anything to happen to her."

"She's my everything." I turned fully toward her. "And I take care of what's mine, Ms. Massey."

The corner of June's lip curled. "That's good. That's very good."

Rose stepped outside and stopped cold, looking back and forth between June and I.

"Everything okay?"

June winked. "Of course, dear. Go on, get to work so you can get home early and relax in time for the weekend."

They kissed cheeks and as Rose crossed the porch, June reached into the house and plucked two ponchos from the coat rack.

"Here. Take these rain coats. Bad storms comin' this afternoon."

25

ROSE

*A*fter breakfast, we'd gone back to my house where Phoenix treated me to his own version of home-made dessert. An hour later, I'd left him there to work on my security system while I went into the office to close out the week. And by security system, I mean renovation. Well, pretty much, anyway. The guy had a slew of people, including his brothers, scheduled to bring something, or install something, over the course of the day. Phoenix promised that by the end of the weekend, my home would be Fort Knox. And I had no doubt it would be because one thing I knew about Phoenix was that if he was passionate about something, he did it with gusto.

Hello, barely being able to walk.

The man was incredible.

I was on cloud nine when I pulled into the office, despite the dark, ominous clouds hanging low in the sky. A light mist hung in the air like a blanket, and true to June's warn-ing, the local radio station had spent the morning news warning of the storms to come. It was adding up to be one of the strongest storm systems of the season, capped off by tornado watches. I'd already promised myself I'd cut out early for the day. Not only to spend more time with Phoenix, but to make sure he wasn't getting carried away with my cabin and installing bullet proof windows and steel doors or something. Instead of my usual six-inch heels and tailored suit, I'd opted for rain boots topped with a long puffer jacket that hung to my knees, and I must say, it felt good.

Almost as good as the soreness settling in between my legs.

Phoenix.

Heat rose to my cheeks as I unlocked the office. I flicked the lights. Not a soul around.

Humph.

The door shut behind me and my nose wrinkled at the pungent smell of stale, old coffee. I searched the room, my gaze landing on a large paper cup rimmed with red lipstick.

That Zoey.

Shaking my head, our conversation from the day before ran through my thoughts

"Who's week is it to take out the trash?"

"Mine. Sorry, kind of got distracted this morning hearing about another murder. I'll take it out tonight..."

Another ball dropped. If Zoey kept this up, Theo might be out two employees. Unless I could keep my relationship with Phoenix under wraps, but somehow I knew that wasn't possible. Phoenix wouldn't have it, which was fine with me because I was already wanting to scream it from the rooftops.

Three orgasms in less than five hours will do that to a woman.

I crossed the lobby—yep, a spoiled, half-drunk coffee with whipped nastiness on top. Not wanting to leave it to fester in a trash can all weekend, I grabbed the cup and pushed out the back door onto the small patio where Theo kept a few chairs and table. I opened the trash can, tossed the cup, and froze.

My brows squeezed together as I raised on my tiptoes and leaned inside, peering at the bright blue handle of what appeared to be scissors.

Blue.

Scissors.

Andrew, Carl.

No. *Way.*

I grabbed a stick from the ground and carefully lifted the wadded papers and candy bar wrappers from the object. Nerves tickled my stomach as the object came into view—a small, sharp pair of scissors with a blue handle... and red stains on the tip.

I gasped and slammed the lid closed, my heart racing as fast as my thoughts.

And as I reached for my cell phone, a towel wrapped around my nose and mouth.

26

PHOENIX

a crack of thunder had me glancing at the clock on Rose's wall—12:15p.m.—then at my phone for the hundredth time since she'd left for work, leaving me to her security renovation.

A flash of lightning lit the walls.

The storms were almost here. I looked out the window at the thick, black clouds moving swiftly overhead. I stepped onto the deck. The air was still, heavy with electricity, and eerily silent. No chirping birds, no squirrels skittering from branch to branch. Nothing. The woods were shadowed, as dark as twilight.

A ball formed in my gut and I wasn't sure why.

"You alright?" Gage asked from the living room floor inside, encircled around a snarl of wires and security cameras.

"Yeah." I stepped back inside and closed the door.

"You're like a lovestruck high school kid. Give the gal a break."

I forced a smile.

Eyeing me, he cocked his head. "Something's wrong. What's wrong with you?"

"Nothing. Well... I haven't heard from Rose in a few hours."

"Were you supposed to?"

"No." I shook my head. "Never mind."

Another boom of thunder, this time followed by rain drops pinging against the windows.

I wanted Rose right then.

Home. In my arms.

I told myself to get a grip and shifted focus to the bookcase where Gage and I had decided to install a motion-activated camera that would alert Rose of an intruder if she wasn't home. Okay, fine, it would alert me, too. Another positive was that Rose could also access it remotely to check inside before coming home. The camera wouldn't avert someone from breaking in but it would give her peace of mind, and that was priceless. Besides, Gage and I had already installed a truckload of things to avert—and capture—peeping toms. Well... everything aside from the bear trap I wanted to hook up outside the perimeter. Gage said no to that. Something about laws...

I walked over to the bookcase and began removing the alphabetized self-help section—an irony that wasn't lost on me. I picked up a book entitled "Own Your Emotions, Own Your Life," and stopped cold. The thick book was significantly lighter than the others. I turned it over in my hands and spotted a small, black circle in the spine.

"Holy shit."

Gage pushed off the floor and met me by the bookcase. I ripped off the clear tape that had been wrapped around the book and flipped it open. The center pages had been cut out and replaced with a mini video recorder.

"Another one?"

My gaze skittered around the shelf.

"The internet's still off." Gage reminded me. "No way it's streaming."

I zeroed in on the red, blinking light. "It's on, though. Whoever implanted it didn't realize the internet wasn't on." My blood turned cold. "And it's new."

"Since when?"

"Since today. This morning. Since Rose and I left for breakfast." I grabbed my cell phone from the counter.

"How do you know?" Gage asked.

"I did a detailed check last night after Rose fell asleep. I went through every book in this case. Someone broke in after we'd left this morning. Someone was watching us." I dialed Rose's number. "Someone was just here. Get your keys."

We jogged out the door as I listened to ring after ring, and no answer from Rose.

Lightning split the sky as the clouds opened up and it started pouring. I ushered Spirit into the trailer that was still attached to Gage's truck.

Gage fired up the engine. "Where to?"

"Kline and Associates. Go."

I kept dialing her, call after call going unanswered, each voicemail sending my pulse pounding faster. I'd promised Rose I wouldn't let anything happen to her. I promised myself I wouldn't fail her again.

"*Christ,* can this thing go any faster?"

"Not in this fucking monsoon. We'll get her."

"Just get there. Fast."

Raindrops the size of walnuts pounded the windshield, the wipers struggling to keep up.

Wind swirled around us, beating against the sides of the truck.

Yeah, the storms were here.

Gage flicked on his headlights. The day had turned to midnight in an instant it seemed, a green-tinted darkness coloring the woods around us.

"Turn on the radio," Gage demanded, his eyes laser focused on the road that we could barely see.

I clicked over to the local news station.

"... *has spotted a possible tornado west of Shadow Mountain, ahead of a string of storms that have already produced verified tornados, damaging winds above sixty miles per hour, baseball-sized hail, and flash flooding. This is not a drill, folks, seek shelter immediately. Go to your safe spot, and keep NWA radio on...*"

"Dammit..." Gage muttered from the driver's seat. The guy could single handedly eliminate a group of tangos with AK47's, but there was something about tornados that made him jumpy. As if on cue, the truck slid around a flooded corner. Gage and I both looked back at the trailer. Still there.

The radio flickered as a bolt of lightning resembling a witch's staff touched the ground somewhere close by.

I clicked on my cell and dialed Jagg's number.

"You better be calling me from your storm shelter cause—"

"I need you to get to Kline and Associates now."

"Dude, have you been outside? It's like the apocalypse. I'm helping the local PD with the roads. There're freaking cars everywhere. They're slammed."

"Jagg." I seethed between a clenched jaw. I was out of patience. "I need you at Kline's."

"... Okay, man, *okay.* On my way."

I clicked off.

"Dude..." Gage's face paled. "Shit..."

I followed my brother's gaping gaze to a massive wall cloud beginning to swirl in the distance.

"Better hit the gas, bro," I yelled over the pounding rain.

Three minutes, and twenty white knuckles later, we pulled up to Kline and Associates and skidded to a stop next to Rose's BMW.

"Check around the building. I'm going inside."

Rain pummeled our shoulders as we jumped out. I did a quick three-sixty check around Rose's vehicle before jogging down the sidewalk to the office as Gage disappeared around the side of the building. The door was unlocked. And that ball in my gut? The thing turned into a damn bowling ball as I stepped inside. Rose's purse sat on the front counter next to her keys.

No Rose.

Despite the storm raging outside, the air inside was quiet, still, an unnerving stillness. I'd felt it before, many times, during my door kicking days. An evil that left a presence.

"Rose?" I hollered as I jogged to her office.

Nothing.

I searched the conference room, the break room, then jogged to the corner office with sweeping windows that overlooked the valley. Unlike the other offices, the curtains in this one were drawn, a dark brown satin next to a row of plaques highlighting the name: *Theo Kline, PSY.D.*

My gaze shifted to the built-in bookshelf that took half the wall, where dozens of books had been removed and stacked on the floor. I stepped over and ran my finger along the edges, something telling me to look further. I began pulling books and tossing them on the floor behind me when a narrow beam of light caught my eye—a twinkling light from behind a stack of encyclopedias. I tossed the books to the ground, squinted into the light, and stared at the tiny peep hole that led directly into Rose's office.

White-hot rage zipped through me.

Theo Kline.

I spun around, my frantic gaze dropping to scattered folders that had fallen out of the books I'd tossed from the shelves. Hidden folders. Scattered around them were dozens of black and white photos of Rose in her home, a few of her stark-raving naked. I shook with fury as I picked up the folder entitled "Experimental Psychology, Theo. L. Kline."

Inside were dozens of pictures of electrocuted and mutilated chickens, each containing detailed notes of the torture that was done, recording bodily stats such as heart rate and temperature, the length of time it took the animal to die, as well as detailing each stage of death. I picked up a handful of pictures of Rose, in her office, getting coffee, at the gas station. Each picture had been dated and time stamped, with notes of events pertaining to the day, such as the time she arrived, the time she took her lunch, what she ate, her demeanor, what she was wearing.

Then, my eyes shifted to another folder labeled "Suitors." Inside, were not only pictures of Josh Davis, but of me as well, including an aerial view of the Steele Shadows Security compound and possible breaching points. Next up, pictures of Carl Higgins in different stages of death, as well as closeups of his melted skin seconds after the electric wires had been ripped away. My stomach rolled. Next were pictures of Andrew's body, taken from a cell phone, presumably.

But the most unnerving thing I found was the transcript of Rose's interview with the department of human services when she was just eight years old, detailing the moment she found her foster mother dead, and how she ran for her life after. Theo's shaky, handwritten notes included *'subject's emotional resolve now slipping. Events beginning to take mental and emotional toll.'*

"Subject's."

Rose was a freaking science experiment. Theo Kline's own, personal science experiment.

The man was out-of-his-mind crazy.

Insane.

Then, I noticed divorce papers at the top of the stack, dated exactly six months earlier—to the day.

"There's usually an emotional trigger that makes someone with a mental illness snap..." Rose's words echoed in my head.

"Holy shit, dude." Gage said over my shoulder.

Just then—

"Rose, where are you? We need to take shelter."

I jerked my head up, spun on my heel and jogged out of the office.

Zoey squealed and dropped the coffee in her hand, sending a funnel of steaming liquid into the air like a fountain. Cameron froze behind her, carrying a bag of takeout.

"What... you're... Phoe—"

"Have you seen her? Rose?" My pulse roared in my ears.

"No, I... no. I'm sorry. What—" A flash of lightning lit the panicked expression on her face.

"Have you talked to her today?"

Gage jogged out the door to fire up the truck.

"No. Cameron and I were both running late today. The storm...we need to... is everything okay?"

"I need you to get me Theo Kline's home address now."

Zoey dropped her purse and ran to the computer. "Is

Rose okay? Is everything okay?" Her fingers flew over the keyboard. "Theo lives at thirteen-sixteen Sycamore."

I pulled my keys. "Is there a basement here?"

"Yes."

"Get there now, take shelter, and lock the door. Don't open it for anyone other than myself or the police."

27

ROSE

a wave of nausea washed over me as I opened my eyes to blurred, swirling colors. Vomit shot up my throat. I attempted to roll onto my side, but was pinned in place. Ice-cold panic zipped through my veins. I was tied down. My ankles and wrists, tied down. I began choking, panic mixing with the vomit filling my mouth, my stomach convulsing until two hands wrapped around my head and turned it to the side. I threw up, spit, gagged, until everything was out of me.

"Better?"

My heart froze. I knew that voice. I blinked the tears away then craned my neck to see Theo Kline, my boss, standing over me in a white lab coat. He stared down at me, holding a clipboard in his gloved hands.

Theo. Kline.

My stalker. I knew it instantly.

"It's from the chloroform," he said. "You should feel better after throwing up."

My eyes widened as the scene around me began to unfold. The first thing I noticed was the smell, chemicals mixed with an earthy, musty scent. And something... burned. Burned toast, maybe? Hair? My stomach swirled again. A trio of lightbulbs dangled from cords attached to a dark, cement ceiling. I was in a basement, somewhere underground. The walls were lined with rotted wooden shelves, each covered with mason jars of various sizes, holding pieces of what I prayed weren't human or animal body parts—although my gut told me they were. At the end of the shelves sat the stuffed animal, Creepy-Ted, and the video recorder that had been hidden in my home.

The sound of a rusty crank broke the silence as my torso was lifted to a seated position. That's when I noticed the wires coming from my arms. It took me a second to realize they weren't IVs and that they were attached to my skin with something sticky. The wires were connected to a large, black piece of blinking equipment in the corner. Black wires ran from it like octopus tentacles, spreading across the stained concrete floor.

And then I saw it. My worst nightmare coming true.

More wires led to my guardian angel, June Massey, who was also tied to a table. Her eyes were closed, squeezed in pain. Her face was pale, lips blue. And under each wire, ran a river of blood and pus from blackened, burned skin.

Tacked to the wall above her head were the crime scene photos of my foster mother, Cheryl, dead, with a needle hanging out of her arm, bile running out of her blue lips, her eyes staring lifelessly into the camera. I stared at the memory I'd spent years trying to erase. The guilt from blaming myself for her death that I knew would never go away. Then, I stared at June, the woman who'd found me in the woods and saved me.

I threw up, again.

A wet washcloth ran over my lips.

"Better now?"

"Let her go." My voice cracked. "Let her go, Theo."

His dilated pupils twinkled. "Ah. That's exactly the point of this science experiment. Everything has led to this final moment."

"What are you talking about?"

"You, Rose, were the perfect specimen for my experiment."

"What?"

"You experienced horrific traumas at a young, impressionable age, and while science tells us these kinds of events would lead to significant neurological impact, you have been able to control the effects. Your will to survive, to overcome, is nothing short of extraordinary. So, I wondered, what would it take to break that resolve? Are you really extraordinary, Rose? Or is it all a cover? Can a human really ever overcome their past? That's what we're here today to find out."

Fear trickled up my spine. The man was mad. Completely insane.

Theo stepped over to the black box. A pitched *beep* echoed against the cement walls as he flipped it on.

"You allowed your foster mother to die when you were eight years old. It was your fault, Rose. You could have saved her. Now," he nodded to June, "you have a chance to save the woman who saved your life. Will you redeem yourself today? Redeem yourself for killing your foster mom by saving June?"

"At what cost?"

"Your own life."

He picked up a wired, brown helmet, reminding me of Medusa. The wires connected back to the box. A cold sweat beaded on my forehead as he carried it to me. And that was it. I lost it. Like an animal, I unhinged, started screaming, crying, pleading. My voice wasn't mine, I was no longer me. I was a woman about to die.

As he tried to secure the helmet to my head, I bucked, fought the binds like a rabid beast.

He punched me in the face.

I stilled, dazed, bile rising to my throat for the third time.

That was the moment. My body fell weak, my heartbeat slowed.

I gave up.

The helmet was strapped to my head. "It's you or her, Rose," he whispered, a low hissing like a snake. "You die, or June dies. It's your decision."

I watched him walk back to the machine, my limbs frozen, my thoughts evaporated. Fear gone, my hope gone. I wondered if this is what the final moments of someone's life were like. An eerie calm. An acceptance that death was coming.

"Tell me, Rose," he said. "Will your survival instinct overcome, or will the guilt you've carried for twenty years kill you? It's your decision. You or June. Save her, or kill her."

The world around me stopped. Everything faded as his finger slid over the dial and he said—

"It's time to decide."

28

PHOENIX

"*F*orget Kline and Associates, I'm going to need backup at thirteen-sixteen Sycamore," I yelled over the roar of hail that was hammering Gage's truck.

There was a rustling on the other end of the phone, followed by shouts and sirens in the background of what I assumed was the latest accident Jagg was trying to get around.

"Where are you now?" He asked.

I glanced at the GPS. "Heading east on highway twelve."

"What's the address again?" The growl of Jagg's truck roared to life in the background.

I rattled off Theo Kline's address again.

"I'll be there as fast as I can."

I clicked off and hurled the phone at the windshield.

"Goddammit, Gage, hurry."

My brother didn't respond, simply pressed the gas, speeding through a storm that had driven everyone else to the side of the road. We couldn't see much past the hail bouncing off the hood. A massive, black cloud colored the rearview mirror.

There was a loud *pop* as a fist-sized ball of hail bounced off the window, followed by a crack splitting across the windshield. A few more hits like that and it was a good chance the thing would shatter. I'd never seen hail so big in my life—and that was saying something being born and raised in Tornado Alley.

"Here. Stop!" I gripped my seat. "Turn here. Snakepit road. It'll cut through the mountain."

Gage slammed the brakes and took the turn because he knew, as much as I did, that every second counted.

"Destination one hundred yards ahead," the GPS warned us.

Leaves and twigs swirled around the truck.

"The winds are picking up, man, I can feel it moving the truck."

But he didn't pull over.

We couldn't. Rose's life depended on it.

Squinting, I leaned forward, trying to make out anything through the whirling storm around us. Suddenly, a deafening *crack* overhead, followed by a *whoosh*.

"Gage!" I screamed.

A massive oak tree split in half in front of us, collapsing over the dirt road seconds before we barreled into it. Two seconds earlier and we would have been dead.

Leaves rained down around us, the branches entangling around the crumpled hood of Gage's truck.

"Dammit. Door's wedged shut!" Gage shouted over the howling wind.

I looked at my brother and the branch that had pinned his door less than a foot from his head. Mine was pinned, too. We were *inside* the tree.

I looked back at the trailer, still upright, then at Spirit bucking, kicking just past the door that had busted open.

"I've got to get out of here, Gage."

He pulled a hammer from his tool bag in the back and handed it to me. "Bottom's up, bro."

I grabbed a jacket that had slid to the floorboard and tossed it to him. "Cover your face."

He covered his dick.

"Not fucking funny. Cover your goddamn face."

I waited until he turned away, then took the hammer to the passenger window. Glass shattered around the cab.

"I'm right behind you..." Gage's voice faded as I climbed out of the broken window and maneuvered my way through the tree like a damn spider monkey.

"Spirit!" I whistled.

A flash of white over the tree. I gripped the saddle and pulled myself on and like the lightning through the sky, we took off through the woods. Hail battered my face, my arms, one popping open the skin below my eye. I wiped the blood and hunkered down against the rain, flapping Spirit's reins.

"Go, go girl, *go!"*

Rain swirled around us, winds beating into my side threatening to throw me off the horse. For all I knew, at that moment, I was in the middle of a tornado. The woods were as black as midnight.

We soared over a fence and took off across a field— sitting ducks for the lightning.

We didn't care.

My breath came out in short puffs against the sudden drop in temperature, my heart a cool pounding reminding me of the moments before executing a raid. Except with this one, I didn't have intel, I didn't have my team at my back, only my sixth sense, SIG, and the sheer resolve to save my Rose Flower's life.

The outline of a large structure came into view. I pulled

the reins and we skirted to the right, parallel with the side of the large house. My eyes darted from point to point, my brain putting together an internal layout based on the outside.

It was an old, decrepit colonial style mansion with four white columns running in front of a porch that led up to double doors. Several shades of stain colored the white paint peeling on the sides. Cracked shingles speckled a waved roof that led to a crooked chimney. Tangled, dead bushes encircled the structure. It looked like something from The Shining. Fitting too, for this mad doctor.

The windows were dark, with only a dim orange glow coming from somewhere deep inside the first floor.

I pulled Spirit to a stop and slid off.

"Stay here."

Double-gripping my gun, I sprinted across the yard and slammed my back against the house.

I paused to listen, pulling my focus from the rain to the home.

And that's when I heard it.

A scream so shrill, so horrifying, the hair on the back of my neck stood up.

Rose.

Allowing my instincts to guide me, I sprinted down the side and rounded to the back. Another scream, this one was muffled. My gaze locked on a row of stone steps that faded under the house.

The basement.

One more scream, although this one faded into a gargled plea.

This scream was from pain.

Adrenaline shot through my body, a kind of panic so

strong that it overcame years of training and calculated judgment. I was tunnel-visioned with one thing in mind—to save the woman I loved.

I sprinted down the stone stairs that led to a locked wooden door. After backing up a few steps, I blew the knob, sending shrapnel and shards of wood through the air as I leapt inside.

Decades of executing hostage raids could not have prepared me for what I saw. The first thing that registered was the smell. The scent of burning flesh. Under the dim glow of a single bulb, Rose was bound to a table that reminded me of where death-row inmates took their last breath. Her eyes were shut, her skin a waxy pale. A wired, leather helmet was strapped to her head. Syringes, vials, and a few blue-handled scissors sat on a silver rolling table at her feet. Next to her, June Massey, bound and wired as well.

And on the other side stood Theo, draped in a stained lab coat, with a nine-millimeter pointed to my head.

"Drop the gun," he said in an eerily calm voice.

"Step away from Rose."

"Drop the gun or I'll crank up the voltage and you'll watch her convulse to her death."

He released one hand on the gun and trailed it along the edges of a black power box. His hand was steady. The man was cool, calm, collected, and bat-shit crazy. An entirely new adversary for me, and one that perhaps was more disconcerting than the most evil doers. There was no predicting what this guy might do next—unlike someone with a suicide belt and a trigger in their hand—because if I had to guess, he didn't know either.

I lowered the gun.

"Kick it to me and raise your arms above your head."

The gun slid across the basement floor. My eyes flickered to Rose, still motionless. Lifeless. Whatever the guy had done to her had incapacitated her. She needed immediate medical attention.

"She's a strong one." Theo said, with a mad twinkle in his eye.

"I'm stronger. Let her go and take me."

His brow cocked. "Well this is an interesting twist."

"Let both women go and take me."

"I don't know Mr. Steele, I think Rose is the strongest of you two. The flush of your cheeks and shortness of breath tell me you're verging on a panic attack. Your adrenaline is being compounded by an inner anger so fierce, it's clouding your judgment and preventing you from making solid decisions. You can't control your emotions, even before getting shot in the head. Your anger—your pride—is your biggest weakness, Phoenix. It's stronger than you'll ever be. So, while you stand here, all two hundred and thirty pounds of muscle, you are quite possibly the weakest person in the room."

The words cut me like a knife, exactly as he'd intended.

Head games.

A wicked smile crossed his face. "Let me prove it to you."

My heart slammed against my ribcage as I watched his fingers turn the dial.

Rose's arm jumped on the table.

"*No!*" I lunged forward.

"*Stop* or I'll do it again!" Theo screamed.

I froze and stared down the barrel of the gun inches from my face.

"See?" Theo cackled a laugh. "See, Phoenix? You're so overcome with panic, you just made a decision that would not only end your life, but hers as well. I'd electrocute her to death and shoot you between the eyes. You'd both be dead. You lose, like always." He took a step back. "The question is, what am I going to do with you now?"

I narrowed my eyes, focusing on the mad man in front of me. If he wanted to play mind games, I was in. Everyone had a weakness, a trigger, and I knew his. There was one thing greater than his obsession with Rose. One obsession that eclipsed all else.

"You're not the only one who's done their research, Theo."

His eyebrows arched in enjoyment. "Please, go on."

"Your lovely ex-wife. Seems no one has seen her for a while."

The slightest flicker of surprise crossed his eyes.

"Interesting, isn't it?" I said. "So I called in a favor. I've got the local PD doing a welfare check on her right now. They're combing her house as we speak."

His eyes slowly rounded.

"They're going to find her body, aren't they, Theo?"

He blinked, digesting this unexpected twist in his little science experiment.

"You killed her, didn't you?" I edged closer. "She divorced your crazy ass and you went nuts. Killed her."

"You won't find her body."

"I might not, but the cops will. And they'll come after you. Whether both Rose and I die here today or not, they're going to come after you. It's all over now, Theo. No matter what happens right now, the wheels are turning. You're busted."

His body began to tremble.

"Give me the gun, Theo."

His hands shook viciously, his pupils dilating against eyes wild with madness.

"No." Tears streaked his face as he shook his head. "No. They won't get me."

And as he turned the gun on himself, I threw myself over Rose's body to shield her from the spray.

29

ROSE

Eight months later...

y heart skipped a beat as I turned off the ignition. Adrenaline, excitement, butterflies swirling in my stomach. I looked at the red folder sitting on the passenger seat of my BMW.

It was done.

Signed.

Done.

A smile curved my lips as I gazed up at the sign above the front door.

Rose Flower Center for Counseling

A pride I'd never felt before swelled inside me as I grabbed the loan documents I'd just signed and pushed out the car door. I'd been a bit trigger-happy by putting up the company sign before closing the loan, but that had been intentional. Put your goal in front of you, every day, to remind you of it. Face it head on.

And I did.

I, Rose Floris, officially owned my own therapy clinic now. My own *business*. And the best part? The best freaking part? *I* owned it. No one else but me. No one else was on the loan. I'd done it all by myself.

And it felt *so* good.

A cool gust of wind swept past me carrying the spicy scent of fall. I inhaled, glanced up at a sapphire blue sky speckled with white, fluffy clouds. A beautiful day, indeed. I pulled the key from my purse, smiling down at it as if it were the golden key to Narnia or something. I slid it into the lock, only to realize the door was already unlocked.

Frowning, I pushed through the front door.

Pop!

The cork of the champagne bottle bounced off the ceiling, pelting me in the forehead.

"Congratulations!" Zoey raised the bottle while Cameron tossed confetti into the air.

Above the front desk was a sign that read, *You Did It*.

Yes, I did it.

I freaking did it.

"Is it done?" Zoey asked, her excitement palpable. "It's done, right?"

I held up the folder. "Signed, sealed, delivered. It's done."

She squealed again, then grabbed three Styrofoam cups and began pouring the champagne.

I smiled, looking around the small rock building I'd purchased outside of the city park. The location alone made the building double what it was worth because it provided endless free marketing on Main Street, and to the families who frequented the park. More than that, though, there was just something about the place. Something calming. A pebble walkway led the way from a rock parking lot shaded by towering trees. The building was warm, welcoming, with dark cherry-oak throughout, rounded entryways, and a beautiful stone fireplace in the new "lobby." It had a magical, fairy, Lord of the Rings vibe when you walked in. In addition to the lobby, there were two bedrooms that I was going to turn into office-slash-therapy rooms, a meditation room, full bathroom, and a kitchen. And in the back was a small room where I was going to start up my *Roseology* podcast again. It was perfect.

And it was mine.

Zoey handed me a bubbling cup with a smirk stretching from ear to ear.

I narrowed my eyes. "What?"

She jerked her chin toward the door that I'd already designated as my office. I looked at Cameron, who was also smiling.

"What's going on?"

"Go see for yourself."

Head cocked, I crossed the lobby and pushed through my office door.

A smile spread over my face.

Hammer in one hand, security cam in the other, Phoenix stood tall on a ladder with a pair of nails between his teeth. He glanced over his shoulder and grinned around the nails.

I grinned back. "What do you think you're doing, Mister? I didn't approve—"

The whirl of the drill cut me off.

He pulled the nails from his teeth and slid them into his pocket. "I'm installing a security system."

"A camera in my *office?*"

He climbed down the ladder. "That's right."

"Hang on a second, Hot Rod. Where does the feed go?"

He ignored me, assessing his work.

"*Excuse* me?"

"The feed goes to a very prestigious local security company."

I set my purse on a folding chair and crossed the room. "Would that company happen to be Steele Shadows Security?"

He looked over his shoulder and winked. "Only the best for Rose Flower."

"So you're going to spy on me all day?"

"Spy?" He turned, winked. "Depends on what you're wearing." He grabbed my waist and pulled me to him.

"Pervert."

"Damn straight." His lip curved as he searched my face, his gaze landing on my lips. His hands slid up the back of my shirt.

"Not here. Not now." I giggled like a schoolgirl. "Zoey and Cam are in the other room."

"Oh, come on. Let's see how quiet we can be."

"*Phoenix.*"

His hands dropped to my butt, squeezed.

I felt a blush sneak up my cheeks as warmth spread between my legs. It was an unavoidable side-effect to being in close proximity to Phoenix Steele, I learned. I pressed my body against his, grabbed his ass, and whispered, "Later."

"I'm going to hold you to that, Love," he whispered, then took a step back.

Love. It was his pet name for me since saving my life.

Since not leaving my side for a single night. Since officially asking me to be his girlfriend.

Since moving in with me a month earlier.

To no one's surprise, Phoenix had offered to buy my new clinic building for me, including a significant "loan" to get the business off the ground. His payment terms had sent me blushing, and his demanded items for collateral sent my panties to the floor and had me doing things that I was pretty sure were illegal in several countries. But as tempting as being Phoenix's sex slave was, I wanted to do it by myself. It was important to me.

I raised the champagne. "Guess Zoey and Cam are celebrating early."

He laughed. "They're on their second bottle, but they didn't want to tell the *boss* that."

I laughed, then said, "There's sparkling water in the fridge if you want some."

He shook his head. "I'm good."

The old Phoenix would have chugged the entire cup of Champagne in celebration.

Not the new Phoenix.

He nodded to the folder in my hand. "Is it done?"

"Yes." I couldn't fight the huge smile that crossed my face.

He pulled me to him again. "I'm proud of you, baby."

"Thank you. Me, too."

"Not just for that." The playful look in his eyes faded to emotion. "I'm proud of the woman you are, the woman you've become. The odds you've beaten. The belief in yourself. I thought I had all that. I didn't. You showed me how to be strong. You inspired me to be better, Rose. I'd be nothing without you."

Tears threatened to sting my eyes. I jerked my chin back. "What is this? What do you need from me?"

He smiled, a flash of excitement touching his eyes. "I need you to come with me."

"Where?"

"Don't worry about it."

I groaned. "Come on, just tell me. You know I hate surprises."

"Yes, I know. Let's go."

He grabbed my hand and led me out of the office, and mid-way through a stolen kiss in the corner. Although Zoey and Cameron hadn't made their relationship status official, the grins they carried when they were around each other did the talking for them. They were a cute couple and I was happy for them.

"I'll be back... I think." I said over my shoulder as Phoenix dragged me out the door. He bypassed my SUV and opened the passenger side door of his Chevy.

I smiled. "How does it feel to have your license back?"

"Like signing the papers on my first business." He winked, then helped me inside, kissed my knuckles, and shut the door.

I watched him jog around the hood, an extra pep in his step. The guy was definitely up to something.

"What's going on, Phoenix?" I asked as he slid behind the steering wheel.

He reached into the console and pulled out a black blindfold.

"Whoa. Just cause I wore it the other night doesn't mean—"

"*Shhh...*"

He slid the blindfold over my eyes.

"Damn you, Phoenix."

"That's not what you said last time you had it on. I believe it was something to the effect of 'put it in my'—"

"*Stop.*"

He laughed. The engine roared to life and we took off. To where, I had no idea. In a weak attempt to keep me preoccupied, Phoenix droned on about his security plan for my office. I zoned out thirty seconds in.

The road turned from smooth to bumpy, and finally, rolled to a stop.

"Hope you don't like those heels."

He helped me out of the truck and I cringed as my new Manolo Blahnik's sank into what I imagined was a very muddy field. A breeze swept through my hair, silk over my skin. I can't explain the sudden warmth that ran over my body, my soul. It was an instant happiness. Like I was exactly where I was supposed to be at that moment.

In my life.

I heard shuffles, maybe a few whispers, and a new scent carried through the wind—freshly chopped lumber.

We stopped.

"You ready?"

I sucked in a breath. "I *think* so?"

The blindfold was removed—and my heart fell to my feet.

My mouth dropped as I looked at the newly constructed horse stables with a sign that read *Rose Flower Equine Therapy Center* over the double doors. It was bright red, with white trim, sparkling under the autumn sun. It was glorious.

Gage, Gunner, Axel, the rest of the Steele Shadows Security team, stood in front. Jagg, and a mirror image of the detective, that I could only assume to be his brother, stood to the side.

June stood proudly in the middle.

Tears filled my eyes. "Oh my God," the words came out in a breathy whisper. "Phoenix." I turned to him. "How did you do all this without me knowing? I can't..."

"Yes you can. Consider this my rent payment for moving in with you. Your therapy clinic is all yours, this is just an extension of it. It's a Steele Shadows Security investment in the community. In those in need of help."

I was at a loss for words.

Gage stepped forward. "We're all going to help. You'll have more than enough volunteers and manpower. Your boy here," he nodded to Phoenix, "convinced us of the healing power of horses, and between his and Spirit's weird-ass love affair," he winked, "I'm on board. We all are. We think it will be a great service to offer our clients at Steele Shadows as well."

I turned and fell into Phoenix, wrapping my arms around his neck. "Thank you, thank you, *thank you.*"

I released and ran over to June. Tears streamed down my face.

She cupped my cheeks. "Congratulations on owning your own business, my dear."

"Thank you, Mama."

I wiped my tears and turned to the group around me, the team of former military veterans who'd helped make my dream come true.

"This center will be focused on treating PTSD, and will be free to all service men and women, and first responders."

I looked at Phoenix. He dipped his chin—*thank you.*

I dipped my own—*I love you.*

"Let me show you around your new digs." He said.

The crowd dissipated as he led me into the barn. It was stunning, something right out of architectural digest, with soaring ceilings and rustic chandeliers hanging from log beams. Everything was polished, dark wood. Black iron gates housed a dozen stalls. Past that, a sitting room with lush chairs and couches positioned around a coffee table over a beautiful paisley rug. June's photographs lined the walls. I immediately envisioned well-to-do men smoking cigars and sipping Brandy there... or perhaps the Steele brothers with a deck of cards and a handle of whiskey. Beyond that were two offices, a fully-stocked equipment room, and at the end, a small kitchen. There was an indoor riding ring and several outdoor paddocks in the back.

It was beyond my wildest dreams.

Little did I know what was yet to come.

We stepped into the indoor ring. Phoenix clicked his tongue, pulling my attention to Spirit, making her way across the dirt floor. I smiled as I met her beautiful black eyes, and I can't explain why, but goosebumps prickled my skin as she walked toward me.

She wore a sparkling golden bow.

I looked at Phoenix, his intense gaze sending my heart pumping double time.

Spirit stopped at my feet and nudged my shoulder.

My gaze shifted to the white envelope dangling from the bridle, then to Phoenix.

He nodded—*open it.*

I unclipped the envelope, opened the flap, and pulled out two airplane tickets. Destination, Positano, Italy.

I gasped.

"Let's start unearthing those roots of yours," he said.

"Phoenix, you didn't..." I flipped the tickets over in my hands. "They're one way tickets."

He smiled. "How does spending the next few months sound? Thought we could escape for a bit before your business officially kicks off."

"That sounds like heaven."

Spirit nudged me again, but this time, angled her head to show a small box secured to the bow.

My heart skipped a beat.

"Open it," Phoenix said softly.

My hands trembled as I pulled the little blue box from the bow.

Tiffany's.

Inside, a four carat ruby enclosed in a circle of diamonds.

A rose.

I gasped, again, this time with tears welling in my eyes. I turned to Phoenix, now on his knees.

"Marry me," he said. "Marry me, Rose. My Rose Flower. Marry me."

I fell to my knees, grabbed his face.

"Yes. Yes, Phoenix. *Yes.*"

A tear slid down his cheek as he slipped the ring onto my finger. A perfect fit.

Cheers erupted behind us.

I turned to see his brothers, his closest friends, my dear June, and began sobbing.

My new family.

～

～

JAGGER SNEAK PEEK

★ Nominated for the Daphne du Maurier Award for
Excellence in Mystery/Suspense 2021 ★

Jagger (Steele Shadows Investigations)

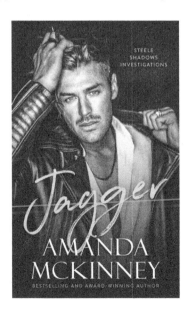

He found her covered in blood.
She promises she's innocent.
The question is... Can he trust her?

Feared just as much on the streets as at a crime scene, Homicide Detective Max Jagger has dedicated his life to one thing—speaking for the dead. Everyone and everything else be damned, including his own demons. During one of the most oppressive heat waves to hit the small, southern town of Berry Springs, the former Navy SEAL is called to a scene where a real estate heiress is found standing over a dead body, holding the murder weapon. The local cops immediately dub it a slam-dunk case, but if Jagg has learned anything from his days running special ops, it's that nothing is as it seems... including this suspect.

Despite her name, Sunny Harper is as beguiling as a fallen angel. Mysterious, clever, completely unwilling to cooperate, and, perhaps his least favorite quality—mind-numbingly intoxicating. When evidence from the scene suggests an accomplice, Jagg begins to believe that Sunny is both innocent and in danger, despite the towns' uproar to lock her up. Torn between his growing feelings for his suspect, he takes Sunny to a secluded lake house where he discovers there's much more behind those enchanting green eyes... including secrets that could take them both under.

With his career on the line and the clock ticking, Jagg must decide if he can trust Sunny... before they both get burned.

Jagger is a standalone romantic suspense novel (no cliff-hanger!)

∾

CHAPTER ONE

Jagg

A thin fog slithered around the headstones like a snake searching for its prey. Or perhaps more fitting for this story, like a virus, spreading, spreading, spreading, slowly consuming everything in its path. But it was too late. The crowd was gone. I was the only one left.

Come and get me, I thought. I'd spent my entire life tempting the devil and always won. Little did I know what the horned fucker had in store for me next.

I tilted my head to the moon. Glowing iridescent clouds crowded the spotlight, waiting for the perfect time to steal its light.

A full moon was coming.

I did not like full moons.

I refocused on the swaying milky mist, my back against a tree, my feet planted in front of me. Uneven rows of headstones—most tilted and unreadable—speckled the rolling hills, once a vibrant green now brown with dying, wilted grass. Even the trees seemed to sag. Berry Springs was in the middle of the hottest heatwave on record, according to the weatherman. The night had ushered in cooler temperatures —cooler, as in low-*eighties*—but no reprieve from the suffocating humidity. It had been six days of three-digit temperatures, and feels-like temps of your-balls-are-guaranteed-to-stick-to-your-leg-all-day. Brutal, if you're unfamiliar. Or neutered.

I shifted, the root poking into my tailbone finally making my ass numb. I was hoping that numbness would climb to my lower back.

No luck.

I popped another pain pill then hurled a rock into a nearby bush in an effort to silence the screaming cicadas, a million maracas shaking between my temples.

Despite the bugs and the ball-plastering heat, I couldn't leave. I stared at that damn trident, etched on the headstone in front of me, until the thing began to blur.

It had been eight hours since the small, southern town had gathered in their black best, weeping, grieving, trying to understand. Colleagues, friends, family, trying to wrap their heads around a new life suddenly derailed by the finality of death.

Cheated life.

Too early.

Way too fucking early.

Shadow Hill was a typical small-town graveyard where everyone born and raised within a thirty-mile radius was buried. Located in the center of town, the cemetery was nestled in a clearing outside of City Park, which consisted of twenty acres of manicured woods and jogging trails just behind Main Street.

I suppose this is where I'm supposed to say I hate cemeteries, like any normal human being. Truth is, I've been to so many over the years that they've lost that haunting luster. Death is the only thing certain in life. I know that better than anyone. Some deaths you accept, a normal course of immortality stolen by time, but others were stolen by six rounds to the chest.

That night was the latter.

I scanned the tree line past the clearing for the hundredth time. The chatter of the town had died down, as most small towns did after eight pm. Trucks, cars, horses had disappeared from the roads with the exception of a few logging trucks passing by. Three, to be exact.

I smashed a mosquito the size of a Volkswagen against my forearm, this one double the size of the last. The blood-sucking bastards were swarming and getting ballsier by the minute, probably attracted to the seventeen layers of sweat that had settled under my white dress shirt. Always white, by the way. I don't do print. Print button-ups are for pussies and men who manscaped.

Although I tossed the suit jacket and loosened the necktie I'd gotten at the thrift shop earlier that morning, my Hanes had been in a constant state of damp since taking my place among the mourners.

It had been a hell of a day.

Not unlike so many before.

I tipped up my whiskey, my throat numb to the burn of the tepid liquid by that point. Tepid? Who am I kidding? It was like swallowing fresh tar. Something I don't recommend. Twenty-four hours of vomiting followed by a two-day hospital stint is how that story ends.

I got that twenty bucks though.

A whisper of a breeze swept over my skin, on it, that familiar earthy scent of a freshly dug grave. A scent that never failed at triggering memories to loop in my brain like a black and white horror movie. One dead body, two, three, four... spinning, spinning, spinning, their eyes locked on mine begging for answers.

I swiped the fresh sheen of sweat from my brow.

I was so damn sick of the heat.

My hand drifted to the tie around my neck, giving it a few more tugs. Polyester, best I could tell. Silk was also for pussies.

I hated ties. A noose invented by some overindulgent silver-spoon prick in the seventeenth century had now become a symbol of status in our society—you know, with the printed-shirt people. A man wearing a necktie was considered to have an importance of sorts, always busy, always on the go. Rushing from one very important meeting to the next, with a quick stop off in the company bathroom to rub one out because his barbie stay-at-home-wife never let him stick a finger in anything other than her wallet. Always in his shiny sports car or slick SUV, a weak attempt to prove a masculinity that ironically dissolved the moment he'd asked his nanny to Plattsburgh-knot his tie after pulling his dick from her mouth. Yes, I'm important, the tie told society, despite being bound and gagged at the jugular.

Ties were like dog collars, in my humble opinion. I hated dogs, too, for that matter. Pitied them, having to always wear their version of a tie—the ultimate noose—slowly tightening over years, going unnoticed by their neglectful owners. The only thing that reminded the dog of years gone by was the deep ache in his back and that damn collar growing too tight.

Hell, I was that dog.

A tissue tumbled across the grass, dancing along the mound of dirt like an evil fairy taunting the dead to rise again. For one last chance. One last fight. One last night in a world that had released them to their fates.

I leaned my head against the tree and contemplated heaven and hell, and good and evil, as I had done so many times before. After years being on the front lines of fighting a concept that has ripped nations apart for centuries, I came to one conclusion: Good is a fluid concept and evil is a guarantee. While good is easily overlooked, our society has turned evil into a separate entity, a faceless label given in an attempt to understand the atrocities that happen on a daily basis. Because something has to be responsible, right? Something, or someone, has to be blamed and held accountable. Evil gives us something tangible to focus our anger on, and therefore, we accept its place on earth.

Genocide, terrorists' attacks, rape, murder, torture, all caused by evil.

Is it?

Or is it simply a passive acceptance, a way to turn a cheek and dismiss a responsibility that society is too scared to address. Too scared to attack head on.

Too scared to look in the face.

That was *my* job. To face the evil and expose it for what it truly was.

I didn't allow myself the luxury of believing in good or evil, simply because they don't come in black and white facts. Declaring someone evil isn't enough to get them locked behind bars. Evil doesn't give grieving families closure.

My job was to speak for the dead.

To bring them justice.

And never, in my career, was that resolve stronger than it was at that moment.

On that note, I decided to get moving. Hunting, probably a better word for it.

I pushed myself off the dirt floor, freezing mid-way like Bigfoot caught on camera. Searing pain shot up my back, waves of nausea following seconds later.

Always the nausea.

Goddamn the nausea.

As always, this pain was followed by a rush of fury. Anger at the realization that I wasn't the invincible man I used to be. Anger that my life had changed in an instant, leaving me with a constant reminder of what had now become the good 'ol days. Anger that I couldn't fight the heavy hand of time. A bitch, time was.

Unlike good and evil, old was one concept I never thought about. I never assumed I'd reach the age to be considered *old*. Records are old, aversion to anal is old, the Karate Kid is old. I'm not old. If I'm being totally honest, I expected to go out years ago in a blaze of glory—in my vision, I'm wearing a sweatband in a mid-air Kung Fu leap with a ball of fire at my back. You know, like Rambo but without the quirked lip... ... who is *also* now old, come to think of it—with one hand flashing the middle finger and the other wrapped around my nuts.

Unfortunately, the universe had other plans for me.

My pain finally dulled to what I imagine a severed organ would feel like. My hand mindlessly drifted to the bottle of pills in my pocket.

Wait until you get home, a little voice in my head whispered.

I straightened fully, cursing my bones, then took off down the graveled drive that cut between the headstones, the blue-glow of the moon lighting my way. I decided to avoid Main Street and cut through the woods of City Park.

The night dimmed around me the second I stepped under the thick canopy of trees. My only light was from the dim lampposts that line the jogging trails. I knew every inch of those woods, that park, by heart. Not only from running the trails every morning, but from responding to countless noise complaints during my beat cop days before becoming a detective. It was a favorite spot among the local teens, their own little Hookah lounge right there in the middle of town.

The clouds drifted over the moon and darkness engulfed me, my senses shifting to hearing and smell only. For a moment, I felt like I was back in my twenties, slipping from shadow to shadow on a black op that usually ended in more than one dead body. It felt good.

God, I missed it.

I stepped onto the jogging trail under the yellow spotlight of a lamppost, and that's when I got that good ol' feeling that I wasn't alone. I paused, scanning from left to right when a soft chiming caught my attention. A distant song, carrying through the midnight breeze like a siren's call. My brow furrowed as I looked in the direction of the sound, trying to figure out where it was coming from. It wasn't music, in the traditional sense anyway, just random creepy-ass chimes, growing louder in the wind. Soft, tinkles of a song.

The clouds parted, moonlight washing over me again as I stepped off the trail and into the woods, following the sound. More chimes, this time followed by a sparkle of lights flashing through the trees overhead. My hand instinctively slid to the gun on my hip as I picked my way through the brush, each flash of light increasing in speed as I approached. Like a freaking discotheque, or maybe a late-night fiesta of dancing cicadas wearing little red hats and shaking their maracas.

The music grew louder. My senses piqued. My hand squeezed the hilt of my gun as I stepped into a clearing.

A massive oak tree sat in the middle of the clearing with long, low branches, snarling around each other like arthritic fingers. A perfect climbing tree—aside from the fact that someone had turned it into a shrine.

Dozens of wind chimes, crystals and strings of broken mirrors dangled from the branches, catching the slivers of moonlight and reflecting in a kaleidoscope of colors on the surrounding trees. I half-expected Cinderella to jump out of a pumpkin—something I would not have minded, by the way. The compliant, blonde maid was my first childhood crush. I mean, the woman could really clean a floor. The difference here, though, was that Cinderella didn't carve Wiccan symbols into tree trunks.

A rotted branch had been positioned at the base of the oak, a circle of candles flickering on top. And hidden among the branches sat dozens of voodoo dolls, their black, beady eyes staring directly into my soul.

∾

JAGGER (STEELE SHADOWS INVESTIGATIONS)

ABOUT THE AUTHOR

Amanda McKinney is the bestselling and multi-award-winning author of more than twenty romantic suspense and mystery novels. Her book, Rattlesnake Road, was named one of *POPSUGAR's 12 Best Romance Books,* and was featured on the *Today Show.* The fifth book in her Steele Shadows series was recently nominated for the prestigious *Daphne du Maurier Award for Excellence in Mystery/Suspense.* Amanda's books have received over fifteen literary awards and nominations.

Text **AMANDABOOKS to 66866** to sign up for Amanda's

Newsletter and get the latest on new releases, promos, and freebies!

www.amandamckinneyauthor.com

If you enjoyed Phoenix, please write a review!

Made in the USA
Middletown, DE
07 March 2024